Adriana Georgescu

In the Beginning Was the End

Adriana Georgescu

In the Beginning Was the End

Introduction by *Monica Lovinescu*
Translated from Romanian by
Dr. *Dan Golopenția*
Edited by *Guy* and *Lidia Bradley*
Notes edited by *Marius Oprea*

Memoria Cultural Foundation
Bucharest, RO

The Aspera Educational Foundation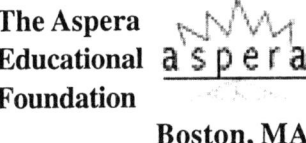
Boston, MA

Cover design by Dora Ionescu
Maps by Iuliana Barnea

Copyright for the English translation and edition: Adriana Georgescu, 1951 and The Aspera Romanian Educational Foundation, 2003

Copyright for the Romanian edition: Adriana Georgescu, 1951 and Humanitas 1992; Adriana Georgescu, 1951 and Fundatia Culturala Memoria, 1999

Copyright for the French edition: Librairie Hachette, 1951

The English text is a translation of the Romanian edition published by Editura Memoria in 1999, ISBN: 973-99523-0-5

The translation of this book into English, as well as its production, printing, distribution and marketing has been made possible by The Aspera Romanian Educational Foundation of Boston, MA, USA. Founder and president: Lidia Bradley; Email: contact@aspera.ro Web site: www.aspera.ro

---

Descrierea CIP a Bibliotecii Naţionale a României
GEORGESCU, ADRIANA
  In the Beginning Was the End / Adriana Georgescu; introduction by Monica Lovinescu; translated from Romanian by Dr. Dan Golopenţia; edited by Guy and Lidia Bradley; notes edited by Marius Oprea - Bucureşti: Editura Fundaţiei Culturale „Memoria", 2004
   ISBN 973-99523-8-0

I. Lovinescu, Monica (pref.)
II. Golopenţia, Dan (trad.)
III. Bradley, Guy (ed.)
IV. Bradley, Lidia (ed.)
V. Oprea Marius (ed.)

821.135.1-31821.135.1-31

A NOTE ABOUT THE ENGLISH EDITION

This English edition of Adriana Georgescu's book, "In the Beginning Was the End", was created as part of the Romanian Oral History Project supported by the Aspera Foundation, and hosted on the Internet at www.memoria.ro.

It is an eye-witness account of the communists' rapid takeover of Romania at the end of World War II and of the workings of Stalinist-type propaganda, a victim's rendition of the first show trial of that period, a memoir of years spent in communist prisons (1945 – 1947), and a tale of escape and exile. To our knowledge, this book, written in 1949 - 1950, was the first to describe the mechanisms by which the Communists effectively destroyed the other political parties and Romanian civil society in the years after the war, as a prerequisite to establishing the Soviet-supported totalitarian rule that lasted in Romania until the fall of the Ceaușescu regime in December of 1989. This description is done by a lucid observer who was not only at the center of events, but, trained as a lawyer and journalist, was also politically sophisticated.

It was also the first book to describe the treatment of political prisoners in the Romanian Gulag. The fate of victims of the early communist repression is portrayed in clear, vivid lines. So is the inhumanity of their interrogators. And yet, in writing about prison life, the author, then a young woman in her twenties, transcends the horrors and finds at times a fresh, even humorous tone. The psychology and language of the common criminals with whom she spends time in squalid, over-crowded cells come to life, rendered with sympathy and warmth.

Adriana Georgescu wrote "In the Beginning Was the End" in Paris directly after her escape from Romania in 1948, with the in-

Adriana Georgescu

tention of "opening the eyes" of Westerners as to what was going on behind the Iron Curtain. Monica Lovinescu[1] translated it into French while it was being written. The French edition of *"Au commencement était la fin"* was published by Hachette in 1951. Forty years later, when, after the fall of communism, the book could finally be published in Romania, it had to be translated into Romanian from French. Humanitas published a first edition in 1992, and a second edition followed in 1999 under the supervision of Micaela Ghițescu of the Memoria Cultural Foundation. The present translation into English by Dr. Dan Golopenția, with input from Guy Bradley, follows the 1999 edition of the Romanian text.

Growing up in Romania in the sixties, hearing one version of history from my parents and being taught a different one in school, I started wondering how the regime change from a constitutional monarchy to a communist dictatorship actually occurred. I must have been about twelve years old when I first heard, from my parents, whispered accounts of Adriana Georgescu's suffering. My father was related to her, and I have fond memories of her mother and sisters, whom we used to visit at Sinaia and in Bucharest. However, even the child I was then could sense, underlying their warmth and friendliness, suffering and fear. After leaving Romania in the early 1980s I was often asked to explain to foreign friends how Romanian communism came to develop its extremely dictatorial form. Presenting Adriana Georgescu's account in English is the best answer I can give.

I met Adriana in 2001 in England. At over eighty, and in spite of the continually recurring depressions she has suffered as a result of her years of torture and imprisonment, her energy shines through her eyes, it resounds in her voice. She has never stopped denouncing totalitarianism: of characters like hers the stuff of resistance to tyranny and manipulation is made. Her book is relevant today, and will be relevant at every point in history when ideology prevails over civil liberties.

This edition benefits from the research of the Institute of Recent Romanian History (IRIR), whose historians Marius Oprea and Stejarel Olaru created and edited the explanatory notes; from the research of the Memoria Cultural Foundation, which allowed us to use the maps of Romania showing the locations of prisons and areas

In the Beginning Was the End

of activity of post-war resistance groups; from the generous advice of Professor Sanda Golopenția of Brown University; from the thoughtful assistance of Mircea Ivănoiu of the Aspera ProEdu Foundation in Brasov and the technical help of Simona Ceaușu, who typed the translated manuscript.

Lidia Gheorghiu Bradley,
The Aspera Foundation, Boston

September 27, 2003

Notes:

[1] *Monica Lovinescu* (b. November 19th, 1923, in Bucharest): literary critic, writer, essayist and radio analyst living in Paris since 1947. A strong voice of the Romanian exile and a harsh critic of the communist regime, she contributed for decades to Radio Free Europe broadcasts. In the 1980's the Romanian political police *Securitate* tried to assassinate her.

INTRODUCTION

I met Adriana Georgescu again in April 1990 in University Square in Bucharest. I knew that she was now living on the other side of the Channel in a British town. That she had changed her name, after a new marriage, to Westwater. That her appearance had been changed not only by the passing of time but also by the incurable trauma of her prison experience. I had followed year after year her evolution and her tragedy. Still she seemed to belong amidst the youth here. When they sang with humour – a humour pierced by bullets – the *"golanilor"* anthem[1]. And then, kneeling, when they picked up another refrain, "Oh Lord, please come Lord, to see what is left of the humans". Between the lyrical-revolutionary illusion of the beginning and the disconsolate premonition of the end was Adriana's real place.

Adriana Georgescu was a symbol of the obstinacy with which Romanian students and youth in general defied the Soviet occupation after the war. Near Mihai Fărcăşanu's[2] unmistakable silhouette leading the Liberal Youth demonstrations, and inseparable from it, was Adriana's golden hair, athletic slenderness, confident laugh. Newspaperwoman, very young attorney, just out of the University, then General Rădescu's[3] chief of staff, the anti-communist resistance found in her an emblematic figure. She was also to become one of the first sacrificial victims of the first show trial in the long series that Nicolschi[4] imposed upon Romania, a series that was to lead to the unfinished symphony of horror at Piteşti[5]. That diabolical stage hadn't yet been reached, but even these initial exercises had been enough to change Adriana's whole existence, henceforth accompanying all the stages of her life with their unending nightmare.

Adriana Georgescu

When we met in Paris at the end of 1948, despite what she had been through, Adriana seemed unchanged. She was still General Rădescu's Chief of Staff, stopping here on the road of exile that was to take him to the United States. Adriana could still laugh as well as before, she hadn't given up hope. Of course it was also true that all of us, students or recent graduates, in Paris in sufficient numbers to turn Boulevard St. Michel into a sort of Calea Victoriei away from Romania, we all shared the same recklessness of our age. I only knew one exception: Virgil Ierunca[6]. He walked among us actively pessimistic and was the only one whom I never heard using at New Year or other holidays the ritual formula, "Next year in Bucharest". I myself had come to Paris with the firm belief that Malraux[7] could be convinced to set up international brigades to free Romania.

But I had come to a Paris that was convalescing after one war and unable to prepare for another, and I was among Marxists, Marxist sympathizers, communists, and other fellow travellers for whom Moscow was an anti-fascist Mecca. Among the representatives of the Great Powers who made up the Nüremberg Tribunal, the representatives of the Gulag were trying the heads of the Nazi concentration camps.

One couldn't talk about the satellite-ization of the East without being labeled a fascist. Our stubborn refusal to admit to the division of Europe and the flagrant injustice of the peace was not dulled by aggressive contact with reality. We printed newspapers, we agitated, we held meetings, we knocked on all the doors, we wanted to open eyes that had chosen to remain closed. Such an out-of-sync attitude cannot be explained only by our youth. A very mature Grigore Gafencu[8] did the same thing at a different level. In the United States Committees of the Captive Nations were formed – we even had two, one led by C. Vișoianu[9], the other by General Rădescu and Mihai Fărcășanu. The legitimacy of regimes that came to power in falsified elections seemed easy to challenge.

The word exile is actually misleading: there are a number of very different types of exiles. Ours was mainly made up of people who had run not to escape, but rather to continue fighting.

And we kept fighting. Without weapons, without those tanks in which we still dreamed of returning to Romania. We fought with our pens, with our words. Only in 1956, when we saw in amazement that the bloody suppression of the Hungarian Revolution took place without any reaction from the Western Powers (a single United Nations plane carrying the General Secretary of the UN to the Budapest airport, in answer to Imre Nagy's[10] desperate call, would have probably been enough to stop the slaughter and to change the course of history), only then did we realize that our wish was in vain. And since then there have been many types of exiles. The ones determined to continue – true courage, said Simone Weil, is to fight when there is no hope – did it, each in his own way, living their life as a hiatus between what was, and what had almost no chance of coming into being. Others more or less adapted. Others assimilated. And in the waves of exile that followed some were strictly "economical". Seldom "political". In 1956 there occurred the first great loss from the first great exile: Grigore Gafencu, while coming back from a radio station where he had launched a last appeal to save a revolution which could have spread beyond Hungary's borders, was brought down by a heart attack.

But it wasn't yet 1956 when I saw Adriana again in Paris. We still lived with the conviction that eyes must be opened. In the cafés of St. Germain-des-Prés, instead of talking about existentialism and looking for Sartre and his cohorts, we came up with a strategy. Adriana would write an eyewitness account, and I would translate it into French. The sooner the better. The urgency was measured by the number of prisons that were filling up in Romania. We agreed that she would bring me every day what she had written the previous night. When she didn't have time the night before, she would write at my house and I would translate it on the spot. "My house" was in fact an attic room ("chambre de bonne" the French call it), the kind poor Parisian students had in those days. And for the first time in my life I was quite poor. But I admit I didn't completely dislike this bohemian lifestyle, which I hadn't known in Romania: university eating halls, rooms without running water, unlit staircases.

There, at 44 Boulevard Raspail, Adriana climbed daily to the seventh floor, and of course there was no lift. Sometimes with three or four pages written in a hurry, sometimes without any so she had to write while I prepared something to eat. Because Romania had broken cultural ties with France we were left without stipends and had only minimal student aid. I didn't really know how to behave when one is left with nothing, but for some reason poverty was connected in my mind with *mămăligă*[11]. So we looked in all sorts of specialty stores for corn flour, which was rather expensive in those days, out of which, I due to my ignorance, Adriana due to her extreme concentration on the manuscript, we made a rather poor mămăligă. We ended up with some lumpy stuff which we complemented with American chocolate. Various American charitable associations sent food and second hand clothing parcels for East European refugees. They shipped it all together so that our chocolate smelled of... moth balls. We smoked and we drank, Adriana tea and I coffee. And we worked.

When she left, usually late, down the unlit staircase, Adriana sometimes dropped the pages that had been translated, or threw them crumpled into the waste-paper basket. They weren't very important to her, she wrote with a single goal in mind: "to open eyes". During our breaks we behaved childishly or even ridiculously: we put Romanian words to the French Partisan song and imagined ourselves in the first battalions that would throw open the prison doors. We projected the obsessive, in those years, images of the French resistance onto the Romanian reality. And after an intermezzo of hallucinations we would start again: she to write, I to translate.

When she got to her first experiences with prison and torture, Adriana put her fountain-pen down. Her whole body started to tremble. Her teeth were chattering. (This trembling has accompanied her throughout her life, it has been her eternal present.) I gave her another cup of tea. I opened the window that looked out over the Paris roofs. But she was still in the darkness of the Bucharest prisons. Before starting to write again, she told me, still trembling, all the things that she couldn't put down on paper. Then gradually she calmed down and wrote, torturously, sparely, allusively about the unnamable. She threw those pages into the fire immediately after I had translated them into French, seemingly believing that by burning them she could also consume her past. The paper turned into ash but her burden remained.

In the Beginning Was the End

But even among her prison memories were episodes that were not tragic. She remembered with humour and tender emotion her prostitute and thief cellmates. In order to translate Romanian slang into French, a friend introduced me to one of his resistance comrades who talked only in argot. Plain, massive, primeval even, seemingly still holding in his hand the machine gun which he hadn't yet completely set aside (he told me he kept his weapons hidden under his bed), a simple and courageous man – he had also been behind bars for honourable reasons – he told me everything he knew. Thanks to him the Dâmbovița[12] felons, thieves, and prostitutes were able to talk just like those on the shores of Seine. A single word remained unchanged: "rag" – the friendly way Adriana's prison-mates called her. I remember it because Adriana and I adopted this name and used it later in our conversations, and after her departure for England in our mail. Never "dear Adriana" or "dear Monica". We used "rag" instead as a sort of a link – unconscious? – between what we were hoping for then and what was never going to happen.

Adriana busied herself not only with the writing of the book, finished in record time due to our rhythm and working style. She was always active. As a member of the Liberal Party. As Rădescu's secretary. She made things clear to politicians, newspapermen, she went to meetings, she kept talking, she kept talking. At the trial brought by the heads of the democratic parties from East and Central Europe against the communist author of a book that was making waves in those days, *"L'Internationale des Traîtres"*, Adriana, in her deposition, warned the West that if it failed to do something for the "other Europe" it would eventually be faced with neurotic societies. Her prophecy, based in part on her own suffering, was confirmed by the state of Romanian society after 1989.

The book was published by Hachette in 1951. I signed the translation with a pseudonym (Claude Pascal). I had a hostage in Romania: my mother. In spite of this she was arrested in 1958, at the age of 70, sentenced to 25 years, and in the end murdered in prison through the denial of medical care. Not, however, because my pen name was deciphered, but absurdly (and what wasn't absurd in communist Romania?) for "espionage". How? By sending me

13

printed silk scarves on which she supposedly drew... military maps. Needless to say, my mother didn't know how to draw maps and I never received any scarves from her.

Despite the leftist milieu, Au commencement était la fin was favourably received in the French press. Adriana assumed that the Romanian Embassy bought the whole edition so that the book wouldn't reach the public. I don't know if this was the case, totally or partially, although such "mass purchases" were used by the communists at the time. In any case the whole edition sold out.

What is left to say is why I think the publication in Romania of Adriana Georgescu's book is salutary and of current interest. Salutary because we suffer, and are going to suffer for a long time, from Romania's image in the media as the Eastern European country with the weakest dissident movement. And, with a few well-known exceptions, this is a fairly accurate description of the last decades. But not of the first decades after the war. The resistance movement in Romania after 1944 was probably more numerous, more unified, and more determined that that in neighbouring countries. And longer lasting. In September 1947 in Vienna, after I had clandestinely crossed a border (even though my passport was in order... but that is another story that I am not going to tell here), I was in the office of a French officer in order to get a new visa in my passport already filled with stamps. Behind his desk there was a huge map of Romania with small flags marking the resistance bases in the Carpathian mountains. The officer wanted to know if I was aware of any other resistance centers. I wasn't. I was aware though of the resistance that was more or less open in society ("civil society" we would call it today; and it existed in those days).

I was the delegate of the Literature Department of the University of Bucharest to a large student congress in May 1947 in Cluj. The communists and the various "fronts" behind which they were hiding wanted to force us to stigmatize and "fire" the professors resistant to the new order. We withstood the pressure so well (universities from the whole country were represented) that the congress ended without any positive results for the communists and with the Royal Anthem being sung in a large hall filled with students. I was lodged in the medical student dormitory, and we plotted in long sleepless nights what tactics to follow. Among the intellectuals there was the same determined attitude. Together with Ştefan Augustin Doinaş[13] and other members of the Sibiu circle[14] we went to see Lucian Blaga[15]. Blaga wanted to know details about how the Bucharest writers and university professors were surviving. His long periods of silence were punctuated by anxiety and determination. "Silent as a swan", Blaga was listening to the future.

I think this initial resistance has to be emphasized in order to reestablish the truth, to honour those who are no longer with us, and to rid ourselves of one of our rare undeserved complexes (so many are justified!).

As far as the current interest of this testimony goes... I assume it isn't necessary to dwell on it. The readers will judge for themselves. For me it was enough to meet Adriana again in University Square in 1990.

There are some essential differences though.

In 1945 we had a civil society, but also the Red Army, in a land abandoned to Soviet "influence". In 1989-1990, the society, with a few well-known and wonderful exceptions, seems ill, "neurotic", Adriana would say. On the other hand, Europe is no longer divided, and the Red Army is busy at home.

In 1945 everything depended on foreigners. Now everything is in our hands. In principle, there is no reason for the beginning to be the end.

Monica Lovinescu
Paris, March 1991

Notes:

[1] *Golan* (pl. *golani*): literally, a 'have-not', a 'vagabond'. After 1990, when President Ion Iliescu, a former high-ranking communist leader, called the students and intellectuals protesting against his government in University Square *golani*, the term acquired a positive connotation, even becoming a badge of honor. President Iliescu later

apologized publicly. Two young folk singers, Cristian Pațurcă and Petre Constantin, known as "Dr. Barbi", composed the so-called '*golanilor* anthem', which was sung by the thousands of protesters in the square. Its refrain was "Better to be a vagabond than a traitor / A hooligan than a dictator / Better to be a have-not than a party activist / Better to be dead than a communist." Many well-known Romanian intellectuals, including Alexandru Paleologu, a writer and Romania's Ambassador to Paris at that time, declared themselves to be '*golani*'.

[2] *Mihai Fărcășanu* (?-1987): charismatic president of the Romanian Liberal Youth Organisation, writer (pen name: Mihai Villara) and journalist (Editor in Chief of *Viitorul*, official newspaper of the National Liberal Party), escaped Romania in 1947 and took refuge in France and then in the United States, where he was a founding member of the Romanian National Committee and then succeeded General Nicolae Rădescu as President of the League of Free Romanians.

[3] *Nicolae Rădescu* (1876-1953): general, Chief of the Great General Staff until October 15th, 1944. Prime Minister between December 6th, 1944 and February 28th, 1945. He tried to quell the communist agitations, but was forced to resign. He took refuge at the British Legation in Bucharest and, in 1946, managed to fly out of the country to Cyprus. His daring escape surprised even the Allies, who, in order to avoid more tension between them and the Soviets, kept him for nine months on the island in a British refugee camp, before allowing him to emigrate to the United States via Lisbon. In Washington, General Rădescu organized the Romanian National Committee (Comitetul National Roman, CNR) in 1948, under the patronage of Michael I, King of Romania. CNR initially consisted of ten members, representing the three main Romanian democratic parties of the interwar period: the National Peasant Party, the Liberal Party, and the Independent Socialist Party and acted as a substitute for a post-World War II Romanian democratic government in exile. It was one of the nine organizations that made up the Assembly of Captive European Nations. After leaving CNR in 1950, due to policy conflicts, General Rădescu founded the League of Free Romanians. He was head of this organization for only a short time, since in 1952 he developed an illness of the lungs that could not be diagnosed. He died one year later, on May 16th, 1953, in New York.

[4] *Alexandru Nicolschi* (1914-1992): KGB officer. After Romania was occupied by the Red Army in 1944, he was charged with arresting the leaders of the democratic parties. He rose to the rank of general and became deputy director of the *Securitate*. He was in charge

In the Beginning Was the End

of special operations of the *Securitate* against political opponents, and directly responsible for the crimes and torture carried out by the communist political police during the first ten years of its existence, participating in person at interrogations considered 'of importance'. It is therefore significant that he personally and savagely tortured Adriana Georgescu, General Rădescu's former chief of staff. Retired in 1961 as a major general. After the 1989 revolution he 'justified' his crimes by saying: "Who knew that 1989 was ever going to happen?". He died on the very day when, after long delays, the Romanian authorities, pressured by the civil society, decided to prosecute him.

⁵ *Piteşti Prison*: best known political prison in Romania. It was the location of the Piteşti Experiment, a process to 'reeducate' political detainees. Of unparalleled cruelty, it was basically brainwashing by torture. The experiment took place under great secrecy between 1949-1952 in a number of Romanian prisons, but was perfected at Piteşti. The *Securitate* presented it as an initiative of the detainees themselves, most of whom were students and members of right-wing parties. Beaten and starved, then tempted with promises of freedom and jobs, a few of the detainees were convinced to torture their cellmates, in order to 'reeducate' them and turn them into useful builders of the communist society. The result: 30 detainees were killed, more than 780 tortured, out of which 100 were left with great infirmities; some committed suicide in order to escape torture, and others went mad.

⁶ *Virgil Ierunca* (b.1920): real name Virgil Untaru, Romanian literary critic, writer and publicist living in France since 1947. Ierunca has been one of the harshest critics of the Romanian communist regime. The *Securitate* tried to assassinate him.

⁷ *André Malraux* (1901-1976): French writer and politician.

⁸ *Grigore Gafencu* (1892-1957): studied law in Geneva and obtained his doctorate in Paris. Member of the National Peasant Party, Romanian Foreign Minister between 1938-1940, later founding member of the Romanian National Committee (Comitetul National Roman, CNR) together with General Nicolae Rădescu and eight other politicians and diplomats.

⁹ *Constantin Vişoianu* (1897-1994): former Romanian Foreign Minister appointed at Titulescu's recommendation as a member of the General Secretariat of the League of Nations in Geneva, ex-minister to Hague and Warsaw, ex-foreign policy counsellor of Iuliu Maniu, participant in the secret negotiations with the Allies in Cairo in 1944. Went into exile in 1946 aided by the American Legation in Bucharest. Led the Romanian National Committee until its dissolution

in 1975. Represented Romania at the Meeting of the European Captive Nations in Strasbourg.

[10] *Imre Nagy* (1896-1958): Hungarian Prime Minister between 1953-55. During the anticommunist uprising of 1956, which he had initiated through his political reforms and his attempt to take Hungary out of the Soviet zone of influence and the Warsaw Pact, he was called back to lead the country. After he was removed from power by the Soviet troops, the communist authorities in Bucharest offered him political asylum at the suggestion of the Soviets. Once he entered Romania, he was arrested and interrogated by Soviet agents at a secret Securitate location. He was then sent back to Hungary, where he was tried as a traitor to the communist cause, sentenced to death and executed.

[11] *mămăligă*: Romanian word for polenta or maize porridge, a peasant staple. In communist Romania, *mămăligă* also became a symbol of the control excercised by the state over the population: *"Mămăliga nu explodează"* or "Polenta doesn't explode" was a phrase that, in the '80s, was often used to describe the resignation of Romanians to their fate under communism. The phrase began to become invalid on November 15th, 1987, when workers in Brașov openly demanded the end of the Ceaușescu regime, and then finally became obsolete through the revolution of 1989, which removed Ceaușescu from power.

[12] *Dâmbovița*: river in southern Romania, 268 km long, running through Bucharest.

[13] *Ștefan Augustin Doinaș* (1922-2002): real name Ștefan Popa, Romanian poet and academician. Between 1996 – 2000 he represented the Civic Alliance Party, the political party of Romanian intellectuals, in the Senate.

[14] *Sibiu Literary Circle*: founded after the Romanian University at Cluj was moved to Sibiu as a result of the Vienna Dictate (1940), which ceded the northern part of Transylvania to Hungary. One of the most fruitful cultural organizations in Transylvania.

[15] *Lucian Blaga* (1895-1961): Romanian poet, playwright and philosopher. Marginalized by the communist regime, who kept him under constant surveillance, as proven by documents recently published by his daughter. After his death first his poems, then his philosophical writings were reissued.

DEDICATION

I dedicate this book to all Romanians who, during the forty years of communist bondage, were persecuted, arrested, tortured and unjustly sentenced to long years in prison.

Adriana Georgescu

AUTHOR'S NOTE

Because this book was written during the Stalinist period, the names of certain people and localities were changed, making it impossible for the communist police to identify, harass and arrest the people with whom I was in contact.

PART ONE

"In the beginning was the end"

I

In July, 1943 a small incident, apparently of no importance, changed my whole life. I was twenty-three and until then my life had followed a quiet course in the direction I wanted it to take, in the exact direction I thought I could give it. I wanted to be a lawyer, and I had just graduated. I wanted to do sports, and I had already taken part in a few national championships in volleyball and table tennis. I wanted to be a journalist, and for the last year I had written the movie column for *Universul Literar*[1]. I was also a nurse in a military hospital.

Then, in July, 1943, on the very day of the graduation exam, it all started. It must have been on a Friday...

I have just learned the result of the exam. My colleagues want to celebrate the event by inviting me out for dinner. I turn them down: I am on duty at the hospital. I leave them and go down the stairs. A colleague catches up to me: „Adriana, please give me your permit."

I give it to him. I seldom have the permit with me. My university friends are much more passionate about movies than I am. I only go once a week, to do my column. When one works in a hos-

---

[1] *Universul Literar* : literary magazine that, during the WWII years, invited contributions from writers and intellectuals irrespective of their political position.

pital, one sees too many dead, too many wounded. And the movies in Bucharest are almost exclusively German...

✢

Night shift at the hospital. Duty in the ward of those near death. In every bed the same closed eyes, the same gasping breath, the same cracked lips that open only to ask for water, and for water again.
At one a.m. another nurse comes to relieve me. I have to go to the operating room. Three operations. The drone of the planes in the sky above the hospital is drowned in the smell of chloroform, in the metallic clatter of the shiny instruments the assistants pass to the chief surgeon, in the sound of gasping breaths that dominate the night as it slowly passes away.

✢

At six in the morning we accompany the chief surgeon to the car that waits in front of the entrance. The crisp air of the morning burns my eyes. In the emergency room a doctor is helping me with my coat, when Gheorghe, a colleague from the newspaper, appears.
– I have to talk to you immediately.
At this hour? What must have happened for Gheorghe to come to the hospital at such an hour?
– You can talk in front of the doctor, he is a childhood friend.
– Grab your purse and come right away. I have to talk to you alone. It's secret.
I take my purse and follow him. Before I leave I tell the doctor:
– I'll be back shortly.
– No, you are not going to come back, says Gheorghe, once the door is closed. They are looking for you... *Siguranţa*[2]. Don't be so surprised. The censors have warned you a few times. You should

---

[2] *Siguranţa:* Security and information service within the Police and General Security Directorate of the Romanian Interior Ministry. Abolished by the communist regime in 1948, when it was replaced by the General Directorate of the People's Security (later known as the *Securitate*), based on the Soviet NKVD. Between 1945 -1948, communist agents who had infiltrated *Siguranţa* acted as a political police force against the democratically oriented political groups and individuals.

have laid low. Why did you have to be so critical of the German movies? The censors agreed to only seven lines from your last column.
— I wrote what I thought.
— The result: police came looking for you at the paper and at home. They are waiting for you at both places.
He seems scared. My legs feel rubbery.
— I'll go say good-bye to the doctor and the nurse.
— Are you crazy? They'll come looking for you here as well. Outside there is a car waiting. You must leave immediately. I always thought you were irresponsible.
I shrug.
— Where do you want me to go?
— We are going to hide you; this is not the moment for conversation. Let's leave before the police get here.
He grabs my hand and pulls me after him. I add:
— You think it's that bad?
Gheorghe stops and says, furiously:
— Listen, you have to decide. Do you want to disappear, or would you rather pay a little visit to the Gestapo?
The idea of the Gestapo scares me. I follow Gheorghe, running without another word. A car is waiting downstairs. Speeding through the city. Grey dawn.

Adriana Georgescu

II

I don't understand what's happening. I have become a brunette. I have false papers and live in Câmpulung[3]. Gheorghe didn't lie. Before reaching Câmpulung I almost fainted from fear a few times. And I used to hate detective stories... I live in a house in a town I don't know. A provincial town, nice and peaceful. A house where I don't feel at home. At least I didn't in the beginning. Now I am getting used to it.

I share a room with a young woman my age, a Jew named Coca. She is also hiding. In another room, four men. In the living room, the owners, Sandu and Jana. Sandu belongs to a resistance group, he is the organizer. After eight at night the house is quiet. We listen to BBC and Voice of America. Jana records the Allied communiqués in shorthand. Afterwards we duplicate them on the linotype. The front gets closer and closer.

On the streets of Câmpulung the Nazi soldiers pass in disarray. At night the four men distribute the leaflets. One of the men, Tudor, has a car. Coca always sits in the car next to the driver. Everybody is happy. I have trouble fitting in. Jana thinks I take too seriously the fact that the police are after me. Maybe she is right.

Still, I am very much afraid, but I don't show it too much. I can't get used at all to the young brunette with my features whom I see in the mirror. To the false papers, in the name of Johanna Müller, even less. A hundred times a day I repeat this name which should be mine. I try to tame it, to make it mine.

Often I think of the hospital that I had to leave so suddenly. Was it bombed? For the last few months Bucharest has been bombed

---

[3] Câmpulung: small town on the slopes of the Southern Carpathian Mountains, ca. 160 km north-west of Bucharest.

In the Beginning Was the End

almost daily by British and American planes. I am not allowed to send letters.

✢

My fellow inmates admire me for attacking the Nazis. I tell them again and again that there was nothing admirable about it. I simply found the Nazi movies, with their slogans, their buzz-words, their racist ferocity, odious and I said that. That was all. Sandu and the men think I will be a political star tomorrow. I know they are wrong. I try to convince them, but in vain. I have never been involved in politics. I only know that I hate the war, this nightmare with which we all struggle.

✢

I turn twenty-four on the 23rd of July, 1944. The first year that nobody wishes me happy birthday. A day like any other, like all the others in the year I have been living in this house. The same frantic, slightly disorganized activity. The men found an abandoned German truck filled with white paper. We are printing twice as many leaflets as before. Tonight, American planes passed over Câmpulung on their way to Bucharest. It was the only noteworthy thing today.

✢

The days are the same, always the same. The town is animated and filled with excitement. The front is getting closer to our borders. I am in a state of uneasy peace, like a body of water regularly agitated by winds. Trapped in this tiresome waiting... I can't think straight.

✢

No more night rides in the car. For camouflage we turn off all the lights after ten. We go to bed early and wake up at four in the morning to listen to the communiqués. All the alarm clocks in the house start ringing madly at a quarter to four. I wake up feeling uneasy every time.

Adriana Georgescu

✦

The night of the 23rd of August, 1944[4], I have just fallen asleep when a pounding at the door makes me jump. Sandu in pyjamas, yells:
– Armistice, girls, armistice! Quick... to the radio. The King is speaking!
Sandu is bouncing like a ball and the yard is lit up. No more camouflage? Maybe I am not dreaming, since Sandu keeps jumping and yelling. Every time he touches the ceiling lamp, which swings wildly.
We run and listen, holding hands, quiet, moved. Only Sandu talks loudly:
– Wonderful! The British and the Americans are our allies. We will fight the Germans, alongside the Russians, you'll see, we'll be free.
We embrace, we are all in a state of mad happiness. We sing all the national anthems loudly: Romanian, the Marseillaise, God Save the King, the American. We would like to be perfect democrats, but none of us knows The International.
Next day when I enter it, the room where we danced and sang all night, seems strangely sad. Empty glasses and bottles on the floor. Shafts of dusty light struggle through the thick curtains. The cigarette butts give off an acrid, musty odour. I open all the windows wide and search for music, any music, on the radio. Anything to interrupt and break this strange and sinister spell. I go into the yard, calling Coca and the rest to help me clean up. The first to appear is Jana, in a night gown. She mumbles, crying:
– Paris was liberated.
Jana spent her youth there. I have never been to Paris, but my throat tightens and the earlier sadness gives way to great happiness. I leave Jana stupefied with happiness repeating: "Paris was

---

[4] 23rd of August, 1944: the day of the coup d'état initiated by the young King Michael I of Romania against Marshall Ion Antonescu, as a result of which Romania broke the alliance with Germany and joined the Allies. From then on the Romanian army fought against Nazi Germany until the end of WWII on May 9th, 1945. Between 1948 and 1989 the communists unjustly took credit for initiating the coup. They proclaimed the 23rd of August as the Romanian national holiday.

liberated," and run to tell the others. I find Coca in front of the door talking to Tudor, who has just arrived. They are both agitated and waving their arms. I yell from afar:
– Paris was liberated!
– I know, says Tudor, but we'll enjoy that later. For the moment try to wake up this fool who doesn't want to understand.
– Why wake her up?
– Because you must go to the countryside.
– You want to get married in the countryside, in an idyllic setting?
– Don't be stupid, the Russians are coming!
– Big news. We know it too, believe me. The Russians are our allies. The war is over. The armistice has been signed. No more camouflage, no more bombing. Here is the full communiqué. See, we are up to date too.
– Another fool! Understand, woman, things are not as simple as we thought. I hope that we haven't been happy for nothing, but, for the moment, everybody goes to the countryside. The Russians are going to pass through Câmpulung. Dress quickly and don't ask me anything. We must leave, I have an order to take you all. An order, understand?

I look at him carefully. He left at dawn happy, and now the look in his eyes has changed. Order? Another move? I don't understand what's going on. I still have in me a sort of light. I can't analyze anything. Nevertheless, I feel that days and nights with a wind of madness are coming.

✦

Half an hour later we and our luggage get into Tudor's car. We don't know where we are going; we don't know for how long we are going to be gone; we don't even know if we can laugh about this new and absurd adventure.

✦

Jana, Coca and I have a quiet room in a peasant's house. In the other room lives an old woman. Her only son is "somewhere on the front". A childhood friend of Sandu. I still don't understand what we are doing here, even though we arrived three days ago. We don't talk much, we watch the scenery, by now very familiar, through the windows. The men commute between Câmpulung and this god-forsaken place. Even when they are here we almost don't see them. The house has no electricity for the radio; they go to listen to the news at the Town Hall and then come to tell us.

✢

The fourth night since we arrived. After all that has happened, every nightfall stirs up our emotions, due to the darkness and to our imaginations running wild. A dull noise, then a light at the backyard gate. We get up. I grab Jana's hand. The Russians? Quiet. Voices, actually only one very low voice, Sandu's. Face drawn, in semi-darkness, it is almost unreal. He has come from Câmpulung and tells us the news very slowly, as if he is afraid we won't hear it.

The Germans have been bombing Bucharest for four days. For a day they controlled Băneasa airport; now they have the one in Buzău[5], and can thus, taking turns, bomb Bucharest twenty-four hours a day. They hit the Royal Palace, the University, the North Station, the neighbourhoods around Cișmigiu[6], they destroyed the National Theatre. More damage than in five months of American bombing! Our troops fight against them around Bucharest, which is surrounded.

Suddenly I am engulfed in visions: Cișmigiu, my street, my streets; dust settling over all that was. Jana is sobbing. Suddenly we don't belong in this room; we all leave, only in our imagination of course. For all the other departures, the real ones, we must first wait for the Russians to pass through.

The rumours that circulate from village to village are faster than

---

[5] Buzău: town ca. 110 km north-east of Bucharest, near the border of Romania's old historical provinces of Muntenia (Wallachia) and Moldova (Moldavia).

[6] Cișmigiu: large park in the center of Bucharest, designed in the 19th century by German landscape architects.

In the Beginning Was the End

the Russians, so we learn about a sort of an invasion of savages very much unlike the allied and friendly army promised by the radio communiqués. We hear about rapes, serial robbery. Maybe they are only rumours. More convinced than us, the men took the car engine out, broke and damaged a few parts here and there, and put the car in the barn between two pigs and a cow. We curse them. We think it would have been better to take the car and go to Bucharest. We make them laugh. They tell us another current rumour, the Russians "rape" three "objects": watches, women and cars.

✦

Jana woke up first that morning. She yells to us to look outside. A number of men riding hunched over small horses, spurring them on; from the horses hang various objects: pieces of carpet, ribbons, dresses, bottles. Some are whipping their horses, yelling.

We are almost amused by the show. They look very much like the pictures in our 8th grade history books: Attila's hordes on their way to Europe.

The voice of the old woman suddenly breaks our contemplation. She seems scared.
– Where are the men?
– At Câmpulung.
Her words remind us that we are in our night-gowns.
– Get dressed immediately. It looks like the invasion of the barbarians. I am going to hide you.

Three minutes later we are ready. We go out into the yard and toward the ice store in the back of the house next to the barn. After she lets us in and has closed the door, the old woman leans for a moment against it and says in a low voice:
– You got in just in time, praise the Lord!

The gate creaks. It's nobody we know, because the dog is barking.

We sit on the ice blocks and cover each other with straw. We mustn't talk. We are so frozen inside that we don't feel the coldness of these ice chairs. The steps in the yard get closer. Instinctively, we grab each other by the hand and form a chain. Each hand almost crushes the other. When the steps move away we release

the hold. We hear the first Russian word: *Davai*[7].
What does it mean? More steps. Pretending that she is quieting the dog the old woman talks loudly, so we can hear her:
– Don't talk. They broke the mirrors in the rooms. They are looking for women. They are drunk. Keep quiet.
The dog barks wildly. A shot from a hand gun. Did they kill the dog? *Davai*. We hear the old woman sobbing.

✢

How long have we been sitting like this, listening to the horses' hooves, the stray shots and these *Davais*? We are paralyzed, inert, afraid. We can no longer keep track of the minutes and hours passing.

Suddenly the door opens. Forgetting prudence, Coca lets out a sort of yell, a deep, throaty sound. In the door frame, lit by a flashlight, are Sandu and the old woman.
– You can come out now.
We get up staggering and try to shake loose the straw covering us. Next to Sandu is a man in a Russian uniform. Sandu laughs sheepishly.
– Stop making these funeral faces. Your host called us at Câmpulung. I went with Tudor to see Şandor. You know, the communist he has been hiding for a month. This officer is a friend of his, a Bessarabian[8].
I asked him to come and "save" you. So here we are.

---

[7] *Davai* : Russian, "come on", or, in this context, "give me".

[8] Bessarabia: historically a Romanian province, part of Moldavia, bordered by the rivers Dnister, Prut, and Danube, and by the Black Sea. The territory was annexed at various times by the Ottoman Empire and Russia, which subjected it to a harsh regime of Russification, especially after 1812. In the secret non-aggression pact signed on August 23rd, 1939 by Germany and the Soviet Union, Hitler accepted the occupation of Bessarabia, then belonging to Romania, by the Soviet army (which occurred on June 28th, 1940). After Romania entered the war in June 1941, Bessarabia was liberated and reintegrated with Romania, but in 1944 Soviet troops occupied the territory again and annexed it to the USSR. Today, the territory belongs in part to the Ukraine and in part to the Republic of Moldova, an independent state that came into being after the dissolution of the USSR.

In the Beginning Was the End

My head is spinning and I lean on the door. I can't follow Sandu's intricate explanations. What counts is that he is here, that the Russian officer came to save us.

Sandu introduces us to the "saviour". The first Russian that doesn't say *Davai*. He speaks Romanian with a strong accent. Blue eyes, cold, impersonal. He apologizes in his own way:

– Evidently, regrettable things happened, but inevitable for any occupation army.

Occupation army?

We follow the old woman into the house to get our luggage. We realize we spent the whole day and part of the night in the ice shed. It must be five in the morning, judging from the pale dawn light. I look at myself in a piece of mirror, my face is very swollen. I am shivering and my teeth are chattering. I look at Jana and Coca: the ice treatment wasn't any better for them either, their faces are round, huge. Coca's face also has a strange greenish hue. She is hobbling, we must help her climb into the truck waiting in front of the gate. The old woman doesn't want to stay behind alone, so she is coming to Câmpulung as well. Going through the yard we see the dog sprawled on the ground, killed by the bullet we heard before. We drag away the old woman, who has started to sob, and climb into the truck.

✢

It has been drizzling for half an hour. The truck is not covered and the rain seeps insidiously through our light clothing. Sandu takes a piece of a Persian rug, shaped like a triangle, from the truck cabin and tries to cover us. The dawn is long this morning, and we are still immersed in a grey light. In the truck, aside from Coca, Jana, Sandu and I, are two Russian soldiers.

Suddenly, Jana starts laughing so loudly that I think she is having a nervous break-down. She points toward one of the soldiers who is admiring with evident satisfaction four watches on his wrist. He checks the time, seemingly comparing the watches, an enchanted, childish smile on his lips. The other seems sadder or older. Anyway, he only has one watch. He gets up, heads toward Jana and asks:

– *Papirosi*?

The second Russian word we have heard in the last twenty four hours. Sandu offers him a cigarette, and I understand the meaning of *papirosi*. But *davai*?

We meet another column of Russian soldiers. There are a few horses loaded with all sorts of objects, pillows on their heads, or covered with rugs, and near them some soldiers, clearly drunk, wobble on their feet and block the road singing to their hearts' desire.

The truck has to stop. Our officer climbs down, takes off his gloves, and starts hitting the drunks conscientiously with his whip; he then climbs back in the truck, puts on his gloves and tells us:

– These are a disgrace to our glorious Red Army.

We start again and speed through empty villages. Houses with open doors, broken windows, seemingly inhabited by ghosts. It's day now, but it is still drizzling.

✢

I have been in bed for the last two days, back in the same room in Câmpulung. The ice treatment didn't suit me. I am shivering, have fever and my face is still swollen.

Coca goes out often with the Russian officer, Tudor and Sandu. Jana goes with them sometimes and at night the two women share the room with me. Coca has decided to join the Patriot's Union, a pro-communist association. Jana doesn't agree, and the two fight late into the night with childish arguments.

Tonight the discussion is heating up and I just can't take it anymore. I get up, put on my coat and go out into the yard. I must go as soon as possible to Bucharest, go back to my life, and find my colleagues, my friends. I have had it with being pushed by events like a leaf in the wind. The current drama of my life seems absurd; I have to put order in my head, which feels like it is splitting.

✢

I take the train with Coca and Tudor. We are squeezed into a third class car. The train stops for hours in small stations to let pass numerous Romanian military convoys heading for the front. At the

In the Beginning Was the End

head of each train a car with the red flag with the hammer and sickle. On the cars, written in chalk: "Long live the Soviet-Romanian Friendship".

Of all the news that circulated on the grapevine in our train, like in a newspaper room, I recall two.

First: Radio Moscow announced three days ago that "the glorious Red Army, after heroic fighting, liberated Câmpulung, chased away the Germans, and was received with flowers by a deliriously happy population."

But I was in Câmpulung. The Germans had left a while ago, there was no fighting, and the population was hiding in their homes after carefully locking their gates. There were, in fact, a few rapes and robberies. Even now "the Glorious Red Army" is responsible, every night, for more of the same. If all the news from Radio Moscow was as truthful as this report, which I was able to check myself...

The second: at Iași, the capital of Moldova[9], Romanian troops, who, following orders, were trying to make contact with the Russian troops, were disarmed by the latter, made prisoners and deported to Russia.

I can't believe it's true; on the other hand I can't convince myself it's pure fantasy either.

The train stops in Chitila[10]; from there we must reach Bucharest on our own.

There are about ten kilometers left. We find a wagon heading toward the city and we settle, Coca, Tudor and I, more or less comfortably amidst the lettuce and the fruit. In the fields, on both sides of the road, corpses putrefy. The uniforms are intact: Germans and Romanians. I don't see any corpses in Russian uniforms. Did they "free" Bucharest like they did Câmpulung?

We cross the outskirts and the working class neighbourhoods... they are almost entirely destroyed. A closet still leans against the only wall of a building without floors. A few women, holding their

---

[9] Moldova (in English, Moldavia): bordered to the west by the Carpathian Mountains and to the east by the river Prut, it is one of the three main provinces of Romania. Not to be confused with the present-day Republic of Moldova, an independent state which came into being after the dissolution of the Soviet Union.

[10] Chitila: small town on the outskirts of Bucharest.

children by the hand, search through the rubble. Telegraph lines and posts form strange geometrical figures, like in an abstract painting. I believe I started crying because Tudor looks at me in a strange way.

I must understand what's happening!

In the Beginning Was the End

III

I have found Bucharest, my house, the shadow of my former life. Dust covers everything. I tear up my false papers, and the memory of my false identity gradually leaves me.

For a few days I immerse myself in this unhoped-for happiness; I straighten everything, clean, touch quietly, taking my time, each object. I restore my soul and my self-image.

And then, suddenly, a strange frenzy takes hold of me that makes me call all over town to try to renew old ties, to reconnect my old life with my present one. I don't find my friends, my colleagues. Has nobody yet returned to Bucharest? After five days as a recluse I realize my wallet is empty. I must find work; anyway, I can't live in this vague and shifting land, lacking reality, that is my current loneliness.

Because the last two nights the streets of Bucharest have been calmer, no more gunshots or cries, I decide to go to my newspaper. There was no answer on the phone, but maybe the lines are cut.

I must have left at nine in the morning on that day.

I walk the streets of bombed houses lit by the autumn sun. The same sun shines on people's faces, people made poor by the bombing and the robberies. They look lonely amidst ruins that seem to ask to be forgotten.

The same sun shines on those in foreign uniforms: the Russians. Men and women soldiers. The women, with round faces and light hair, have old fashioned shoes with high heels. Some wear decorations; strange petticoats show sadly from under their uniforms. They are silk nightgowns. I stop, amazed: one of them has a bra over her military uniform. I feel a sudden pang in my heart and forget the army that robs and steals. I only see these awkwardly stylish women. I try to imagine their life, the clothes they used to wear before the uniforms. Maybe they never had anything but a uniform. I can't distinguish one from the next, they seem to me interchangeable.

I leave and cross Cişmigiu. Autumn is already in charge here. A few steps before I reach the newspaper's building, my heart starts beating wildly.

On the first floor I bump into somebody who starts yelling:
– You are alive!
I recognize Gheorghe in an officer's uniform.
– Don't go. There's nobody there. I don't know if the journal can continue. All the editors have been mobilized.
– I wanted to restart my column.
– You want to work?
– Yes.
– Come with me to *Viitorul* [11].
– It's a political journal.
– So what?
– I have never been involved with politics.
– What the hell did you do in Câmpulung?
– Leaflets!
– You don't think that's politics?
– No, politics is a subtle mixture of deals and lies.
– It's a rather limited point of view. Come anyway to *Viitorul*. Maybe you can do the movie column even in a political paper. Even if you don't find work you can see the office; it looks very much like ours; all, including the director, are young and know how to write.
– All right, let's go. Anyway, I have been looking for well-informed people who can explain the political situation to me.
– We'll do everything to make your mind clear.
And we leave, arm in arm, laughing.

✦

We climb two floors and enter a small room. Only one table. With an ashtray overfilled with cigarette butts in front of him, a man writes and pays no attention to us. Gheorghe says hello... the man keeps writing and smoking. Gheorghe motions to me to sit

---

[11] *Viitorul* (The Future): official newspaper of the National Liberal Party.

In the Beginning Was the End

down and disappears next door. I am almost grateful to Gheorghe for leaving me alone, and to the important and quiet man for keeping writing without looking at me.

I rediscover the atmosphere of a newspaper office and I am very moved. One can't explain this atmosphere; you feel it or you don't, that's it. Paper crumpled in balls on the floor, smoke-saturated air, cigarette butts, the man writing hurriedly... the whole forms a unity that helps me find myself more than the past eight days of loneliness and reflection.

Gheorghe opens the door and motions to me to follow him. I leave the man devoured by the sacred fire and enter a better lit room. Gheorghe introduces me to two young men who are talking. The first, wearing glasses, offers a cigarette. The second brings a chair and invites me to sit. They keep talking.

– You know very well that on August 28th Radio London aired a long commentary about the *New York Times* military column.

– Baldwin[12]?

– Yes, Baldwin. He thinks The Reich will be not able to replace the thirty Romanian divisions and its own units lost in this fight. According to him, Romania switching sides is one of the decisive blows suffered by the Reich.

Gheorghe breaks in:

– Also on September 15th Radio Moscow aired a commentary from the *Yorkshire Post* about the armistice signed between the Romanian Government and the governments of Great Britain, the United States and the Soviet Union. The commentary says that the armistice is not inspired by the idea of revenge. The Soviet government wants only one thing: the security of Romanian territory.

– The writer from the *Yorkshire Post* didn't see the entrance of the Soviet troops into Bucharest. On the morning of August 31st in Bucharest there were only German prisoners. And not one German soldier capable of fighting! Under these conditions, why did Radio Moscow announce that very evening that Bucharest had been liberated? Liberated by whom?

---

[12] Hanson W. Baldwin (1903-1991): military expert for the *New York Times* and author of several books on WWI and WWII, won the Pulitzer prize for his reporting in 1943.

– Don't you know how Câmpulung was liberated? I was there, and...

Gheorghe scowls at me, as if to say: "You are an idiot who doesn't understand anything. Shut up!"

I sink deeper in my chair and shut up. The man who looks like a Protestant pastor with glasses raises his voice.

– I realize our country is defeated, but this doesn't justify lies. Why does Radio Moscow announce they liberated towns that weren't occupied in the first place? Look, I have here a report describing the Radio London program of September 25th, which contained Sam Watson's article from the *Manchester Guardian*. It can already be clearly seen that Romania's switching sides will have extraordinary repercussions for the whole of South-East Europe. Bulgaria's position is becoming very precarious: the German-oriented Sofia regime fell in one night.

My courage is renewed, even Gheorghe's furious looks can't stop me. I break in:

– Excuse me, but I would like to know exactly how the coup d'état on August 23rd happened.

The pastor-like young man explains in a professional tone:

– Immediately after the democratic block was created, the King[13], Maniu[14] and Brătianu[15] entered talks with Great Britain

---

[13] Michael I of Romania (b. 1921): King of Romania between 1927-1930 (under regency) and between 1940-1947. In 1944, at the age of 23, King Michael secretly negotiated with the Allies and proceeded to lead the coup against Marshall Antonescu, thus aligning the country with the Allied forces, and, according to some historians, helping to shorten the war by six months. For this act, King Michael was awarded the Legion of Merit by the United States and the Order of Victory by the Soviet Union in 1946. However, on December 30th, 1947, under threat of civil war, King Michael I was forced by the communists to abdicate. He took residence in Switzerland and was not allowed to return to Romania until 1992.

[14] Iuliu Maniu (1873-1953): leader of the National Peasant Party. Prime Minister of Romania in the interwar period. Arrested by the communists in 1947, he was sentenced to life imprisonment and died in the Sighet prison, located in the north of Romania, on the border with the Ukraine, where the communist authorities imprisoned the former Romanian political elite.

[15] Gheorghe Brătianu (1898-1953): leader of the Liberal Party, professor and politician. Arrested by the communists in 1950, he died in the Sighet prison, as did numerous other democratic politicians.

In the Beginning Was the End

and the United States, and Lucrețiu Pătrășcanu[16], in turn, with the Soviet Union, to prepare the armistice. In April 1944, Molotov[17] had declared that "The Soviet Union has no intention to annex Romanian territories, to change the existing social order, or to intervene in Romania's internal affairs. The Soviet government considers, on the contrary, that it is imperative to reestablish, in concert with Romanians, Romania's independence, to free her from the fascist German yoke."

– I know Molotov's statement. I also listen to the foreign broadcasts. What I would like to know is how the coup d'état on August 23rd took place.

They seem to take me for a naive girl or an idiot living on the moon. The young "pastor" continues, slightly irritated:

– I am afraid I can't tell you anything new. On August 23rd the King ordered Antonescu[18] arrested. The palace guard was quite small, and Bucharest was occupied by the Germans.

The new government, headed by Sănătescu[19], informed the Reich's embassy and the commander of the German troops in Bucharest that our country wished to end, by agreement, its relations with the Reich, and that the Romanian Army, ready to defend itself, will not initiate any unilateral actions. The Romanian government would allow German troops to retreat from our territory.

---

[16] Lucrețiu Pătrășcanu (1900-1954): lawyer, communist leader. Minister of Justice during 1945-1948. Accused by his fellow communists, at Stalin's command, of nationalism and conspiracy against the communist government, he was arrested, submitted to an investigation that lasted five years and culminated in a well-publicized show trial, then condemned to death and executed in 1954.

[17] Veaceslav Mihailovici Molotov (1890-1986): real name Skriabin, Soviet politician. Close collaborator of Stalin and one of the main organisers of the mass repressions that took place from the '30s to the '50s. On August 23rd, 1939, Molotov, then foreign minister of the USSR, signed, with Joachim von Ribbentrop, foreign minister of Germany, the German-Soviet non-aggression treaty that established respective zones of influence (the Ribbentrop-Molotov pact).

[18] Ion Antonescu (1882-1946): Marshall of Romania and head of state from 1940 to 1944. He was sentenced to death by the communists and executed in Bucharest after a period of detention in Moscow.

[19] Constantin Sănătescu (1885-1947): army general. After the coup d'état of August 23rd, 1944 he was named Prime Minister and remained so until December 6th, 1944.

41

Adriana Georgescu

The Commander of the German troops gave the King formal assurances not to undertake any hostile actions against our troops. The result? A few hours later, German units attacked and disarmed Romanian units and fired on civilians. The German air force bombed the capital, destroying whole neighbourhoods and especially targeting the Royal Palace. Thus the Reich put itself in a state of war with Romania. As a result, the King ordered Romanian units to fight against German troops on our territory. Currently nineteen Romanian divisions are engaged alongside the Soviet troops against the Reich. Churchill declared in the Chamber of Commons that the armistice, signed on the 12th of September in Moscow, offered Romania favorable conditions. This is a fair summary. Is this what you wanted?

I don't have time to reply. On the doorstep a fairly young man with grey temples smiles at us.

– Still arguing? I always find you making the same comments about the same problems.

Gheorghe introduces me to the director of the paper, Mihai Fărcăşanu, president of *Tineretul Liberal*[20]. I am unable to cut off Gheorghe, who is telling the story about the leaflets in Câmpulung and "my great activities in the resistance". It's absolutely stupid and I want to hide in a dark corner. Mihai Fărcăşanu seems very interested and says he followed my movie columns:

– However, they were becoming completely illegible, he adds.

Gheorghe tries to defend me:

– Sure, they went through censorship.

– Well, miss, if you don't intend to upset the censorship of the Allied Control Commission...

– Allied, that is Russian, breaks in Gheorghe.

– Allied, that is Russian, continued a smiling Fărcăşanu, you can work with us.

– I hope that the Soviet movies are better quality and I won't have to upset anybody, I say, happy to have found work.

– I am sorry, but somebody else is doing the movie column. I need a reporter at the Ministry of the Interior.

– Reporter? But I don't know how to take pictures!

---

[20] *Tineretul Liberal* (The Liberal Youth): organisation of the National Liberal Party.

In the Beginning Was the End

– You won't have to photograph anybody. You will take the news from the Interior Ministry and edit it for the paper. Think about it and give me an answer tomorrow. And he extends his hand. Even before I leave the room they start talking again about the armistice.

✢

I am walking on the street feeling disappointed. I don't see myself becoming a political reporter. I must look for work again. Sad and upset I reach *Calea Victoriei* [21]. I can't cross due to a column of demonstrators waving red flags and yelling: "Long live the Red Army! Long live democracy! Stalin! Stalin! Long live the liberating army!" A young man, red flag in hand, pushes me. He yells louder than the rest: "Long live the Red Army!"

After all the discussions at the paper, I blurt out:

– You couldn't find Romanian flags? Our soldiers fight alongside the Russians. Is this what you call democracy?

– Comrade, grab her. She insulted the Red Army and democracy. You are under arrest. Fascist!

I find the situation funny and I start laughing. People on the street stop and try to pull me from the hands of "the democrats", who grab me and drag me, yelling: "Fascist! Fascist!" As they take me with them, I try to make myself heard:

– I agree to go with you to the police; the inspector will tell you that you can't arrest people without an order.

They don't reply, so I raise my voice louder:

– Do you want to identify yourselves? No? Then you will identify yourselves at the police station.

– What police, you dirty fascist? We will take you to the Russian "tribunal" and shoot you.

– You have read too many detective stories.

– We don't read detective stories! They are decadent. But we will take you to the Russian "tribunal" and shoot you.

– We are in Romania. I don't see a connection between this and the Russian tribunal.

---

[21] *Calea Victoriei*: boulevard that crosses the centre of Bucharest, location of many important public buildings.

Adriana Georgescu

A voice from the crowd yells:
– It's a communist commando. When you see a policeman ask him to intervene and stop these hooligans. You are wasting your time talking to them.

I don't see any policemen. On the way people stop, astounded. We probably form an odd group: I, my hair in disarray, struggling, and the four young men dragging me, waving red flags. I start to lose my patience:

– Listen, I am a lawyer, I know that nobody can be arrested without an order.

– You are a fascist.

– How do you know?

– You said that this is not democracy.

– Yes, I did and I repeat it. You are free to demonstrate for the Red Army and for Stalin, but in my opinion, I think you can also demonstrate for the Romanian Army which is fighting together with the Red Army. It's my opinion and I have the right to express it, even if you don't agree.

– You don't have the right to talk like this.

– I am using the same tone of voice you are using. Instead of being on the front, you are marching in a disorderly manner on Calea Victoriei yelling. It's your right to love the Red Army.

– So you don't love the Red Army, you dirty fascist!

– I didn't say that. But...

– Comrade agitator, don't let her talk. She is under arrest!

– In its declaration, Sănătescu's government promises a democratic regime, in which public freedoms and citizen's rights will be respected. You have communist representatives in Sănătescu's government!

– Yes, but we want to have more.

– Wait for the elections.

– Before the elections we want a completely communist government.

– But the communist party doesn't have more than a thousand members in the whole of Romania! Were you born in Romania?

– Aha! You are racist.

– I am not racist. I only think that with such shock teams you are helping neither the communist party, nor the cause of Romanian-

Russian friendship. You must in fact prove to us that Russia is our friend.
– Of course she is our great friend and ally, her army liberated Bucharest.
– Let's forget this false detail, but you....
– Comrade agitator, shut her up. She will talk at the Russian "tribunal".
– I don't understand Russian.
– Your sentence will be translated.

Trying to out-yell each other, we reach Piața Victoriei where I finally see a few policemen. I call to them and try to free myself. The policemen intervene. I show them my papers and a policeman asks the four agitators, suddenly quiet, to do the same. The enlarged group heads toward the police station, the four agitators protesting.

– Comrade policeman, we have orders from the head of the demonstration to take this fascist to the Russian "tribunal".
– You will talk to the inspector.

I breathe more easily, relieved. They have let go of my arm, I walk slightly ahead of them. My agitators don't seem eager to get there. After he asks us to write our statements, the inspector talks to the four "agitator comrades from Shock Troop Nr.5".

– I read in your statement that the young lady is reactionary, a fascist and an agent of Anglo-American imperialism. Russia is still an ally of those two countries, isn't it?

"The comrades" reply in unison:
– The Anglo-Americans are imperialists.

The inspector doesn't seem to want to keep the discussion going and asks us to go home. I ask him for a policeman to escort me. The team starts yelling again:
– You can ask for all the policemen in the world to escort you. We'll find you even in a snake's hole. Dirty fascist!

The inspector wants me to help write up a report about the threats. I refuse and leave the police station.

I get home around four in the afternoon and decide to become a political reporter for *Viitorul*. Next day I start my new profession.

IV

I divide my time between the tribunal, the Ministry of the Interior, and the newspaper. Meanwhile the Sănătescu government is replaced and on the 6th of December General Rădescu becomes prime-minister.

There is a new team at the Interior Ministry: Rădescu is also minister for internal affairs. Of the four undersecretaries, one, Dimitrie Nistor, is liberal, another, Teohari Georgescu[22], communist. I go to the Interior once a day and become used to seeing ministers in the flesh. I also see what's going on in Bucharest, and that is a lot less fun.

The communists hold demonstrations almost daily. The members of the trade-union committees are not elected by secret ballot, but instead by raising of hands. In factories workers protest, asking for a secret vote. The communists then call in armed agitators to assist at the vote by raising of hands. The workers don't have arms, and even if they did, it would be useless.

Soviet patrols are all over. The Romanian army is on the front. The communist party, backed by the Red Army, can do as it pleases.

After the trade-union committees have been replaced by this democratic procedure, terror comes into play. Workers with three absences at demonstrations are fired without notice. The Chamber of Labour postpones all claims *sine die*, and the right to strike has been abolished because "the country is in a state of war and works for the army"...

---

[22] Teohari Georgescu (1908-1976): typesetter, communist from before the legalization of the Romanian Communist Party, Interior Minister (1945-1952). He coordinated the political repression in Romania until 1952, when, following internal power struggles among several communist factions, he was expelled from the party, arrested and investigated (1952-1955). He was rehabilitated by Nicolae Ceaușescu in 1968.

The workers are dragged a few times a week to various demonstrations to ask for a new government and to proclaim death to the Reaction. "Reaction" means anything that is not communist.

At all the meetings of the Council of Ministers the communists in the government deny responsibility for creating this "state within state". And the communist radio station *România Liberă*[23] calls daily for the "democratization" of the army... the same army that is mentioned daily in Marshal Stalin's releases.

✢

The news I have brought for the last week has caused panic at the newspaper. In Moldova, a Romanian province bordering Bessarabia, which had again been taken by the Russians, famine and typhus are raging. The communist shock teams are taking advantage of this to do some good work. Not only in factories, like in Bucharest, but also in local administrations. In each district there is a legal prefect and one named by the communists. Thus there are two prefects, and also two police forces. The land is reallotted by the same shock teams, who want to carry out land reform before the return of the Romanian troops to the national territory. The local population, starving, ravaged by typhus, watches helplessly without much understanding. The methods are indeed completely new.

In the latest meeting of the Council of Ministers, the communists were accused of being responsible for the anarchy reigning in Moldova. The Council decided to send a fact-finding committee into the field in order to reestablish the rule of the law. The communists (who only had one answer to all the accusations: "We are not responsible"), were forced to accept this solution before consulting with their Central Committee. They put two more conditions before agreeing to take part: no journalists were to accompany the committee, and a delay was requested so that they could be vaccinated against typhus.

---

[23] *România Liberă* (Free Romania): official newspaper of the communist Antifascist Patriotic Front, which first appeared clandestinely in January 1943. On August 24th, 1944, the newspaper became legal and henceforth openly expressed the views of the Romanian Communist Party.

The watchword of this meeting of the Council was: "Keeping the absolute secret".

✤

The absolute secret was not kept, and next day the head of *Viitorul* looks for a volunteer to go to Moldova. A volunteer who will be, in theory, the secretary of the liberal minister on the committee, and, in fact, the special envoy of the newspaper. Why a male and not a female secretary? I volunteer.

Three days later, at six thirty in the morning, I introduce myself to Dimitrie Nistor, undersecretary at the Interior Ministry, whom I know because I interviewed him a few days earlier.

Twenty cars are lined up in front of the Interior Ministry. In them are not only representatives of the parties in the government "of wide democratic concentration", but also doctors, agronomists, and technicians who are to reestablish "democratic order" in Moldova.

I give my luggage to the driver and climb into the liberal minister's car, together with the undersecretary of the Army, General Puiu Petrescu, and a socialist undersecretary, who seems very preoccupied with his party's organization in Moldova.

It's very cold – we are in the middle of December – we cover ourselves up as well as we can. Dimitrie Nistor explains to me the situation in detail as we go through destroyed villages and frozen fields. The trip seems endless.

We stop in Focşani[24], the first district capital where we are to "reestablish order". The official speech is given by the legal prefect. The communist one is not there. Dimitrie Nistor gives the government's message. District elections not being possible for the moment, two members from each party represented in government are invited to talk with the guests from Bucharest.

The committee sits behind a large table. In front, ten chairs are lined up waiting for their occupants: two from each party: national-peasant, liberal, communist, socialist, *Frontul Plugarilor*[25].

---

[24] Focşani: town ca. 160 km north-east of Bucharest, in Moldavia, not far from Buzău.
[25] *Frontul Plugarilor* (The Ploughmen's Front): small political organisation founded by Petru Groza. It joined the National Democratic Front and was dissolved in 1953.

But, at the last moment, some other people, chairs in hand, show up. They introduce themselves, shouting down the din in the room after their arrival:
Two representatives of the Communist Youth;
Two antifascist women;
Two representatives of the General Confederation of Labor;
Two from the Patriot's Union.

I begin to understand. Since the Romanians had been showing little enthusiasm for the Communist Party, almost overnight there mushroomed a series of organizations, with neutral names, intended to attract the unsophisticated. When people discovered that some of these organizations were fronts of the C.P., the ones that left were arrested by the shock teams. Amateurs beware!

Now, the representatives of these new parties were in front of the committee. The committee – with the exception, of course, of the communists – protests, maintaining that the presence of the "mushroom parties" is illegal since they are not represented in the government.

Emil Bodnăraş[26], the C.P. representative on the committee, starts shouting:

In the name of the Communist Party... blah, blah, blah... long live the Red Army... blah, blah, blah... Long live its glorious leader, Marshal Stalin... blah, blah, blah... In the name of the Central Committee of the C.P., I nominate X for prefect and Y for mayor.

Uproar. The communists are chanting: "Stalin, Stalin". From the street we can hear the steps of the Russian patrols watching over the committee.

I am sitting a little to the side to take notes. I sense a presence behind me. Somebody is leaning over to see what I write. I turn my head. A young woman with green eyes and a calm demeanor. I look at her, wondering:

---

[26] Emil Bodnăraş (1904-1976): army officer who deserted the Romanian army in order to join the Soviet secret service. After being trained by the Soviets, he secretly returned to Romania, where he was arrested and sentenced to ten years in jail. He escaped in 1943. Actively involved in the coup d'état of August 23rd, 1944 as a representative of the Romanian Communist Party, he was Secretary of Defense between 1947-1955 and played a decisive role in the restructuring of the Romanian army based on the Soviet Red Army.

— I am Ana Toma[27], comrade Bodnăraş's secretary. And you?
— Mr. Dimitrie Nistor's secretary. Can you explain to me why Mr. Bodnăraş and his fellow party member, Mr. Vlădescu-Răcoasa, disappeared a few minutes before the start of the meeting and why their return was followed by the appearance of all those people with chairs in hand? Don't you think that by acting this way Mr. Bodnăraş is trying to influence the committee, which, thus, becomes useless?
— Comrade Bodnăraş is free to contact party representatives.
— You know very well that the other delegates don't act in this way.

Ana Toma doesn't answer. She sits not too far from me and starts to take notes. My notes will become newspaper reports, which I'll phone in to Bucharest, and which will appear in *Viitorul*. Ana Toma's notes will be discussed, worked over by the Central Committee and sent to Moscow. Just a matter of nuance.

✢

Second stop: Botoşani[28]. Same routine. During the discussions, we can't get anything from the communists but the same slogans, which by now we know by heart. At lunch, in order to establish a relaxed, working atmosphere, we don't discuss anything. Anyway, I always arrive when it is time for dessert. I come from the post office, where I phone in my report. I always list at the end of the report the names of the newly elected prefects and mayors. They were, without fail, members of FND (National Democratic Front[29]), in other words: communists.

---

[27]Ana Toma: communist activist before and after the legalization of the Romanian Communist Party, wife of Sorin Toma, Editor in Chief of the communist newspaper *Scânteia* and an NKVD secret agent. She became Ana Pauker's chief of staff.

[28] Botoşani: town ca. 420 km from Bucharest in the north-east of Romania, at the center of the historical Romanian province of Moldova (Moldavia).

[29] National Democratic Front or *Frontul Naţional Democratic (FND)*: political coalition launched by the Communist Party on September 26th, 1944 with the publication of a common platform. Although it was asserted that the new alliance would represent the views and opinions of all left-leaning parties and organisations, in reality its aim was to allow the communists to control and assimilate the other political groups.

At the other end of the line, my colleague from the newspaper wonders:
– Why does the FND win all the votes?
– Very simple. Listen. The communists don't want secret ballots. They seem to like voting only by raising of hands. And even with secret ballots, the intruders invited by Bodnăraş, who arrive with their own chairs, form an overwhelming majority.
– Are the other ministers asleep? Why don't they protest? Why don't they return to Bucharest instead of continuing with this useless trip?
– Because the election of mayors and prefects must be ratified by the Council of Ministers after they return. One positive result could be a deep understanding of the operating methods of the C.P. As for the sanitary investigation...
– The Red Cross sent medicine...
– The communists take their cut from the sanitary trains and trucks. The medicine is then sold on the black market. Many of those trucks are commandeered and sent to Reni and Russia.
– Well played, I say. How is Bodnăraş?
– Always gloomy. His favorite topic of discussion: "How I escaped from the Aiud prison[30]." He doesn't say anything about his time in Moscow. Shouts with conviction the party watchwords. Wears a very reactionary golf suit. Appearance more German than Russian.
– The bottom line?
– Zero. If the Russians hadn't opposed district elections because of the state of war...

✢

The routine is the same in each district, disgustingly the same: in front of the committee, representatives of the democratic parties express their point of view about reorganizing the district, naming, usually, apolitical, but well-prepared people. The communists and their

---

[30] The Aiud prison: one of the harshest prisons during the communist regime, situated in the town of Aiud, in the county of Alba, Transylvania. Considered a maximum security prison, it was located in an old jail built by the Austrians at the end of the 18th century.

followers recite a lesson they know by heart, the watchwords being Stalin and the glorious Red Army. Real parrots.

Iaşi, the capital of Moldova. Bodnăraş nominates Mr. Alexiuc for prefect. Mr. Răutu, from the National Peasant Party[31], stands, scared:

– Listen, Mr. Bodnăraş, we cannot go on like this. It is not possible to nominate in Iaşi, the cradle of Romanian culture, a man with only an elementary education and who is also not from the district. It's against all our laws.

– You mean, against all reactionary laws?

Everybody starts shouting. And suddenly, seemingly by pure chance, bullets shatter the windows, ending up in the walls. They are shooting above us, there are no wounded. The meeting is adjourned without reaching an agreement.

As I am about to leave to phone in my report, the driver bursts into the hall and blurts out, with a desperate air on his face:

– Miss, when these scoundrels started shooting, I ran. They ransacked the car and took your luggage and overcoat. I saw them, I wanted to chase them, but they started shooting.

I especially regret losing my "travel journal" with my impressions of Moldova, I intended to use them for the conclusions of my articles. The luggage, the coat... no big deal. Professional risks of a special envoy.

✦

I was left in a blouse. Ana Toma loans me a red sweater and a windbreaker.

Ana Toma is a good mate. She is a communist by conviction; did two months in prison, suffered for her faith, and for that she probably intimidates me a little. We get along fairly well, if we avoid political discussions. But it's almost impossible to avoid political discussions.

---

[31] The National Peasant Party, or *Partidul Naţional Ţărănesc*, came into being on October 10th, 1926, when the Peasants' Party, founded in 1919 and led by Ion Mihalache, joined the National Party led by Iuliu Maniu. Mr. Maniu became president of the newly formed entity. On the center-right, the NPP represented the interests of the developing middle-class. In 1946 the NPP won the national elections, but the results were falsified by the communists, who abolished the NPP a year later and put its leaders in jail.

In the Beginning Was the End

In the evening, after what happened at Iași, we share the same room. Despite being tired – after leaving Bucharest I haven't slept more than four hours a night – we can't fall asleep. Inevitably, we start talking. I try to explain to her that by continuing on this path the C.P. risks not having any deputies in the future parliament. Once the war is over, there will be free elections, and then... Ana Toma gets angry:
– It's foolish on your part. You are poor, you work to live, I don't see why you are in a capitalist party.
– The Liberal party made the first agrarian and socialist reforms in Romania.
– That's stupid, you know. You have no future with the liberals. Our party needs young, energetic people. Join us.
– Listen, let's not start again with this discussion that we both know by heart. And, I added laughingly, anyway, you know that I hate slogans.

Quiet. After five minutes she wants to restart the conversation, but I pretend to be asleep.

✣

Next day, after phoning in my report, I find the whole committee very agitated. Emil Bodnăraș shouts louder than the rest:
– Who is the special envoy from *Viitorul*?
– I am.
– I didn't expect this from you. I thought you were loyal. In *Scânteia* [32] there is not one note, not a single line about this mission entrusted to us by the government.

To hear Bodnăraș talking about loyalty is quite funny.
– You talk to me about loyalty, you who call followers, whom you have bought the day before, in order to obtain a majority of the votes, you who name unknown prefects from a list furnished previously by the Central Committee? You are getting angry be-

---

[32] *Scânteia* (The Spark): one of the most important communist newspapers in Romania. It appeared only clandestinely and sporadically before August 23rd, 1944, and its importance before and during the war was much exaggerated by later communist propaganda. Its first legal issue came out on the 21st of September, 1944. It ceased to exist in December 1989.

cause I dare to be a journalist. Your party mate, Mr. Lucreţiu Pătrăşcanu, the Minister of Justice, declared in the amnesty decree that public freedoms were reestablished after August 23rd. Freedom of the press is among them. I don't see anything shocking in the fact that my paper is telling this story.

I think I succeeded in making him completely mad.

– You have chosen the worst possible path. You are young, energetic, and are wasting your time with the Liberal Youth that is rotten to the core. I didn't think you were such a reactionary. If you aren't careful you'll end up very badly.

I keep laughing. Bodnăraş' "you'll end up very badly" doesn't scare me. He is a communist. So what? The war will end, the Russians will leave and, without their backing, the communists won't get a single vote in a thousand, for sure. Their attitudes during the last few months, the things that took place under our very eyes, are the best anticommunist propaganda in the world. Emil Bodnăraş can shout all he wants. He makes me laugh. We need to resist until the Russian troops leave. Afterwards this nightmare will end in one night.

✤

Brăila[33]. The last stop before going back. Ana Toma invites me to join her at a Christmas tree celebration organized by her party. She hasn't lost hope of converting me. I am tired of all these useless discussions. Our discourses are so different that conversation is not a dialogue, but two monologues, clearly separated, like two parallel lines. We will never meet. I refuse to join her.

She seems amazed. I tell her that I am not feeling well, that the typhus epidemic depresses me, that urgent measures must be taken to stop it, instead of all these endless discussions. Unperturbed, she answers that the typhus was brought to Moldova by the fascists and the reactionaries. She looks at me with the same impassive face she had yesterday when listening to the reports of the desperate physicians: in each district there are at least ten thousand cases of typhus, the famine is so great that the peasants are

---

[33] Brăila: town ca. 200 km from Bucharest in the south-east of Romania, port on the Danube.

In the Beginning Was the End

making bread out of the tree bark. I repeat these facts, but instead of answering she starts talking about Ana Pauker[34].

She is her best friend. No, not friend, her guardian angel. Generous, without ambitions, Ana Pauker didn't enter the government because she prefers to work from the shadows for the good of the Romanian people. Listening to Ana Toma, one can almost see the image of an apostle walking barefoot, in rags, in order to serve the Romanian people and sacrifice herself for them. I shrug. I am too tired to answer. I let Ana Toma go alone and write conclusions about the trip for the newspaper.

A knock in the door. I am afraid it's Ana Toma again, here to indoctrinate me. No, it's some children with a big star, made of colored paper, showing the manger. They stand in the middle of the room and start singing naive carols announcing the birth of Christ. I think I must have started crying, because they stop singing and look at me astounded. I give them apples and biscuits and they leave. It's snowing. I light a cigarette and start writing again, feverishly.

✢

Return to Bucharest. My newspaper mates carry me triumphantly through the office. It's a success. *Viitorul* was the only paper to be informed about the situation in Moldova. Mihai Fărcăşanu comes and gives me a solemn hug. I feel like I am becoming a great character, but I can't get myself in the right mood and laugh as I should. I can still hear the voice of a communist who, taking me for one of them, gaily offered to show me the prefect's office in Brăila.

– Welcome comrade, he said.
– Thanks comrade, I replied, playing the game. How are things going?
– Rolling. The Red Army is backing us strongly...

---

[34] Ana Pauker (1894-1960): Romanian Jewish communist leader, imprisoned in the interwar period. Freed on the basis of a prisoner exchange agreement between Romania and the Soviet Union, she left for the USSR, from where she returned to Romania with the Soviet troops. Together with Vasile Luca, Teohari Georgescu and Gheorghe Gheorghiu-Dej, she headed the Romanian Communist Party in the post-war period. Foreign Minister of Romania (1947-1952), she was removed from power in 1952 by her fellow communists with Stalin's agreement.

V

I start again my daily route from the Ministry of Interior to the newspaper and back. The weather remains frosty and I wear a windbreaker. I can't afford a new overcoat though. I try to compensate by bundling up in a number of sweaters of different colors.

Wearing this rather odd outfit three days after returning I show up at the Chief of Cabinet of the Interior Ministry. He receives me smiling, which is rather unusual for him. He shakes my hand and congratulates me for my Moldova feats. Lucrețiu Pătrășcanu is also present and gives me a sidelong glance.

The Chief of Cabinet tells me:

– I am going to introduce you to General Rădescu.

I had felt that I had moved up in rank, but not quite that much.

– Do you think General Rădescu would grant me an interview?

– You'll see. Take a seat.

– But you told me, a month ago, that audiences have to be arranged a few weeks in advance.

– We'll make an exception for you.

It starts becoming all too real. I mumble:

– Couldn't you make an appointment for tomorrow? How am I going to show up in front of the General in three-quarter length stockings?

– Do you want to interview him, or don't you? I warn you: don't call him "Excellency". He doesn't like it. Call him "Mr. General".

General Rădescu never gives interviews. It's an unhoped-for opportunity. Still I insist.

– Make an appointment for tomorrow; I would like to think about the questions to ask him.

But the Chief of Cabinet isn't listening to me anymore. He pushes a button, and calls. Lucrețiu Pătrășcanu glances at his watch and leaves, saying he will return in half an hour. The Chief of Cabinet

In the Beginning Was the End

disappears also into the adjoining room. I am left alone in the office, where two phones break, at regular intervals, the rather official silence. I would very much like not to be here! The door opens wide, I hear my name pronounced solemnly by the Chief of Cabinet, who remains standing stiffly in the doorway.

I enter the Prime-Minister's office. Behind a desk laden with papers, a tall, thin, gray-haired man, in uniform, without decorations. I have in front of me the man who wrote an open letter to Hitler's representative in Bucharest, Baron von Killinger, to protest against the German occupation of Romania and who paid for this with a year of internment. I have in front of my eyes the man who at this moment is confronting the Russians and the C.P. He controls the Ministry of Interior, and because of his firmness the communists haven't been able to get hold of all the key posts and arrest at will all who resist them. If we dare smile, live, and fight, it is because he is here. It is thus perfectly normal to feel so intimidated. For his part, the General seems quite amazed:

– Are you the special envoy of *Viitorul* in Moldova?
– Yes, Mr. General.
– For a special envoy, you are quite young.
– I am twenty-four, Mr. General.

I am more and more intimidated, and don't have the slightest idea how to start the interview.

– Judging from your reports, you seem very concerned about the situation in Moldova.
– Yes, Mr. General.
– The Germans were looking for you and you were hiding?
– Yes, Mr. General.
– Liberal Youth has brave, energetic people.
– Yes, Mr. General.
– Mihai Fărcășanu has managed to gather around him, at *Viitorul*, a team that make this paper one of the few with standing.
– Yes, Mr. General.

The Chief of Cabinet opens the door and announces Lucrețiu Pătrășcanu.

– I congratulate you, miss. You are doing very well.
– Thank you, Mr. General.

The audience is over, and I haven't been able to get the interview. I can just see it: two columns, on the first page... "Yes, Mr.

General. No, Mr. General". I felt paralyzed, like a soldier presenting arms. I bump into Lucrețiu Pătrășcanu, who enters. The Chief of Cabinet asks:
— Do you have a fever?
Maybe my face is very red.
— I have big news for you.
— Did they give us co-belligerence?
— Not yet. Do you want to be Chief of Staff at the Interior Ministry?
— Are you making fun of me?
— Not at all. We need somebody energetic like you.

I don't understand why, from one day to the next, everybody thinks of me as "somebody energetic ". The Chief of Cabinet continues:
— We'll work together. Give me your address. Tomorrow morning, at eight, I'll send a ministry car for you.
— Can I continue working at the paper?
— Sure.
— OK.

As I leave, I try to maintain a proper attitude and tell myself that my paper will, definitely, be the best informed from now on.

✢

My colleagues from the paper celebrate the event by giving me a coat. By subscription, of course.

✢

Since I have become Chief of Staff I haven't managed to read any books. Instead, I read the daily press and radio bulletins and all the papers. To be a perfect Chief of Staff you have to smile all the time. When I have a headache, I smile. When I am penniless, I smile. When I am ill, I smile. A true life-style. A smile is the most necessary and precious weapon in such a job. If I didn't smile, the opponents of the government would think the situation is desperate. Anyway, all the smiles in the world couldn't improve it.

I don't have a free moment. It's a struggle to find the time to go

In the Beginning Was the End

to a press conference called by Petru Groza[35], Vice-President of the government and chief of *Frontul Plugarilor*.
I arrive late. I get out of the car in front of a huge villa. A lackey opens the door. The Chief of Protocol announces, moving a very theatrical red curtain:
– Representative from *Viitorul*.
I go into a sumptuous salon, twenty people stand up. Only men. I see some well-known journalists. Petru Groza, all smiles, receives me and says, shaking my hand:
– Always clever, these liberals. They send us a woman journalist. Beautiful also. Miss, take a seat next to me. We'll preside over the meeting together.

Petru Groza has a square head. He looks like a peasant dressed in city clothes, making desperate efforts to seem at ease. He is one of the richest men in Romania, but his main claim to fame is a month spent in prison, from where he got out due to Iuliu Maniu's intervention. If he had relations with the communists during the war, he did it mostly for personal advantage and to increase his fortune. He took advantage of the persecution of the Jews and the nationalization of their properties: a bank and a liqueur factory became his. This in turn for a few meetings held by the communists in his house during the war. Due to this "fight for the people" he became *persona grata* in Moscow. Not intelligent. The classical psychology of the parvenu who, suddenly inheriting a huge fortune, wants to become famous and have his picture in the papers. Moscow made his dream possible, and Groza shows his gratitude by blindly following orders he does not even try to understand. I sit next to him, annoyed by his jokes that I don't appreciate in the slightest. Petru Groza continues the meeting by insulting Maniu and Brătianu. For the rest, more of the same, all the non-communists in the government get their share of the classic insults: fascists, reactionaries, rotten bourgeois, etc. Finally he gets to the point of the conference:

---

[35] Petru Groza (1884-1958): lawyer, owner of country estates, factories, banks, and hotels, long-time president of the Romanian industrialists' association. Although not formerly a member of the Communist Party, he was a sympathiser and became Prime Minister of Romania between 1945-1952, and President of the Great National Assembly between 1952-1958.

– Transylvania will not be granted to us until Romania has a democratic government. The same goes for co-belligerency.

Nicolae Carandino, head of the paper *Dreptatea*[36] intervenes:
– Co-belligerency will be granted for our military effort. We have already lost 65,000 soldiers in Transylvania. Transylvania belongs to us, you know it, Excellency. You also know that Transylvania was taken by Hitler in July 1940. Have you forgotten this, Excellency?

The journalists applaud. Petru Groza turns red and says, laughing:
– I see you are Maniu's favorite colt. We'll see who is right. Because, you know, gentlemen, I have a very favorable horoscope. I was gifted with a good wife, good children, and a good fortune.

And, throwing a meaningful look at a picture placed in full view on the table showing a famous music-hall star smiling broadly:
– And for the rest I can't complain either.

Moment of general stupefaction. The heads of the largest newspapers in Bucharest have come to this press conference. I think it is the first time they hear and see a minister like this. But, unruffled, Petru Groza continues his insults. We all have the impression we are hearing the editorial of the C.P. newspaper *Scânteia* being read aloud. After he finishes playing his political part, Petru Groza offers us a glass of wine. We go to a dining-room in authentic Renaissance style. Petru Groza's modest "glass of wine" turns out to be champagne and caviar. Petru Groza plays the host, encouraging us:
– Help yourselves, help yourselves. There is more, you know.

He comes to the group I am in and starts telling off-color jokes. I find a reason to excuse myself, and go down the stairs. I cross paths with Miron Constantinescu, editor in chief of *Scânteia*, who says, ironically:
– The liberals have had it.
– Sure, in such a proletarian house!

I finally breathe the cool night air. I am divided between nausea and a desire to laugh. I ask myself if this person treats the grave matters in front of the Council of Ministers in the same fashion.

---

[36] *Dreptatea* (The Justice): official newspapaer of the National Peasant Party, abolished in August, 1947.

In the Beginning Was the End

Petru Groza being too stupid to be funny, I consider the night totally lost. Back home, I write a dull note for the paper. If I wrote to my heart's desire I would be censored by the Allied Control Commission. "Allied, that is Russian", as my colleagues at the paper would say.

✦

When I arrive that morning at *Viitorul*, I find the office turned upside down. Mihai Fărcășanu is calling right and left. Gheorghe is talking with some workers, doors are slammed. I run to Fărcășanu who explains to me between two phone calls what happened.

Some communist printers have decided, on their own, to be censors, and, as they didn't like some of the articles, have refused to print them and have decided in a night meeting to suppress the paper.

We don't even have time to get upset. We have to hurry. Within an hour we have reached by phone and bicycle courier enough young members of the party who know something about printing. They come running. After another hour, the two office rooms are filled with volunteers. I go with them into the basement where they divide up the work.

I only came for half an hour, but end up staying two. I leave at a run for the Interior, promising to spend the night with them helping.

Next day *Viitorul* is printed, and I see off the team of volunteers that does the distribution.

I breathe relieved as if after a night of struggle. I fall into a chair, but get up immediately as if pushed by a spring. I must be at the Interior at eight. I run there, drink coffee after coffee, and, while the phones ring at regular intervals, I automatically make appointments and wear my eternal smile to receive "comrade minister" Teohari Georgescu, who, as always, scowls at me while asking to see the General.

✦

Monday, February 12th, I arrive at the office very tired. I had planned to rest the day before but I was busy all day with the speech

General Rădescu gave at the Aro cinema. The meeting was supposed to take place at the Scala cinema, but the communists, who had decided to hinder the speech by all means, hired some people for 2000 *lei* a head, plus the money for the movie ticket for the last evening show. Afterwards, the spectators, instead of leaving, stayed put. Just like that. Around midnight, a truck bearing the inscription "Patriotic Defense", stopped in front of the theater. A few volunteers unloaded food, and the people in charge distributed it in the hall "for the night". Warned, the police let them sleep quietly in the hall where the prime-minister was to speak the next day. So General Rădescu spoke at the Aro cinema, a few hundred meters away from the Scala. Those who came to listen to him had only to make a few more steps. Thus they could listen to the Prime-Minister summarize two months of government. Well played.

The foreign press correspondents who first went to the other hall started their articles like this:

"In a stifling atmosphere, about a thousand men keep drinking *ţuică* [37]. The people in charge climb on the seats yelling: «Hey, comrade, do you have enough bread?»"

My desk is laden with newspapers and, as the General has not arrived yet, I start writing the press bulletin for him. The communist press violently attacks Rădescu and his speech. I look it over. The same well-known arguments. I read the communiqués and sum up:

"In the Tatra Mountains, Romanian troops advance."

The phone rings. A newspaper head. Wants to know if there is anything new with co-belligerency. No, nothing. Everybody is obsessed by this matter. Today, three long articles in *Dreptatea*, *Viitorul* and *Scânteia*.

Dreptatea writes:

We made commitments and we will keep them. No matter the sacrifices, and efforts. We want to be appreciated for our efforts to fulfill our commitments. We want Romania and her brave people to be given co-belligerent status. A country whose war effort is considered fourth after that of the United States, Russia and Great Britain, a country that was the first to break with the Axis Powers,

---

[37] *ţuică*: Romanian home-brewed plum brandy.

In the Beginning Was the End

a country that thus contributed to the changes in Bulgaria and Finland, a country that joined the brave and glorious Red Army in the greatest offensive in the war to date...

Same tenor in *Viitorul*:

To recognize Romania's co-belligerent status is to give moral support at the right moment to our people, whose deeds bring great service to the allied cause. We trust the spirit of equity of the Allies and hope that at the impending conference of the three great powers Romania's just demand will be examined and will receive the answer it deserves.

Obviously *Scânteia* has a different opinion. I know its point of view, as I heard it expressed by Petru Groza himself in the last days. I read the editorial anyway.

Does Romania currently observe the provisions of the armistice? Of course not. Although, regarding the armed fight, the People make sacrifices by being on the front and in the factories working for the war, almost nothing has been done for democratization, because the Reaction keeps creating hurdles everywhere...

Teohari Georgescu's Chief of Staff interrupts me to tell me that his "comrade minister" wants to be received immediately by the General. I promise to call once the General arrives and go back to the bulletin. The General finally arrives and, while bringing him papers to sign, I tell him that Teohari Georgescu wants to see him.

– He can come.

I call and, five minutes later, Teohari Georgescu enters. I have seen him regularly for a month, but I don't know why today I pay more attention to him: short, bald, obsequious and cheeky at the same time. He doesn't stop, as he usually does, to talk about his great generosity, never proven anyway. Today, he seems in a hurry. I show him into the General's office. Teohari Georgescu greets him in a way that reminds me of a paper accordion suddenly deflating. I foresee a stormy audience because, aside from the affair with the Scala cinema, occupied yesterday by the communists, he has again given orders that run counter to the decisions of the last Council of Ministers.

When, after half an hour, Teohari Georgescu exits the adjoining room, he is red and even more stooped than before. He smiles while passing at Gheorghiu-Dej[38], "the comrade minister" from Communications, who is waiting in my office for his turn. Gheorghiu-Dej has intelligent eyes and an open face. In Moldova, Ana Toma talked about him enraptured: "He is so handsome!"

As he enters in turn to see the General, I motion in vain to him to extinguish his cigarette: the General is ailing and can't tolerate smoke. Gheorghiu-Dej pretends, as always, not to understand. Maybe it is his way of getting back because the General always ends up winning. And, as the audience starts next door, I try to finish my press bulletin.

✢

Two days later, a call from Mihai Fărcășanu to let me know that the incident with the workers is over. I wonder how:
– They came this morning and told me that their salaries are too low and that is why they stopped printing the paper.
– That's an excuse! They never mentioned their salaries when they decided to suppress the paper. Anyway, their salaries were calculated according to the current norm in all printing-houses.
– Exactly, it's a pretext. Invoked now, a week after stopping work. But I took advantage of it. I increased their salaries. They were quite disappointed. You understand?
– Sure.

Sure I understand, I understand it all. The staged occupation of the Scala, Bodnăraș's maneuvers in Moldova, the methods of the communist shock teams, and the politics carried out by the Central Committee of the C.P. Only, for the first time, I feel that the fight is unfair: on one side them, supported by the USSR, with munitions, arms and the Red Army to back them; on the other side us, without arms, munitions, without soldiers in the country, with bare hands and our will to live, to survive. I don't know why, all of a sudden I feel very tired.

---

[38] Gheorghe Gheorghiu-Dej (1901-1965): communist from before the legalization of the Romanian communist party, member of the Central Committee and of the Political Bureau (1945-1965). In June 1952, after his rivals Ana Pauker, Teohari Georgescu and Vasile Luca were removed from power, he became President of the Council of Ministers (1952-1955), and between 1961-1965 he was President of the State Council. He led the party and the country as a stalinist-type dictator, a stance he maintained even after Stalin's death.

In the Beginning Was the End

The phone again. And as I get ready to announce Lucreţiu Pătrăşcanu to the General, I shrug, I almost forgot: he is not here with us. Calling back, I ask in a firm voice for Lucreţiu Pătrăşcanu to come immediately: the General is expecting him.

✢

I have to accompany the General to all the official receptions and, when he cannot go, to represent him and his cabinet. Every time I come back depressed and disgusted with the tense and phony atmosphere. Behind every word, behind every smile of the Soviet officers or important members of the C.P. we feel clearly the dagger strike. In the shadows, something is being plotted. And we, in turn, have to take it, to seem at ease, be friendly. This little game doesn't fool anybody, but it must be played. Requirements of the job.

Today I accompany the General to a reception given by the Soviet embassy. Vinogradov[39] is there. He walks toward the General and shakes his hand effusively. The interpreter is nearby and I hear the translation: "General Vinogradov heartily congratulates General Rădescu for the way he is running the country." I move away and head towards the other end of the hall, where Mihai Fărcăşanu motions to me. I pass behind a group: Bodnăraş and Ana Toma surrounding Ana Pauker. Ana Toma stands straight and stiff, and Bodnăraş almost salutes. Two children on a visit, chaperoned by a dour governess they are afraid of, would not behave any differently. After I pass, Bodnăraş leans toward Ana Pauker and whispers something in her ear. She looks at me now. Ana Toma's guardian angel seems rather angry for an apostle. I finally reach Fărcăşanu. Behind us, Petru Groza introduces René de Weck, the Swiss ambassador, to a Russian general, accompanied by the unavoidable interpreter.

– Mr. René de Weck, the Swiss ambassador, says Petru Groza.
The Russian officer doesn't seem to understand.
– What country?
Unperturbed, René de Weck, replies:

---
[39] L. P. Vinogradov (1895-1967): Soviet general, Deputy Head of the Allied Control Commission in Romania (September 1944 - March 1945.)

– Switzerland. You must know it. The country with the watches. Luckily they are behind me and I can laugh to my heart's desire.

Mihai Fărcăşanu is in a worse position; he makes a few grimaces and adopts a distracted air. He says:
– Bodnăraş and Ana Toma seem to be coming here. I am going! And disappears. I turn and see that Ana Pauker has left. Now, Bodnăraş smiles and Ana Toma shakes my hand.
– You moved up, I hear from Bodnăraş. I told you that you were going to end up badly.

I laugh without replying.
– No, no, breaks in Ana Toma. Let's not lose hope. Why don't you visit me?

We could have a quiet talk.

She hasn't given up trying to indoctrinate me. And, as I still don't say anything:
– Let me give you my address.

But, before she has time to do it, we are told the movie is starting. The pleasures continue. I say good-bye to the two "comrades" and find a seat next to the head of the cabinet. A "cultural" movie starts: a documentary in which some huge snakes wolf down house rabbits and small insects.

Is it a symbol? Lack of tactfulness or just simply a reply to the last documentaries presented by the British mission, documentaries in which "freedom" was the keyword? Anyway, the warning seems barely disguised.

We return to the salons. Champagne flows; the pill must be sweetened.

Viitorul has been suppressed by decision of the Allied Control Commission, "Allied, that is Russian".

✢

The official functions cannot distract our attention from the increasing number of tragedies taking place under our eyes. The most recent is the deportation of Romanian citizens who are ethnic Germans to the work camps in the USSR. We watch, helplessly; this time, nobody has any power. The decision is made and executed directly by the Russians, they accept neither interventions nor appeals. The operation is directed by the NKVD. Romanian soldiers

In the Beginning Was the End

continue to die in the Tatra mountains. The Romanian Army is once again cited in Marshal Stalin's daily order, but co-belligerency is still not granted. We all hope that it will be granted at the Yalta Conference! But the Yalta Conference ended on February 11th and we don't know what was decided.

And thus we come to the end of February 1945.

VI

Entering the General's office, on the morning of February 23rd, I still have on my mind the attack aired yesterday against him by Radio Moscow "in the name of the Romanian people". The General has not arrived yet. I put on his desk the keys to Teohari Georgescu's office. To prevent total anarchy, the State Under-Secretariats were dissolved by the Council of Ministers. Ten days had passed since then, and Teohari Georgescu still continued to come to the office, to make appointments and give orders, as if nothing had happened. The General had therefore asked me to close Teohari Georgescu's office. His Chief of Staff was calmly reading the morning papers. I asked him to take his papers and leave since I had to lock the room. Instead of replying, he started reading in a threatening tone an article on the first page of *Scânteia*.

– Listen. Maybe this will make you think it over. *"Telegram sent by Teohari Georgescu to the prefects and mayors across the country: «By decision of the council of the National Democratic Front, I am and remain in the function I have been entrusted with. I especially bring to your attention the following: do not execute the orders given by General Rădescu and directed against the people. By his dictatorial attitude, General Rădescu has proved himself to be the enemy of the people»."*

– Why do you read me this? It only proves what we already know: that Teohari Georgescu opposes the decisions of the Council of Ministers. Since when has the National Democratic Front, which is only a political organization, had the power to keep ministers in office?

– Since the armistice.

– Excuse me, but that is not true. The King gave General Rădescu a mandate to form the government. This government is legal, and only it can give legal orders.

In the Beginning Was the End

– Rădescu is the enemy of the people.
– That's your opinion, and I don't share it. In any case, Rădescu has not presented his resignation to the King. He is the head of the government.
– He'll be dismissed.
– That's news to me. Who told you? Till then, please, leave the room. I have orders to lock it to prevent your chief from making a fool of himself.

The Chief of Staff stood up, pale. He was waving *Pravda*[40].
– Haven't you read *Pravda*? Obviously, you don't know Russian. I am going to translate for you: *"At the Aro meeting General Rădescu showed his true face. He is an anti-democrat."*
– What about Scala? And the occupation of the hall by the communists. Is that democratic?
– You know we have the means to open the door you are closing today.
– To force the door, you mean. If Teohari Georgescu wants his keys all he needs to do is ask the General for them. They will be on his desk.

The Chief of Staff walked toward me, stopped a step away and said in a suddenly low, threatening voice:
– You are indeed too imprudent, miss.
– I think you are even more so.

He bowed slightly and said, in his everyday voice:
– Goodbye, miss. See you tomorrow.
– Tomorrow, you are not going to be here.
– Exactly. I hope to see you at the formal lunch at the Military Circle. And, this lunch is hosted for the government by the Allied Control Commission.
– I know, but I don't see why you will go: Teohari Georgescu is no longer in the government.

He is on the doorstep now and stares at me:
– Till tomorrow then, miss. At the Military Circle.

When I relate the scene to the General, he replies:
– They'll probably go. As for me, I'm not going.

---

[40] *Pravda* (The Truth): official newspaper of the Communist Party of the USSR. It continues to be published in Moscow.

Adriana Georgescu

✢

Next day, heading to the ministry, I see the street-cars covered with posters: "Death to Rădescu", "Death to Fărcășanu", "Arrest Rădescu", "Down with the government", "Long Live the USSR", "Long Live the Glorious Red Army".
And this Red Army reminds us at the end of the day that the slogans are all too real. Today Soviet tanks cross the city. February 24th is Red Army Day.
I arrive at the ministry. The General is ailing and I am told to suspend all appointments. Radu Ionescu, the head of the Secret Service, enters the room and says calmly:
– I ordered sandwiches for everybody. And tea.
Then, without adding a word, he goes in to the General. I am so astonished that for a moment I don't even answer the phone that is ringing. When I do, I hear Gheorghiu-Dej's voice.
– I want to talk to the Prime-Minister.
– I am sorry, it's not possible. The Prime-Minister is ill.
– But he must come to the Military Circle lunch.
– Unfortunately he won't be able to come. The doctor forbids any movement. You know that for the last few days he has been living in the ministry.
– I am not interested. He must come to the luncheon.
Since returning from Moscow Gheorghiu-Dej has a very self-assured voice. I excuse the General once more, and close just as Petru Groza enters cane in hand.
– I came to take the Prime-Minister to the Military Circle lunch. How will he be dressed? Military or civilian?
– Home clothes. He is ill.
– He isn't dying, I hope? Says Petru Groza, smiling.
– Just the flu.
– I must see him at all costs.
– He won't be able to accompany you.
– Just between us, I would rather have you accompany me, beautiful.
For Petru Groza, all women are "beautiful". I try to control my irritation.
– Thank you, Excellency. I am on duty today.
– If I was a woman, I wouldn't work that much.

In the Beginning Was the End

I remind him of one of the key phrases from his speeches: "Women must be in the work force."
– Yes, but if you don't announce me to the General, you are just a saboteur.
– I only follow my superior's orders, Excellency.
– Is this your last word?
Petru Groza likes definitive sentences.
– Yes, Excellency.
I breathe relieved. He leaves slamming the door.

✢

Radu Ionescu hands me a cigarette. He has left the adjoining room and is talking without looking at me.
– Do you smoke? I just told the General that I have so many volunteer agents that I'll soon have to fire my personnel.
– Those who joined the C.P. pressured by the trade-unions?
– Yes.
He takes another drag of the cigarette and then, suddenly, crushes it in the ash-tray.
– The communists have orders to attack the Interior Ministry today.
– What does the General say?
I can't control the trembling of my voice.
– He is very calm. Anything new here?
– Gheorghiu-Dej has called, and Petru Groza has just left. They wanted to take the General to the luncheon at all costs.
– Did you ask yourself why lunch and not dinner?
I shrug. I avoid talking as much as I can. My voice is trembling too much.
– The communists have orders to attack immediately. Immediately is a few hours after lunch. Obviously it would be better for them if the General wasn't at the Interior at that time. That explains Petru Groza's coming in person.
And, seeing that I keep quiet.
– Come have a sandwich.
– No.
– Yes, you need it. There is also tea in the big audience room.
No time to answer. The phone. I pass the receiver to Radu

71

Ionescu. The colonel that liaises between the government and the Allied Control Commission is calling from the Military Circle to ask if the General has left the Interior.
– The General is ill. He won't come.
And Radu Ionescu concludes:
– It won't be long now. Go have a sandwich and come back immediately.

✦

Back in the office. I only have time to swallow a cup of tea as I watch through the window the trucks loaded with demonstrators passing through Palace Square. On the trucks, huge red posters with the portraits of Stalin and Ana Pauker.
A colleague runs into the big room and calls me.
– Quick, quick, into your office.
I climb the stairs at a run and arrive breathing hard. The Chief of Cabinet hands me the receiver.
– Continue receiving the communiqués. All the prefect-offices in the country are being attacked. Keep the General up to date. I'm going to the Military Cabinet.
He leaves and the phone rings again.
– Craiova[41] here. The prefect-office is being attacked.
The call ends. I want to run to tell the General. The phone rings again.
– Focşani prefecture. They are firing on us.
The call breaks again. I run to the General. He is standing watching through the window. He turns toward me:
– What is it?
– Craiova, Focşani. They...
The General shouts:
– Down! Lie down!
Two windows are shattered. The bullets go into the wall. The General is still standing. The voice of the chief of the guards, who entered the room, is swamped by the uproar from outside. The General's office is suddenly invaded. Everybody is running. The phone keeps ringing. I rise to go answer it. Take two steps. More noise of shattered glass.

---
[41] Craiova: town ca. 230 km west of Bucharest, in the south of Romania.

In the Beginning Was the End

— Down!

I finally reach the phone, but I can barely hear. Outside the crowd is roaring.

— Brăila prefecture. We are being attacked.

From next door I hear the voice of the chief of the guards.

— Mr. General, shock teams are trying to assault the Wilson street entrance.

— Order the guards not to shoot. Quick.

The phone:

— Roman[42] prefecture. They are firing on us.

I run into the General. The chief of the guards, who is running out, pushes by me. I lean on the door so as not to fall.

Suddenly, a blast makes us all freeze. I hear the General shouting for the first time:

— Who gave the guards the order to shoot?

The chief of the guards has returned:

— Nobody, Mr. General. The guards have recently returned from the front. They know they have the right to defend themselves when attacked.

— This is not the front!

The voice of the Chief of the Military Cabinet precedes him:

— Mr. General, the arms were loaded with blanks.

In my office, one of my cabinet colleagues faints.

— The doctor is on the first floor, says Radu Ionescu.

I go looking for him and in the corridor I bump into three Russians in uniform. They all speak Romanian and shout, one louder than the other:

— You fired into the crowd!

Suddenly calm, I answer:

— You'll get all the information at the Military Cabinet. This way please.

I go back, without looking for the doctor. My colleague is still on the floor! Somebody throws some water in his face. The Russians keep yelling in Romanian. The Chief of the Military Cabinet takes them to the General. I leave for the doctor again. When we return, my colleague hasn't yet recovered.

— Heart attack, says the doctor.

---

[42] Roman: town ca. 300 km north-east of Bucharest.

While he leans over the body stretched out on two chairs, I go to the General. The Russians have left. The General is talking with Radu Ionescu. He stops for a moment to tell me:
– Put on your overcoat. It's cold.
Through the broken windows the air is flowing in waves.

✛

It gets dark. For a while, my office is calmer, I just have time to light a cigarette when I hear a song rising from the street. I run to the window, followed by all those in the office. We open the window wide, glass shards fall on the floor. We see a motionless mass of people singing the national anthem in Palace Square. Behind me, somebody picks up the refrain. To my right, a colleague cries. It's a melody, a simple melody; but this melody has for the last few months helped us to hold our heads high, to resist in an occupied land. The great expanse from the Royal Palace fence to the Interior Ministry is filled with men and women who didn't come in trucks and who don't bear placards. A strong shout: "Long live the King", repeated in unison. I think I see, hanging from the fence, Mihai Fărcășanu in his habitual leather jacket. He motions, he is probably talking, because the crowd stops shouting and singing. And again, in a single voice: "Long live Rădescu." Next door, the General has opened the window also. They are singing the national anthem again. And suddenly a car splits the crowd which parts in two fast waves. I hear rattles and cries. The car passes again. They are machine-gunning the crowd right and left. The cries intensify. I don't see the car anymore. Radu Ionescu fires off an order. Somebody shouts:
– The communists are firing into the crowd.
The General runs into the corridor. We run after him and go out into the Square. People are running right and left, out of their minds. In the middle of the square, the General fires off orders to the soldiers. We start picking up the wounded and are soon relieved by medical teams. Ambulances transport the wounded: men, women, children who had stopped for a moment on the street to sing the national anthem. The groups are forming again, denser now. The ambulance I am standing next to is soon surrounded by youths with clenched teeth, watching the wounded being lifted on stretchers by

the medical teams. A woman cries. Another rocks a dead person in her arms. And little by little, the song is heard again throughout the Square. Tenacious, hard, strong.
Somebody grabs me by the hand.
– Come, let's go back. I was looking for you.
It is the Chief of the Cabinet. How long did I stay singing with them?
– Where is the General?
– He just left too.

✢

On the stairs, I cross paths with Radu Ionescu; he tells me in a hurry:
– Upstairs is a Russian commission. Go quick. This time, they want to see you.
He shows me a small package in his hand:
– The first examinations of the wounded. Russian-caliber bullets.
He goes down two steps and turns again toward me:
– We identified the C.P. car. And tomorrow they will accuse us of wanting to massacre the people.
And, as I remain petrified on the stairs:
– Come on, go now! The Russians are waiting for you.

✢

The Russians are waiting for me indeed. They want to take me to the Russian police to give a statement.
– Regarding what?
– Did you lock Teohari Georgescu's office?
– Yes.
– Well, about that.
I throw an inquiring look to Gug Constantinescu, the head of foreign relations, who is waiting for the General to give him a decree signed by the King for the Foreign Ministry. He motions to me to say yes.
– I'll go tomorrow.
– Why not this evening?
– I am on duty.

– We'll come by tomorrow to take you.

And they leave, while Gug Constantinescu whispers:

– Go, go. As for you, you are not going to go. You'll make the statement here, and give it to them. The General is waiting for you.

When I enter his office, the General is writing. He asks me to keep his door closed for everybody, no exceptions, and gives me instructions. He hands me the paper for Gug Constantinescu, who says, before leaving:

– Agitated day, isn't it?

I remove from my desk all the complaints from the relatives of the deported ethnic Germans. X has been in Romania for fifty years; Y, from the time of the Teutonic knights; Z is not even of German origin. The deportations continue. In closed freight cars, like the Jews, in the German days. And yet, after the first moment of fury, Antonescu was able to stem the wave of deportations, and even to stop it. But now!

I call the Radio Station.

– Do you have ten minutes on the 10 o'clock evening news?

– Sure. What's happening?

– Please be so kind and send a liaison team and a sound engineer to the Interior Ministry. The Prime-Minister wants to address the country.

The Chief of the Cabinet enters:

– The car is waiting for you. Go home and try to get some sleep.

– I prefer to remain here.

– This is not about your preferences. Tonight only one team will be on duty, exclusively male. Go and rest. Maybe we'll need you sooner than you think.

I take my handbag and overcoat, and go down. In the car, next to Ivan, the driver, is an armed soldier.

Has a state of siege been declared?

✢

In my room it is very cold. I plug in the radiator, turn on the radio, and take off my overcoat. As I put water for tea on to boil, I hear military marches. Somebody knocks at the door. It is Rodica, the friend with whom I share the apartment, who has heard me come in and wants to know what happened. While I am telling her what I saw, she makes the tea. In the middle of the story, the military music stops and the announcer's voice comes on. I stop. The news program starts with a communiqué from the Grand General Staff:

In the Tatra Mountains region, Romanian troops have occupied Peak 1225. The German troops have fiercely defended every piece of land, bloody fights have taken place.

Quiet. The announcer again:

Attention, Attention! Keep listening. In a few moments the Prime-Minister will address the country. Do not change the station.

The tea is getting cold in the cups. I try to light a cigarette, I burn match after match without success. Rodica paces through the room. We hear another "Don't change the station", and then, immediately, the General's voice.

"A handful of ambitious scoundrels, headed by two foreigners, Ana Pauker and the Hungarian Vasile Luca[43]*, are trying to subdue the Romanian people and, to achieve this, have not hesitated to use terror.*

But, as in the past, our nation has always fiercely defended its existence. It will not be overcome by a handful of cowards."

Rodica comes near me. She whispers:

– Finally, he dares. Somebody dares to tell them the truth!

I motion to her to be quiet.

"They pretend to be democrats, but continually trample democracy. They want to assassinate the country. On our territory, their crimes are innumerable. I will soon have the opportunity to talk to you in detail about them. Tonight I will talk only about what happened today, to thwart all the craven charges they are trying to bring against the people and me, in order to better cover their crimes.

At Craiova, they attacked the prefecture..."

Rodica is sitting next to me. I put my arm around her shoulders.

---

[43] Vasile Luca (1902–1963): communist from before the legalization of the Romanian Communist Party, of Hungarian origin. He lived in the Soviet Union from the beginning of WWII and returned to Romania in 1944 with the Soviet Army. Member of the Secretariat of the Central Committee (1945–1952), Finance Minister (1948–1952). In 1952, when his protector Ana Pauker fell from power, he was imprisoned. He died in jail.

The calls that punctuated my day are still ringing in my ears: "This is Craiova, this is Roman, this is Focşani ..."

"Finally, in the capital, their crimes are even more serious. They fired on the Royal Palace and two bullets entered the office of the Palace Marshal.

They fired on the Police Prefecture.

They attacked the Interior Ministry, where I was, a bullet breaking the window and entering my office.

Three quarters of an hour ago, people that were demonstrating in support of the King in front of the Royal Palace were machine-gunned from a car. There are two dead and eleven wounded.

This is a summary of what happened this very day.

The people guilty of these crimes do not have the courage to admit their responsibility and are trying to blame it on the army, for allegedly provoking them.

I declare this to be false. The Army received my most categorical order not to attack, and executed it.

Moreover: the Army received the categorical order to defend itself only when attacked. In this case, the Army fired in the air only.

I would have wanted to stop even this.

The dark souls of those without God and country did not hesitate to burden themselves with these sins.

These are the facts, these are the people who did it.

We must all rise, like a single person, to face the danger.

I and, beside me, the Army will do our duty to the end.

As for you, remain at your posts."

Rodica jumps up, gesticulates, talks without stopping.

– For months we have been waiting for somebody to say this. We are free, isn't it true that we are free now?

She keeps crying.

The phone: the Chief of the Cabinet.

– Did you listen?

I motion to Rodica to be still and, especially, to be quiet.

– Yes, I would have liked to have been with all of you.

– He was stronger than I expected. Prepare all your socks, sweaters and woolen gloves.

– Why?

– While the General was talking, Bogdenko's[44] adjutant an-

nounced that his chief wants to see General Rădescu.
– So, what?
– What do you mean so what? Bogdenko is even more powerful than Vinogradov. I told you: prepare your warm things for Siberia.
– Funny.
– Not very. Seriously, restore your strength. You'll need it. This is only the beginning, and it's already very serious.
– Is the General going to Bogdenko?
– Sure. Don't you know him?
– How is he now?
– Calm. I have to go. Good night. Go to bed right away.
I hang up, and Rodica comes over quickly:
– Interior?
– Yes.
– What's happening?
– Nothing else but what you heard in the speech. I would like to sleep.
She leaves, I take a sleeping pill with some cold tea.

✦

I am still heavy with sleep and don't know what time it is. Next to the bed, the phone has without doubt been ringing for a while.
I lift the receiver.
– Finally. I didn't think you were going to answer.
I recognize the voice of the Chief of the Cabinet.
– In ten minutes the car will be waiting downstairs. You must come immediately.
– What happened with Bogdenko?
– He asked the General why he attacked Ana Pauker, who is a General in the Red Army. I'll tell you when we have more time. Come quickly! We are waiting for another commission.
I put my clothes on, don't bother combing my hair, grab my handbag and run down the stairs. Ivan is waiting. I glance at my watch: six in the morning.
– The Chief of the Cabinet gave me the morning papers for you

---

[44] V. L. Bogdenko: Soviet admiral, very probably chief of the Soviet information services in Bucharest, his official function was that of Deputy Head of the Committee for Enforcing the Armistice with the USSR.

to read in the car. You know, miss, they didn't allow the papers to publish the General's speech.

And he starts cursing. I calm him down and get in the car. The back seat is filled with papers. On the way, I open the communist paper *România Liberă*. Big headlines:

Events in Romania. Soviet public opinion cannot watch with indifference the fight between democratic and fascist factions in Romania. It is not only a matter of Romanian domestic politics.

Trying, obviously, to prepare the Soviet intervention. How far will they go? Under headlines in big red letters, a caricature shows Rădescu looking at himself in the mirror and trying a fascist salute. Behind him, portraits of Hitler and Mussolini, whom he takes as mentors. Two days ago, in the same paper, the same big letters have already announced:

Soviet condemnation of Iuliu Maniu NDF platform and the role of the reactionary clique of Rădescu's government.

We reach the ministry. The door-keeper tells me, opening the door:

– What a Sunday, miss! The ministry is full with allied commissions and sub-commissions.

In my office are two representatives from the British mission and two from the American mission. I ask them to follow me and lead them through all the offices to show them the bullet holes in the walls and broken windows. They seem dumbfounded.

– But, from where did they shoot?

– From one of the apartments in the building across the street. The apartment is occupied by a Soviet officer. Emil Bodnăraş visited it often. Two, three times a week, usually evenings.

They stop talking. Don't want to show their indignation. Russia is their ally. Reports will probably be sent to London and Washington. We go down to Palace Square. I show them the bloodstains and tell them what happened last night.

– It's a new type of democracy. What do you think?

– There was no fire into the demonstrators from the Interior?

– We were attacked, and the communists forced the Wilson street entrance. The guards fired blanks.

– There were some wounded though?

– In the confusion, yes. They weren't wounded by bullets. And anyway we are the first to feel regret for this. Should we have let

In the Beginning Was the End

the ministry be occupied by the communists?

They turn quiet. I continue:

– Anyhow, these few victims will be shown by the communist press, but they won't mention anything about the other victims killed by them in the Palace Square. Did you see the result of the examinations of the wounded and the caliber of the bullets?

One of the English answers:

– This morning, Radio Moscow called the General "the Butcher of Palace Square".

– Then the nickname will be taken up by the communist press tomorrow and made into a slogan.

And, as he nods:

– Do you know the result of the Yalta Conference?

Silence. I continue.

– If you want to follow me, I'll show you to the General.

The General is sitting at his desk. His face is drawn. All night he did nothing but receive Allied Commissions, one after the other. While the audience is taking place next door, Radu Ionescu hands me the radio bulletins.

– You have no idea, but everything you saw yesterday was only a dream.

Listen to the Moscow broadcast. You'll see what actually took place.

I read:

During the afternoon, Romanian military units massed in the Interior Ministry fired into peaceful demonstrators.

– What Romanian military units?

Radu Ionescu looks at me smiling:

– I would like to know that too. The guard has about a hundred people. But listen, that's not all! Read this as well:

By order of the Soviet commander, all Romanian soldiers and officers on Romanian territory were disarmed.

– Starting with the Royal Palace guard. I must see the General to tell him. Is he alone?

– No. The American and British commissions.

– Maybe they'll be interested also. As things are going, if they don't intervene... You want to announce me?

Alone, I start reading the papers again.

Adriana Georgescu

✢

Next day, February 26th, big headlines in *România Liberă*:
Criminal Rădescu answered with machine-gun volleys the peaceful demonstration of over 60,000 antifascist citizens. Rădescu has tried to start the civil war.
The people's executioners must be punished.
"România Liberă" from February 27th doesn't even conceal its source:
The fire against the demonstrators ended only after the intervention of the Allied Control Commission, announced Radio Moscow.
The Allied Control Commission was at the Military Circle luncheon while this happened. How could it intervene?
In the same paper, in heavy letters:
New overwhelming evidence against the butcher Rădescu. The massacre was prepared using Göring's methods. Complicity of Maniu-Brătianu.
Rădescu answers the Crimea Conference with assassinations. How Rădescu turned ministries into fortresses.
And, under a caricature in which the General is decorated by Hitler, again the sacrosanct pronouncement:
Radio Moscow announced yesterday details about General Rădescu's provocative attitude on February 24th.
Reading the next headline I can't help laughing:
The only historical equivalent of Rădescu's staged crime is the burning of the Reichstag.
Personally, I did not see the burning of the Reichstag. But I saw how a C.P. grey car machine-gunned those who dared to sing the national anthem.

✢

Also on February 27th, I wake in the middle of the night: a call from the Interior Ministry.
– Get dressed quick. You don't know who just arrived in Bucharest...
I mumble, still heavy with sleep:
– Who?

In the Beginning Was the End

— Vîşinski[45] himself.

I sit up in bed. Suddenly, I am awake.

— Where is he?

— I told you: in Bucharest.

— I understand. But where is he at this moment?

— He has just left the Royal Palace. Come quick. You'll be the liaison with the Palace. The car will be at your place in ten minutes.

I only have time to stick my head under a faucet with freezing water. Vîşinski, the prosecutor of the Moscow trials... probably the Kremlin has decided to act sooner than we expected.

At the ministry the reports and an impressive coffee pot are waiting. Radu Ionescu tells me, while lighting his cigarette:

— Drink your coffee quickly. You probably won't be able to sleep for the next few days.

— Did Vîşinski see the King?

— Sure. He went directly from the airport to the Palace. This was the scene: on one side the King and the foreign affairs minister. On the other, Vîşinski and the interpreter. Vîşinski asks for the immediate removal of Rădescu's government, disloyal to the Soviet Union and butcher of the people. He shows the King a list with the members of the new government. The complete list, you understand, brought just like that from Moscow. At the head of the list, Groza.

— And the King?

— He refuses. He tells Vîşinski that the demands of the USSR will be taken into consideration, but he must follow the constitution and consult with the political leaders in the country. To follow parliamentary procedure.

— And Vîşinski?

— He leaves, asking him to hurry up.

— Were the representatives of British and American missions present?

---

[45] Andrei Ianuarievici Vîşinski (1883-1954): Soviet politician. In the '30s he became notorious as the chief prosecutor in the Moscow show trials. In 1940 he became first deputy of Molotov, the Soviet Foreign Minister. His first visit to Bucharest took place in November-December 1944. He was sent by Moscow to replace the Sănătescu government. Later, during 1944-1946, in various visits to Romania he directed the internal social policies and the foreign affairs of the Bucharest regime.

— Do you believe that Moscow warned London and Washington before sending Vîşinski? You are very naive! Or still asleep. Moscow wanted a sensational turn of events.
— What's the King going to do?
— How should I know? He'll probably try to temporize, to give London and Washington time to intervene. Now, are you fully awake? Good. Stay in touch with the Palace.
— I will go to see Mircea Ioaniţiu[46].
— Go immediately.

✦

Mircea Ioaniţiu is the King's private secretary. He confirms the story word for word and seems to be full of hope.
— It's not possible the Anglo-Americans will accept such total interference in our domestic affairs. The Yalta agreement can't be just simple comedy.
And, seeing that I remain quiet:
— You should put on your coat. It's cold.
And points to the broken windows and bullet holes that decorate, just like at the Interior Ministry, the walls.
— I alerted Burton Berry[47] and Marjoribanks[48]. Tomorrow London and Washington will be up-to-date. I hope to give you better news then.
— What does the King say?
— He is firm. He awaits, like all of us, the Anglo-American reaction. Let's keep up hope. Till tomorrow!
I run back to the Interior Ministry. I sit at my desk, my eyes focused on the phone. While he was seeing me off, Mircea Ioaniţiu promised to call me as soon as he had news.

---

[46] Mircea Ioaniţiu (1921–1990): private secretary to King Michael I of Romania (1944-1947). After the King's forced abdication, he took residence in the United States and worked for the Free Europe Committee.

[47] Burton Y. Berry: U.S. diplomat at ministerial level, representative of the United States to Bucharest, sent to Romania in November, 1944.

[48] James Marjoribanks: Consul and Assistant to the British Political Representative Ian Le Rougetel, in Romania between September 1944 - January 1946.

In the Beginning Was the End

✢

The next day, the demonstrations start anew. The communists send all the public servants on the streets to yell: "Death to Rădescu". Of course all demonstrations take place in the Palace Square. Everywhere big posters, everywhere the same placards.

The General spends his time in talks with Maniu, Brătianu and Titel Petrescu[49].

The papers intensify their attacks. But none of them inform the people about Vîşinski's presence in Bucharest.

I commute between the Palace and the Interior Ministry. No reaction from the Anglo-Americans. Mircea Ioaniţiu shrugs.

– Burton Berry has been trying for two days to see Vîşinski, but he doesn't reply and remains invisible.

Not completely invisible, though. He opens the window. Heavy Soviet tanks cross the Palace Square, preceding a Red Army battalion marching to the sound of a band.

– Wonderful directing. Full scale intimidation. What do you think?

– You know very well that the Red Army controls some of the key buildings in Bucharest.

Returning to the Interior Ministry, I see three more Russian tanks parked on one of the side streets.

I haven't closed my eyes for two days and fall asleep involuntarily, head on my desk in my office.

✢

The press campaign is hysterical now and no longer tries to hide anything. The March 1ˢᵗ *România Liberă* finally announces the arrival of Vîşinski in Bucharest. On the same page, next to his picture, heavy headlines:

Rădescu's government must resign, broadcast Radio Moscow yesterday. Will the criminal be dismissed from his position?

---

[49] Constantin-Titel Petrescu (1888-1956): one of the Presidents of the Romanian Social Democratic Party (1945). He refused to work together with the communists, which led to his arrest and imprisonment. He was freed after publicly declaring his support for the communist movement.

A call from the Royal Palace. Mircea Ioanițiu:
– Nothing from the Anglo-Americans.
Three hours later another call:
– Come immediately.
I run to the Palace. Ioanițiu, pale, meets me.
– Vîșinski just left here. He doesn't want to wait anymore. He gave the King the list with the new government and accompanied it with a blow from a fist on his desk. Leaving, he slammed the door so hard that pieces of plaster fell down. He wants the answer this evening.
I probably turn pale myself, because Ioanițiu hands me a chair.
– Sit down.
– No, I'll go back to the Interior Ministry.
– We are waiting for the General here at the Palace.
I mumble:
– So, this is the end?
– I am afraid so. The Anglo-Americans have left us twisting in the wind.

✦

It's getting dark when the General leaves the Palace. He holds in his hand a small chain that Queen Elena always wore on her wrist. While the King asked him to resign, the Queen handed the chain to the last defender of the Romanian monarchy.
He plays, lost in thought, with the chain, and tells me:
– Go to your office and take all your things. Go rest. Now, you'll have time.

✦

Next day, March 2nd, *România Liberă* can finally announce the good news:
Rădescu the executioner was driven from power.

✦

We are sequestered for twenty-seven hours in our offices at the Interior Ministry. The Chief of the Cabinet is court-martialed. We, the rest, are authorized to go home, but must remain available to the police for any additional inquiry. General Rădescu is at the British Embassy.

✥

On March 6ᵗʰ, the Groza government is formed. I don't need to read the names of the members. Those names were already on the list placed, nine days ago, by Vîşinski on King Michael's desk.

✥

I renew my habit from Câmpulung, I wake up in the middle of the night and listen to the BBC and Voice of America.

Today, Rodica called some friends from a neighbouring apartment, who do not have a radio, to listen to the broadcast. There are six of us gathered around the radio.

The BBC plays the three muted chords. We are all quiet. A war communiqué. The announcer reads immediately afterwards the list of ministers in the Romanian government. No commentary. But one comes at the end of the broadcast: Northern Transylvania returned to Romanian administration by decision of the Soviet government.

✥

There are fewer demonstrations on the rain-swept streets. The wind has torn the posters from the walls. A few tatters hang sadly here and here. I can only read "Death to...". Soon other names will surely complete the message. Teohari Georgescu is Interior Minister. My former colleagues from the paper, whom I meet at the Liberal Club, talk now simply of the "Soviet Control Commission", "Allied, that is Russian" has been dropped. The attacks against the opposition are more and more violent.

One day, going to the Liberal Party Club, I find my former colleagues very agitated. They think that the outlawing of the opposition parties is only a matter of months away now.

I ask them:

– And then, what will we do?

They look at me, and one of them tells me calmly.

– Listen, you are not going to start having doubts about us, are you. We'll keep fighting.

I go to him. We shake hands quietly. One of us starts laughing. And then, suddenly, a great happiness erupts and engulfs all of us. We are young, strong in our desire to be free, and have just rediscovered this together. Going outside, we continue laughing in the bright spring light.

In front of the neighbourhood CP quarters a very old woman looks at a great portrait of Stalin in a glass case. She asks a man who is leaving the building:

– Tell me dear, who is this?

Like real loafers we all stop to hear the answer.

– It's Stalin, answers the communist. He is the one who drove away the Germans from our country.

– God bless him, says the old woman. When is he going to chase away the Russians too?

The youngster, furious, snaps "stupid old woman" and goes away. The woman remains dumbfounded in the middle of the street. And then one of us goes to her and whispers very softly:

– Soon, mother, soon. Right after the war ends.

In the Beginning Was the End

PART TWO

"I, the undersigned, declare..."

I

On July 29th I am leaving General Rădescu's house pushing my bicycle by the handlebars. Two cars stop suddenly and trap me between them.
– Bicycle papers. We have information you stole it. Get in the car. You are under arrest.
– Why don't you dare to tell the truth? You are arresting me because I am leaving General Rădescu's house. I am his lawyer.
I open my handbag and hand them the mandate... and the bicycle papers.
– We don't need the mandate. You are under arrest. Get in before we make you.
I shove the bicycle at them and start running down the boulevard. I run by a clock showing eleven thirty. I still have half an hour till lunch. I have to lose them and deliver the message hidden in my hair, which is made up in a bun. I feel somebody grabbing me.
– Don't shout. Don't turn your head.
I turn my head and see on the opposite sidewalk a familiar figure. I shout:
– Horia!
A hand grabs my throat and starts squeezing.
– Don't shout.
I shout to the person crossing the street:
– Tell the Liberal Party office that I have been arrested.
A completely unfamiliar voice answers:

89

– But what is your name?

I kick the two men holding my arms. I manage to free myself for a moment. I run toward the person that answered me. It's not my friend. Just someone who looks like him. A hand grabs me from behind and covers my mouth. I struggle. I am suffocating. I am lifted, I keep struggling. I hit my head on the car door. The car starts. My head is heavy. Is my bun undone? I feel in my ribs, to the right and to the left, two pistols.

– If you make a single move, we shoot.

I try to touch my bun. I change my mind, and don't do it.

– If you shout, we shoot.

The car stops at the Interior Ministry. The doorman is the same. He greets me, astonished. A second car stops behind us. On top my bicycle. They make me climb to the first floor. Nobody in the corridors. We pass my former office, then Teohari Georgescu's office. They push me into Radu Ionescu's former office. Standing, a fair-haired man. Two more men who are smoking.

– Finally the terrorist!

I start laughing. I am pleased they haven't searched me and that my bun is not undone.

– You probably mean to talk about yourselves. You arrest me on the street without a warrant. From a legal point of view...

The fair-haired person comes toward me.

– You better shut up. You want a taste of Siberia? After locking Teohari Georgescu's office you still want an arrest order?

– So, because I locked the office I am a terrorist? It's all clear.

– You are cheeky. We are going to have some fun.

He raises his hand. One slap. Two. Three. I lose count. Finally he stops.

– Who are the people the General asked you to see on his behalf? Who are your contacts?

My cheeks are burning and I taste blood in my mouth. I can't talk. I hand them my mandate. They snatch my purse.

– How many fliers did you distribute?

I shrug.

– We are going to make you talk, don't worry! We'll do anything for that. We've been watching you for quite a while.

He pushes a button. Two soldiers enter the room. The fair-haired man takes my watch and my belt. The soldiers push me toward the

In the Beginning Was the End

door. At the desk, the three men search through my purse.

At the end of the second corridor I see the toilet. I ask for permission to go. The two soldiers look at each other. One of them says:

– It's against the rules. But go. We'll wait in front of the door.

I go inside, close the door, flush, and undo my bun. The piece of paper falls on the floor. I pick it up and tear it into tiny pieces. I throw them down the toilet. I wait a moment, and flush again. No traces of paper. I redo my bun. Flush. Go out. All this time I keep coughing.

Are they going to notice the change in my hairdo? No. They keep pushing me further. We go down the stairs. In the basement, I am entrusted to some civilians, two of them.

– The detained stopped on the way?
– No.

I breathe relieved. The soldiers are not communists then. One of the them adds:

– Lock up.

Another corridor. A series of cells. Now and then, a shout. A hand on my shoulder:

– Here.

A door opens... I am pushed into the darkness. I don't see anything. I try to sit down. I can't. I want to turn. Impossible. The room is the size of a coffin, a stand-up coffin. I want to lean on the wall. I am startled: the walls are covered with wet, cold metal. I am thirsty, my head is heavy. I hear steps. Quiet. Then another noise, very strong, very close: my heart is pounding. Gradually, I start to see, dancing in front of my eyes, red stars, yellow circles, more yellow circles. The circles are turning, and turning....

I recover. I am stretched out on the cement floor in the corridor. I touch my face; my hair is wet.

– Alright. She opened her eyes. Take her to first floor.

Two civilians lift me. Pistols in my ribs. They hold me by the underarms, and push me. I don't understand anything. Where are the soldiers? Why am I being shoved? They open a door, and push me inside a room. An open window. Air. Outside it is dark. The same fair-haired man:

– What connections did you make from the Palace Square office?
– None.

– If you want to live, sign here.

He hands me a sheet of paper. The letters dance in front of my eyes.

– I can't read. And, even if I could, I am not signing anything.

– You'll regret it. Soon all the tools of the reaction will tear their hair out and cry with sorrow.

– I am not signing anything.

The fair-haired man blindfolds me, pulls my hands behind my back and puts on handcuffs. The first ones are too big.

– Should we give up on the handcuffs, comrade?

– No. For her, we don't spare any effort.

They all burst into laughter.

– Let me try these.

Somebody turns my wrists. The handcuffs are tight. They are heavy. I feel as if I am going to fall on my back. I slide down the stairs even though two men are holding me. I feel the cool air. We are probably on the street. They throw me inside a car. The car starts. Revolvers in the ribs.

– If you make a single move, we shoot.

Are the pistols loaded, I wonder? The car seems to go for a long time. A sudden brake. Noise of gates opening. They must be iron gates. Somebody opens the car door and pushes me.

– Let's go, get out. We're there.

✦

They pull off my blindfold in a room that looks like a train compartment. Way up, next to the ceiling, a small, square, shut window. To reach the window, one would have to climb up to the upper bunk, where I see a figure that turns her back toward me. Two swollen, dirty feet show out from under the blanket. I feel the revolver in my ribs.

– It's forbidden to talk. You understand?

The guard closes the door. I sit on the bed. The bed is a very cold board. My eyes hurt. I try to sleep with the light on. I get up.

– How do you turn the light off?

The figure in the upper bunk turns slowly. The face is lit by the strong light. A round, young face. Red splotches on her cheeks. She looks toward the glass eye in the door. She puts her hand slowly to her face, and sliding it, presses a finger to her lips. I understand.

In the Beginning Was the End

We should not talk. They could see us. I lie down again. On my stomach, because of the handcuffs. I try to keep my head to one side so I can breathe. Steps in the corridor. A metallic noise. Chains? More steps now, they stop in front of our cell. The door opens:
– Get up.

I want to stand up, but don't quite make it and fall head first, onto the board. The guard laughs loudly. He pulls me by the arm.
– Let's go, come on beautiful.

I no longer feel my arms; in their place, a heavy pain. We cross a corridor. Cells. Same observation eye on all the doors. An endless row of frog eyes watching me. An office. Four men. One short, fat, with a moustache. Another sharp, rat-like muzzle. The others are talking with their backs toward me.

– Look! She looks good, the layabout, with those bracelets. Those are the kind of bracelets all the reactionaries will be wearing soon. You didn't hide behind your back the gold bracelets you were wearing at the American receptions. Even though they were just as heavy.
– I never wore gold bracelets.

I would like to tell them that I was too poor to buy gold bracelets, but I change my mind. What for? I see my purse on the desk. I look at it with affection, like at a human being. The only thing that connects me with the outside world. The man that looks like a rat takes a package of Pall Malls out of my purse.

– If you would be so kind and tell us which American officer gave you these cigarettes, I'll have the handcuffs taken off.
– I bought the cigarettes for five hundred *lei* [50] a pack.

My arms pull me backwards with all their weight. The rat-like man picks up a key from the desk and comes toward me.
– You are going to sign this paper.

The noise of the key in the handcuffs. I straighten up a little, but my arms hang down even heavier. The rat-man goes away and sits down. Another one gets up and heads toward me. I move backwards and lean against the wall. He grabs me by the wrist and pulls me toward the center of the room.
– Who said you could lean? Sign.

He pushes me toward the desk. On the sheet of paper the letters are dancing, dancing. "Detainee's inventory."

---

[50] *lei* : Romanian currency.

– Aside from the purse and bicycle, I have nothing.
They all start laughing, aside from the rat-man who spits at me:
– All the reactionaries are stupid. The inventory is what you have on you.
Another one breaks in:
– You are quite slow. Let's go, undress.
I take a step backwards. I have goose pimples.
– Let's go, undress!
I am frozen, my legs are shaking. I move backwards one more step. I regain the wall, and lean against it. Two of them get up and come toward me. The rat-man yells:
– You can't lean against the wall. Undress!
The two grab me. I struggle. They laugh. The room is spinning around me. My head gets stuck in the dress they have pulled up. My slip slides down. I cannot help it, I close my eyes and lash out with my feet and fists right and left. Somebody grabs me and hits my head against the wall. I hear the noise. One more slap. They let me go. I open my eyes, turn, regain the wall, stick to it. They laugh again and throw me a pair of overalls. I bend down to take it. My head is pulled by the floor like by a magnet. I can't grab the overalls. A man picks them up and hands them to me.
– So, reactionary whore, we are going to dress you like a doll. You make a lot of fuss, but we are kind, we are patient!
The overalls are dirty. They smell foul, they make me nauseous. I gather them at the neck so they will not slide down my shoulders: they are too big!
– If you sign here, we'll let you go.
It's not the sheet with the inventory any more. A typed sheet of paper: "I, the undersigned, declare that..."
– I can't read.
A revolver is pointing toward me:
– Sign, or we'll kill you.
– Do it, come on, do it!
I cry. A moment of silence. The rat-man puts the pistol calmly on the table, comes toward me, hands me a chair:
– Sit down.
Then he unclasps my hands that I am holding tight at my neck and pulls the overalls down by the right arm.
– Look, her shoulders are tanned, the fascist whore!

His spit flows from my shoulder down my back. I burst into laughter. Why am I laughing and not crying? I laugh, laugh with tears, cannot stop.
– She is hysterical.
I keep laughing while we walk down the corridors. The cell. Through the window I watch a pale dawn. At least I think it is dawn. I fall on the board. They didn't handcuff me. What do they want me to sign? What do they really want? I close my eyes. I feel like my head is swelling, quickly, quick like a balloon while my legs are stretching. And my teeth, my teeth are growing. I open my mouth. From each tooth grows a plank on which men in boots are walking. I hear their steps reverberating inside me. I am thirsty.

✦

It is very warm in the cell. The overalls stick to my skin. They smell so badly it makes me feel sick. Anyway, I have not eaten or drunk since they arrested me. Yesterday? Was it yesterday? The door opens. Two guards who seem huge to me. One of them holds in his hand a sheet of paper and points at me with his finger.
– 55.
Then, addressing the figure above:
– Are you up, Iulişca? Good, 54 is also OK.
They put on my board two metal bowls and a cup of water. In each bowl, a ball of polenta. From the upper bunk first one foot, then the other appear. The woman climbs down onto my bed. For the first time I see her standing. The same overalls like mine, but torn at the belly. A huge belly. Pregnant! The face is very young. Not one wrinkle, only red splotches. She takes her kettle and starts chewing loudly to cover her voice. She tells me simply:
– Budapest.
She is Hungarian then.
The door opens. Another guard.
– Iulişca, come. Outdoor time.
I swallow the dry, hard corn-mush with difficulty. I stretch. How long did I sleep? Did I really sleep? The door opens, and the guard lets in a blue-eyed man with a rather peaceful air. The first who says good-day to me. He sits on the edge of my bed, takes my hand.

– Why don't you want to sign?
– Yesterday, I couldn't even read. I couldn't have held a pencil in my hand.
– Some friendly advice: sign everything they ask you to.
– "They"? Who are they? At least you speak Romanian without an accent.
– Did you distribute T fliers?
– I distributed many fliers. T was one of them.
– Why did you do this?
– If the press was free, it wouldn't have been necessary!
– I advise you not to repeat this. You have nothing to gain by being cheeky.

He leaves. The sun shines in the cell and hits the lamp that is still on. I am unable to concentrate. Two bed-bugs are crawling on the opposite wall. They are free to crawl. How long have I watched them? The door opens again.

– 55. Air-time. In the yard you are not allowed to turn your head. Look straight ahead. Understood?

They first take me to the toilet.

– Leave the door open.

I want to hit him, hit myself, hit everybody. I control myself, leave the door open. We go down the corridor in the opposite direction. We go out into the yard. Above, I notice a big building. The prison resembles a barn. The yard: a square space, two sidewalks. I drag my feet from one end to the other of the sidewalk. The big building in front seems empty. Doesn't look familiar. I would very much like to know where we are. On the other sidewalk, steps. I want to turn my head. A moist hand on the back of my head.

– Look straight ahead or I'll take away your air-time.

The sun burns. It must be noon. My feet get heavier and heavier. The overalls are soaked in perspiration. The sky is very blue. Not one cloud. Not a single one.

Sound of gates opening. A car enters the yard. The rat-man gets out and starts yelling:

– Who gave "air" to this rotten reactionary?

The guard hits me with his fists a few times. The rat-man keeps yelling:

– Bitch, viper, whore...

In the Beginning Was the End

The guard takes me back to the cell. Iulişca is on her bed again. Expressionless face. I stretch out. What if she gives birth here? The hours pass, or don't they? Iulişca keeps quiet. She is probably looking at the ceiling. I count the sound of steps in the corridor in order to fall asleep.

✢

Outside it is dark and the steps on the corridor do not stop. Time seems loaded with the sound of steps. A blast. A shout. Above, Iulişca is not tossing from side to side anymore. She is probably asleep. Steps. The door:
– 55, for interrogation.
I feel cold all of a sudden. In the office, new faces.
– You need anything?
– No.
– Cigarette?
A package is extended. I take a cigarette. Somebody gives me a light... I take the first puff and everything starts spinning around me. I move a few steps backwards to lean against the wall.
– You are not allowed to lean.
I feel like throwing up.
– You admitted you distributed T fliers.
– The fliers replace the papers you suspended.
– You are not pleading in court.
– I noticed.
– I notice mostly that you are cheeky. You know that the T fliers claimed that the Anglo-Americans wanted a just peace and the Russians a Russian one.
– The Anglo-Americans didn't send their foreign secretaries to impose a government on Romania. Without elections.
– You are reciting the lesson you learned from the butcher Rădescu.
– No, we all think this way.
I expect to be beaten. But they don't leave their chairs.
– What was discussed at Maniu's last week?
– Last week I was in Sinaia.
– You are going to give a statement about what was discussed two days ago with the other tool of the reaction: Mircea Ioaniţiu.

– I didn't see Mircea Ioanițiu two days ago.
– How did you meet him?
– We were university colleagues.
– Sit down and write about what you discussed with the King's secretary.
– I didn't discuss anything with him.
– Where is Mihai Fărcășanu hiding?
– I don't know.
– The summary of the discussion between Brătianu and Burton Berry?
– I don't know.
– The summary of the discussion between Maniu and Mețianu[51]? If you talk, we'll let you go.

I pretend I am reflecting in order to summarize. They want to compromise the whole opposition with my statements.
– I have nothing to write. I don't know.

The one looking out the window moves toward me.
– You are going to listen now to what I read. Then you are going to sign. If not, I'll kill you right here.

"I, the undersigned, declare that I agreed with Mircea Ioanițiu, the King's secretary, that the arms cache must be entrusted to Vintilă Brătianu. Following conversations between Maniu, Brătianu, Burton Berry and Mețianu, conversations that I was charged with relaying to Rădescu, it was decided to start a subversive organization named T, for Terror. The purpose of this organization is to eliminate the heads of our democracy put in place by the struggles and sacrifices of the people, and to throw the country into the claws of fascists. The supreme chief of the organization is General Rădescu."

I don't protest and let them read further. They are naive to tell me all their plans in advance. Why do they want to stage this affair? I am quite lucid. The investigator continues:

"I admit that I swore the following oath: «I swear not to tell anybody, at anytime, about the existence of this organization and of those members whom I know. If I ever break this oath, I may be

---

[51] Silviu Mețianu (1893-?): British army captain of Romanian origin. He parachuted into Romania in 1943. Taken prisoner, he was freed in August, 1944, and joined the British Military Mission in Bucharest.

In the Beginning Was the End

considered a traitor and shot. I take this oath of my own free will and not under duress.» The signal for action is to be given by General Rădescu, at the King's behest."
I can not refrain any longer. I want to laugh.
– It's useless to keep reading all these lies. They are too brazen.
– Reactionary bitch, if you don't sign we'll shoot you.
I shrug.
– You are wasting your time for naught.
– You filthy terrorist, you are going to sign.
– No, you are the terrorists.
Slaps. Punches. I struggle. They throw me to the ground. They step on me.
– Sign! I'll kill you! Sign!
One of them immobilizes my arms. Another, my legs. A third takes out of a drawer some sort of a sleeve tied at both ends, and filled with... what?
– You'll sign?
I keep quiet. He bends over, ties a heavy handkerchief over my mouth and whips the air with the sleeve. The air whistles.
– You'll sign?
I look at the sleeve waving above my head. I don't say anything.
– Well, then, hold her.
The first blow lands on my thigh. The second, in my face. Everything is spinning, whistling. I struggle. They all yell. And I? Bite, bite the handkerchief in my mouth. The thigh, the thigh once more. The circles. The yellow is spinning, spinning, coming closer. I pass out.

✦

How long have I been lying in bed? Did I have a nightmare? Iulișca's head is very big. No, her belly. What if she gives birth? The light... I want to turn. My thigh is burning. I touch it. The overalls are stuck to the skin. I try to get it unstuck. I cry. I cannot sit up. I touch my skin. My hand is wet: blood! Steps. They stop. The door. A man in white. In his hand a syringe. He comes close, pulls at my overalls, bares my arm. Gives me a shot. I shiver, I am cold, don't know how to hold my head. It gets lower, it gets lower, it swells. I sink.

✢

I wake up, still numb. It's light outside. On the bed a ball of cornmush. I try to get up. I think I remember that... did I dream? Was I really in those corridors? It seems the rat-man was handing me a sheet of paper. What did I sign? Did I sign anything? I don't know. I want to stand up, but can't. The shot. What was in the vial? Did I really dream? Did I really sign? Are they going to arrest them?

✢

A few days must have passed. I don't know how many. I lost track. Only one thought: after the shot, did I sign anything or not? Did I dream or not?

Once a day I am dragged to the toilet. The door stays open. The guards roar with laughter.

– You look well! Like on the day after the wedding night. My, you are beautiful.

✢

I sit on the edge of my bed, my legs hanging. I look at my feet, they look like Iulişca's now. Swollen, dirty. I am thirsty all the time. Here, the water has a strange taste, brackish, nauseating. I only get a jug a day.

Today again, the sound of steps stopping in front of the door.

– 55, for interrogation.

So, I didn't sign all the statements. Even with the interrogation coming, I feel relieved. On the desk, new objects: spotlights. They turn on and off, pointed towards my eyes. Questions and answers are dictated to me. I refuse to write. My eyes are burning. Even if I close them. I feel points of fire under my eyelids.

– Write: "At the underground meeting were Brătianu, Maniu, Burton Berry, Mihai Fărcăşanu, Vintilă Brătianu[52], Mircea Ioaniţiu..."

---

[52] Vintilă Brătianu (1914–1994): one of the leaders of the Liberal Youth, participated in several anti-communist demonstrations and was sentenced in absentia to life in prison in 1946. He managed to evade the authorities and leave Romania in 1947. In exile, he joined General Rădescu, first as a member of the National Romanian Committee (*CNR*), then of the League of Free Romanians.

He goes on. Names, names. More than fifty.
I mumble:
– Full house, right?
The rat-man yells:
– What do you mean?
– That all these people would fill a big room. Too many for an "underground" meeting.
I manage to think even as the blows are raining down on me. They want to destroy the entire opposition, to attack even the King. My part in this play: to give statements that would allow the arrest of the main politicians. In the case of a likely Allied protest note, my statements would help.
They keep hitting me. I shout:
– I won't sign anything, anything.
I am led to a smaller cell without a board to stretch on. Cement floor. It's very warm. I crouch on the floor. The door opens.
– You are not allowed to sit. Don't lean. Stand up or walk.
The light is not as strong. The cement is wet.

✦

Again in the office. The spotlight game starts again.
– We have here Țețu's[53] statements that certify that you were the liaison between him and Rădescu. Here they are. How did you meet Țețu?
– We were university colleagues.
– Do you know that Rădescu was not allowed to see politicians?
– Țețu was not a politician.
– You mean, the acting head of a subversive organization is not a politician?
– What subversive organization?
– The T organization, of which you stated you were a member.

---

[53] Remus Țețu (1918-?): lawyer, one of the leaders of the Liberal Youth. He edited the manifesto-magazine *Văpaia* ("The Flame"), which sharply criticized the Soviet occupation and the communists. He was arrested, tortured, and sentenced to seven years in prison. He managed to escape and emigrate in 1947, joining General Rădescu as a member of the League of Free Romanians.

Adriana Georgescu

I breathe relieved. Probably the statement I signed after the shot. It could have been worse.
— Are you dumb?
I start laughing.
— Shut-up. There's no reason to laugh, you dirty whore! You admitted in your statement that you carried out Țețu's orders and swore an oath in front of him.
Me, swearing an oath in front of Țețu, the scene is irresistible. I laugh almost heartily.
The rat-man comes over. He carefully takes my head between his hands and starts striking it against the wall. In my mouth a taste of blood. Somebody yells:
— She is crazy, fit to be tied.
The rat-man takes the same sleeve out of the drawer. I lose consciousness...

✢

I am lying on the board. Iulișca is next to me. Crying. For the first time I see her crying. She grabs my hand every time the steps seem to stop in front of our door. Then she starts making signs. She wants to talk to me. She puts her hands on her belly, then points with her finger toward the corridor. She then points at me. She now holds in her hands an imaginary bottle and pretends to drink, drink. Her eyes grow large, frightened. I make an interrogative gesture. I don't understand, I don't want to understand. She is trying to use sign language. I would have never thought that a game learned in kindergarten might serve in such a moment, and especially for such confidences. I follow her with difficulty. She probably doesn't know Romanian well and mangles words: guards... drink; they can't... leave the prison... after the investigators leave... She starts shaking, is not able to continue. She puts a hand on her belly again, keeps pointing at me with the other.
Suddenly it is very hot in the cell. I jump up. I hold my head in my hands, make two steps, reach the door. I turn, make four more steps, reach the wall, turn, make four steps, reach the door, turn, four more steps, reach the wall, turn...

In the Beginning Was the End

✦

The night passes more slowly. I cannot sleep at all. The door opens, two guards pull me by the hand. Interrogation office. The rat-man is not there; neither are the others. Only the guards and, on the table, bottles of booze.
I understand now Iulişca's hysterical shaking. Where did they take her? To another cell? Interrogations. At night when the interrogators are gone. Those that smell of alcohol. Those that are not allowed to leave the prison...

✦

Another interrogation. My legs feel heavy. Like I am wearing chains.
– Write, write:
That Rădescu is the head of the conspiracy;
That Maniu is the head of the conspiracy;
That Brătianu is the head of the conspiracy;
That the Americans are the heads of the conspiracy;
That the English are the heads of the conspiracy.
I yell:
– Why don't you write instead that female prisoners are at the guards' disposal?
Slaps, punches. Revolvers pointed at me.
– The Russians want to investigate you.
– Maybe they are more civilized than you!
– You are going to go to Siberia.
– *Scânteia* writes that Siberia is very beautiful.
– We will kill you right here.
– Do it, let's go, do it! I've had it, had it!
The rat-man strikes the desk with his fist.
– Sign.
– No.
I am thrown into the cement-floor cell. My legs won't hold me up anymore. I crumple to the floor.

Adriana Georgescu

✤

I come back to my senses. Two men lift me and prop me up.
– Write, write: "I declare of my own free will that:
I wanted to kill Ana Pauker;
I wanted to kill Gheorghiu-Dej;
I wanted to kill Bodnăraş;
I wanted to kill Teohari Georgescu;
I wanted to kill Vasile Luca.
– Don't you think these are too many?
Slaps.
– All reactionaries of your kind will be soon in prison.
– This is a prison or a brothel?
– We will kill you right here.
– That's all I want. Please, do it.

✤

Days and nights. Nights and days. How many have passed? The night interrogations continue. During the day, visits from the man with gentle eyes. What was his role?
The last two days they have been more nervous.
– Sign, sign.
Now, nothing in the world would make me sign. It's all the same to me. At night the same nightmare, always the same. Sometimes I dream that I died and I feel light, light. When I awake, I hear shouts, gun shots. I am afraid especially of the sound of steps. When they get close. When they stop in front of the door.
Once more, the man with gentle eyes. He brings me a glass of milk.
– In two days you are going to go.
– Where?
– You'll see!
Milk, a slice of bread. I swallow the milk, don't manage to chew the bread. My teeth are loose. They keep dragging me night after night to interrogation. Same questions. I don't even answer anymore. Insults, revolvers, slaps, punches, the sleeve, then the head against the walls, always the head against the walls, all these leave me indifferent!

One evening the rat-man:
– If you start telling all sorts of things at the trial, you'll be back here again. And we'll take even better care of you.
"Trial". I am startled. The first opening. There will be a trial. I will be able to talk.
Would I really be able to tell it all?

✢

Finally a shower. I was allowed to take a shower. I asked, every time the man with the gentle eyes entered the cell:
– I would like to take a shower.
Why did he grant it now? Because of the trial?
I am alone in a big room that smells bad. The cement is slippery. An open window. Sounds of cars. The street. People passing up and down, they are free to pass up and down. Voices in front of the window.
I wash. I have scabies.
I would like to look out on the street, I would like to look out on the street. I put on my overalls. I hit the glass with my shoe. Shards. I see the street. Soldiers in wagons, probably coming back from the front. A wagon stops in front of the window. A soldier yells at me:
– Are you German?
Probably thinks that only Germans can be arrested.
I start crying and I am not able to answer. The guard enters, sees me crying in front of the broken window, doesn't shout, says only, pulling me by the hand:
– Let's go, come on!
I shuffle into the corridor and keep crying. The guard doesn't push me. I think I will never be able to stop crying. "Are you German?"
Interrogation again. In the office, unknown faces. A man throws me the dress.
– Take off the overalls.
I have difficulty dressing in front of them. They watch me with a strange hatred. My right arm is blue. My back hurts. Not even putting on my dress pleases me. It belongs to a different time, a different world. I will never again be part of that world. Why didn't

they shoot me, why?
A night without interrogation. Next day the door opens.
– Come.
We go out into the yard. They blindfold me. The car. Same pistols in the ribs. And, like when we came, we drive endlessly. Where are they taking me?

In the Beginning Was the End

II

An agent removes the blindfold. I am in the same office at the Interior Ministry. How much time has passed since I was here for the first time? A month? More? Less? The fair-haired man is no longer here. The agent that led me gives my handbag to an employee. Inventory. I am handed over, with papers in order, by the Secret Service (the future *Securitate*[54]) to the Interior Ministry. So the barn-like prison was *Securitate*.

I go to another room. I am undressed and searched by a woman. Now they make me go downstairs. Towards the lock-up? The soldiers entrust me to another guard. We start down a corridor. We arrive.

A cell twice as big as at the *Securitate*. An old woman on the floor; slobbering. Another, middle-aged, lying on the bed. The cell has a wash-basin. I run and turn on the faucet. Water, finally fresh water. I wash, drink, I wash.

I have the impression that I'll never again be able to wash enough!

✦

I pace the cell, up and down, limping. All the pain has become concentrated in my right thigh, I can't touch it without crying. We talk in whispers. The two women – mother and daughter – are Russians. The daughter speaks German and I manage to understand what she is saying. They ran away from Odessa. During the mother's epileptic seizures, I retreat into a corner. I am afraid she

---

[54] *Securitate*: common name of the General Directorate of the People's Security Service. Repressive organization set up by the Romanian Communist Party in 1948, based on the Soviet NKVD, and used to destroy political opposition. Until 1989, the Romanian Communist Party imposed *'the dictatorship of the proletariat'* primarily through the strict control and terror engendered by the *Securitate*, which was considered by the Party to be *'the edge of its sword'*.

might strangle both of us. She seems really crazy, she mumbles meaningless sentences, in which Stalin's and Hitler's names recur frequently, shouts, tears her hair out, rolls on the floor in convulsions. The guards open the door to better watch the scene. It seems to amuse them greatly. One of them moves forward into the cell, and the old woman grabs him by one leg of his pants with her skeleton-like fingers, and pulls, pulls. Even with all the blows they give her, the other guards manage only with difficulty to free their mate. The old woman seems to have concentrated all the strength in her body in the claw that grabs anything within her reach.

The guards have locked the door. The old woman is still lying on the floor, foam at her mouth.

✢

I couldn't close my eyes all night. The old woman had two seizures. I feel that her madness is gradually enveloping me and, when she starts shouting, I feel like accompanying her in a low tone. I wait for the interrogation that does not come. Every hour I put my head under the faucet and let the water run, run. Soon it becomes an obsession. At the first shout of the old woman, the shout that announces another crisis, I run to the wash-basin.

Gradually I see the dawn light. Steps in the corridor. The changing of the guards. After a few minutes, I hear muted sounds through the wall. The Russian runs over and glues her ear to the wall. She listens, then motions to me to come closer. A man's voice says in German:

– Has a new one come in there?

I answer in Romanian:

– Yes, what's going on outside?

– I don't know. What is your name?

– Adriana Georgescu.

– You? Because of you I am here.

I am suddenly covered in cold sweat. Who is he? Did I pronounce his name? The injection? The voice is completely strange to me.

– Who are you?

– Ion Marinescu.

– I don't know you.

In the Beginning Was the End

– Me neither. I was passing on the street when they arrested you. You called to me and....

Steps in the corridor. They stop in front of the cell where the voice was coming from. They open the door, enter. We can talk no longer.

I run to the wash-basin. I let the water run over my face, my hair, my arms. The yellow circles start spinning again in front of my eyes. I thought it was Horia. I had called to him. They arrested him because of me. How long has it been? How long has he been here? It's absurd, absurd. He isn't guilty. But how can I make them understand? Innocent, innocent.

I probably shouted because the old woman raises her face towards me and grins. Nobody can do anything. It's absurd, this is all absurd.

✣

Once the corridor is quiet I run to the wall and call, knock, call. Ion Marinescu does not answer anymore. Did they take him away? Where did they take him? I just have time to get away from the wall as the door opens. The guards are bringing the soup. The old woman laps, like a dog, at the yellow liquid that runs down her chin, throat, hands. Her daughter, sitting next to me on the bed, looks at her almost indifferently and says:

– They are going to send us home. Do you know what that means: to send us there?

I nod affirmatively and try to quiet her.

– No, you don't. You cannot know. Nobody can. Freedom there is worse than prison here. I loved three people. My husband: he disappeared; they came and took him one evening, he must be in a camp. My brother: the Germans killed him. And this, my mother... you can see for yourself.

– Aren't you afraid to talk like this?

– Fear? No, I am not afraid. I've had it with always being afraid. They'll kill me anyway.

– Maybe they won't kill you.

– You talk like a communist. You are naive. Aren't you a communist?

— If I was a communist I would be free now.
— No. Everybody thinks that in the beginning. I also believed. I fought for them. It would take too long to explain. I was a teacher.
— Listen, shut-up. Maybe they can hear us.
— I told you. I've had enough of always being afraid. Another of their big discoveries: fear! Fear of talking too much, fear of not talking enough, fear of talking in your sleep, fear of strangers, fear of your children, fear of your husband, fear of yourself. That's the worst: fear of yourself. I decided after leaving Odessa not to be afraid anymore. I say everything on my mind. Everything, to everybody.

She leans towards me and tells me mysteriously:
— I have discovered something: if I am not afraid, I am free. You can tell everybody, even here, that you have met Varvara, the one who is no longer afraid. It's going to become more and more uncommon, a person who is not afraid. You can tell them my secret. Tell them: "Varvara has discovered the secret of freedom." You'll remember, won't you? Tell them like this, Varvara...

She gets more and more excited and talks loudly. The old woman, in turn, has started yelling, asking for the death of Stalin and Hitler. She is on the brink of a crisis. Varvara, the one who is no longer afraid...

Automatically, I get up and put my head under the faucet. I let the water run, run...

✦

My teeth are shaking. During the old woman's epileptic seizure, I start shaking, and my teeth are chattering in my mouth with a dull noise. Varvara has fallen into a state of total apathy.

I move close to her and try to console her:
— You'll see, one day all this is going to change.
She shakes her head and tells me in a flat voice:
— There isn't going to be a tomorrow.
But yes, there is going to be a tomorrow. There'll be a trial.
What's going on outside? Why don't they call me for interrogation anymore? Two days since I came here. I have been here for two days.

I would like to open the window, but it is sealed shut. There is a

In the Beginning Was the End

horrible smell in the cell. The old woman cannot go to the toilet and goes on the cement floor. The guards do not allow us to clean it, and the feces are piling up. I feel like throwing up all the time... The door opens. Two guards motion to me to follow them. We leave. We enter an office where a man is signing some papers.
– "Transferred to the Martial Court."
I am handed to some soldiers, with whom I go downstairs. I thought I was going to interrogation. I didn't say goodbye to "Varvara who is no longer afraid."
When we go out into the street in front of the ministry, I remember the words she told me, panting: "I've discovered the secret of freedom."

+

The soldiers lift me into a truck and then jump in too. There are about thirty people in the truck. I recognize four colleagues from *Viitorul* and, in a corner, I see Țețu, who shouts:
– Adriana!
The agents yell:
– You are not allowed to talk to each other.
The truck starts. All the men stare at me with their teeth clenched. I probably look like death. Their eyes are full of fear. We are so busy talking with our eyes that we only glance at the streets we pass, at the people who stop to look at us.

We go by a clock: it's six o'clock. There is a heavy, sultry heat. Somewhere a storm is brewing.

The truck stops. We are at the Martial Court. A soldier helps me climb down and takes me to an office. On the door is written "Martial Court Commander." A colonel, sitting behind a desk, looks at me and asks me in a neutral tone:
– Were you General Rădescu's chief of staff?
– Yes.

He writes something on a sheet of paper and hands it to one of the *Securitate* agents, who remains standing, behind his chair.
– Goodbye, miss. Thank you.

From one prison to another, the tone has changed suddenly. The soldiers take me into the yard. The men are lined up two by two. On each side of the row, armed soldiers. The soldier that accompa-

111

nies me shows me a place in the row:
— Here, miss.
I am next to an aged man, with a drawn face. We cross the yard. While walking, the man next to me tells me:
— I am Antim Boghea, socialist.
The soldier doesn't try to impose silence. The man continues:
— Are you Adriana Georgescu?
I whisper:
— Yes.
— You are limping. Did they beat you?
— Yes.
— Me too.
— Who are the others?
— I don't know, we'll meet them.

The line stops in front of a barbed wire fence. Must be the border between the barracks and the prison. A soldier opens a gate and lets us pass one by one. We enter a big room with some thirty beds. The men run towards each other and ask:
— Who are you? And you, and you?
A soldier comes to me:
— Miss, next door if you please.

I didn't have time to find out the names of all the men. I tell them good-evening, and follow the soldier next door. It's almost like a private room, with a real bed, clean sheets and a barred window to the street. I run to the window. A street-car passes very close and I can see the figures moving inside. I can also see people going in and out of the store across the street.

I don't know how long I sat at the window watching the moving, living street. I turn out the light and go to bed, for the first time in how long, in a real bed. The soldiers are on guard in front of the barracks. I am suddenly filled with a feeling of safety, and fall asleep very quickly.

✢

Next day, the soldiers come to take me for finger-printing. An agent sticks my hands to my wrists in a black substance and tells me, while turning them:
— These are wires, not fingers.

In the Beginning Was the End

– You try a rest-cure at *Securitate*, and yours will look the same.
He doesn't say anything and hands me a rag soaked in gasoline, with which I try in vain to make my hands regain their natural color. I give up quickly and motion to the soldier that I am ready. He tells me, while leading me back:
– During the day you can stay in the same room with the men.
When I enter the room, the men are roaring with laughter. One of them jumps up holding some newspapers. A colleague from the paper shows me to a seat.
– Make yourself comfortable so as to better enjoy the bed-time story we are going to read you. Listen to *România Liberă* of August 30th:
Sensational discovery of the terrorist and fascist T organization. Numerous arrests among the Liberal and National-Peasant youth. Under the political control of the leaders of the two historical parties. The T organization tried to eliminate the democratic leaders of the government and the people. The discovery of fascist propaganda material. The terrorists confessed. General's Rădescu's role.
Another hands me the paper.
– Look closely at the picture.
A photograph under heavy headlines:
Printing house and arms and munitions storehouse of the T organization.
– Arms? Munitions?
– At the trial it is going to be easy to prove they are not our arms. They just finger-printed us. They need only compare them with those on the arms.
A man climbs up on a chair and asks for quiet:
– As regards the arms, I am going to tell you a very nice little story, also very true. When they came to arrest me, they turned the house upside down. There were a few fliers in a corner, but they probably didn't think that that was sufficient. They kept searching everywhere. Finally they found two ashtrays in the entrance hall.
New roars of laughter. The man gestures, asking for quiet.
– Yes, two ashtrays! During the air raids, we left the city with a friend that had a car. In the fields around Bucharest we found a few exploded hand-grenades. I brought two of them home and made them into ashtrays. The agents took them as evidence. If it wasn't

for the interrogations, this story would have been really funny!
If it wasn't for the *Securitate* interrogations...

Another man asks for quiet and reads in turn:

The circulation of clandestine, fascist fliers and of a propaganda sheet named Văpaia[55] *had already aroused suspicion that there were subversive political groups.*

Following arrests and investigations, the democratic authorities have found the secret printing house where this organization was printing their fascist sheet. The printed material and confessions of the accused have shed light on the plans of this organization and their political accomplices. The organization intended to eliminate members of government by terrorist means. The terrorists confessed they wanted to kill the president of the Council, Petru Groza. The head of the Organization, Remus Țețu, declared that he received instructions directly from General Rădescu. Țețu edited the underground newspaper Văpaia, *with a circulation of 1,500 to 2,000 copies, at "his underground residence".*

I laugh together with everybody else, and tell Țețu:

– Listen, brother, let's get it straight: 1,500 or 2,000 copies, there's a little difference.

Țețu does not seem to enjoy the joke and shrugs his shoulders. The man keeps reading:

It's interesting to note that Maniu's statements were printed on the same Boston linotype that was used for Văpaia. *The recruitment of organization members was made according to the Iron Guard system, with mystical oaths in a mysterious setting. Members who broke their oaths were to be shot.*

– Oh, well, Țețu dear, you are becoming a very important figure. I can just see myself kneeling in front of you and taking the

---

[55] *Văpaia* (The Flame): manifesto-magazine edited by Remus Țețu, which criticized the Soviet occupation and the communists. The Romanian edition of "In the Beginning Was the End", which was translated from the original French edition, uses the name *Flacăra* when referring to this manifesto. In Romanian, 'flacără' and 'văpaia' are synonyms for 'flame'. The leaflet referred to here is not the better known publication *Flacăra* that was founded in 1948 as a cultural magazine of the communist trade unions' writers and journalists. The latter *Flacăra* began its activity by denouncing 'reactionary elements' in Romanian culture and by praising Soviet achievements. It became an instrument by which the Romanian Communist Party imposed its opinions in all cultural matters.

In the Beginning Was the End

oath. Mystical setting. You wear a mask, and I kiss the hem of your sacred robe.

The one who spoke lies in bed laughing so hard he is crying. And, as Țețu does not reply:

– Why the hell are they staging this terrorist affair around a simple flier? The press is talking exclusively about T. A soldier just told me that every radio broadcast starts with: "T stands for Terror."

– They are ridiculous, breaks in another. How can they do this? Elections will take place and they won't be able to remain in power.

Antim Boghea breaks in:

– Let's not be too happy, and especially let's not be so optimistic. If they make such a noise about a flier – and excuse me Țețu dear – a rather childish one, which doesn't contain anything serious, then they'll probably work even harder on the elections, which will be free only in name. You are all still children. I am an old socialist, and I know their methods well. When they needed it, they staged large trials without even the pretext of a demonstration. It's possible that this story has been cooked up for the international conference that will open in London on September 11th. The Russians probably want to show the Allies that the only truly democratic party in Romania is the Communist party. As for the others, they are all fascist, as will be shown by the Bucharest trial. Yes, this must be the Russians' aim. But I misspeak: not the Russians, but the Stalinists – the Russian people, that's different, they don't have a word to say.

We stop laughing. Antim Boghea's words weigh heavily. I take the paper in turn and continue reading aloud:

General Rădescu's role. It follows from Remus Țețu's and Adriana Georgescu's statements, and also from the presence in the organization of some of the General's close collaborators, that Rădescu was the brain of the organization, to which he regularly sent instructions.

I stop reading to shout:

– What close collaborators? Aside from myself, I don't see anybody else among you. And anyway, I never signed such a statement.

– Keep reading.

It also follows from the statements of the members of the organization that Maniu and Brătianu were aware of the plans and ac-

tivities of the terrorist organization.

Also aware of its existence: Bebe Brătianu, Professor Danielopolu, Mihai Fărcăşanu, Carandino, and other members of the reactionary clique. The terrorists will answer for their crimes in front of the Martial Court, but nevertheless we must not ignore the political role played by Maniu's and Brătianu's cliques.

The merger with remnants of Antonescu's followers and of the Iron Guard, and the use of fascist methods are simply the unavoidable consequence of the political views that Maniu has always held, and this should not be ignored by public opinion, despite the fact that Maniu is not in the defendant's box.

The uproar starts again. A young man shouts:

– In other words: even though we weren't able, despite all the methods used, to extract from the accused the statements necessary to bring Maniu and the others to the defendant's box.

One of my other colleagues from *Viitorul* comes near me while reading:

Georgescu Adriana: lawyer, member of the Liberal Youth, former Chief of Staff at the Interior Ministry, distributed clandestine publications, was a member of the T organization, was the liaison between Ţeţu and Rădescu. Proofs: her own statements, and also Ţeţu's.

– Look at the whole list. Only next to your name is the word "proofs". Why?

And continues:

– You were the only one who personally knew Maniu, Brătianu, and Rădescu. They are probably counting a lot on your statements. "Proofs". If they write this, they probably don't have them. If they had them, Maniu, Brătianu, and Rădescu would by now be jailed next door. But they aren't.

And, after an hesitation:

– Tell me: what did they do to you there?

Deep silence in the whole room. Everybody is staring at me. I whisper:

– You'll find out at the trial.

Then, in the continuing silence, I take a few papers and go next door.

In the Beginning Was the End

✦

I am alone in my room, my head on the window bars. Yesterday Istrate Micescu came to see me. He is one of our great lawyers, an excellent solicitor, an authority of the bar, from which he was removed.
– Seventy-three lawyers have signed up to defend you. I'll be the seventy-fourth. I'll be a witness.
He tells me that Maniu, Brătianu and Titel Petrescu understand the whole affair perfectly. By arresting the young members of their parties, the communists want to show the international public that these parties teach their members fascist methods, and thus discredit them. As for the Romanian public, it understands the situation and waits for the elections. This is a trial staged for foreign countries. We must be strong.

After Istrate Micescu left, I went over to find the men and tell them about the conversation. We opened the window wide, and started singing the national anthem. On the street passers-by stopped, as did some cars and a tram. The whole street was singing with us. Five minutes later, the military prosecutor entered the room together with two *Securitate* agents. One of the agents shouted:
– Close the window! As for the singer, take her to Văcărești[56] to quiet down and think about what is waiting for her after the trial.

I am the singer. The military prosecutor didn't say anything. I am waiting to be transferred to Văcărești prison.

✦

In a car, between two soldiers who offer me cigarettes:
– Why are they sending you to Văcărești? For singing the national anthem? Too bad you didn't have the time to kill them!
– The newspapers are saying stupid things.
– Didn't you want to kill the heads of the government?
– No, I don't think I could kill anybody.

---

[56] The Văcărești prison: close to Bucharest, it was located in the monastery of the same name. A prison hospital functioned there until 1960. After the prison was closed, the monastery, a monument of medieval architecture, was demolished by order of Nicolae Ceaușescu in the mid 80's.

– Too bad.
– Yes, too bad.

✢

The soldiers stop the car and buy fruit and cigarettes. They get back in and offer me the pack.
– For you.
Suddenly I feel free and shake their hands.

✢

We stop in front of the prison. A big sign: "Ilfov Women's Penitentiary". I climb the stairs holding the package the soldiers gave me under my arm. I have been here once for a common law client, a young woman accused of a crime. My first success: she was acquitted.

I can see her again, her head resting on the bars, with a gesture that became familiar: "I am innocent, you know, I am innocent". She was crying.

The guard is different now. When we enter he is shouting at some gypsy-women who are sitting on the floor and breast-feeding their children.

The soldiers hand me over to the guard.
– Preventive custody until the trial.
Before leaving, they tell me:
– Good luck, miss!
The guard assumes an important air:
– So, you are the terrorist. I'll take you to Mrs. Director.

He opens the door on the right and tells me to enter. In the room, three women, one of them quite fat, sitting behind a desk. And, since they are sitting and watching me, I say:
– Good-day.
The fat woman shouts:
– Here we don't say "Good-day". We say: "Respectful greetings, Mrs. Chief Warden".

I am not able to control my nerves at all. I laugh with tears. The Chief Warden yells while the guard, bending toward her, whispers something in her ear. She comes to me and pushes me toward the

In the Beginning Was the End

other two women who fingerprint me.
I hear a choir singing somewhere inside the prison "Our Father, who art in heaven...".
The Chief Warden asks me how I, "a young woman with such a gentle air", could lead a band of terrorists. I explain to her that, aside from four young men whom I haven't seen in a rather long time, I only met the others at the Martial Court. She starts shouting again:
– You are a "hypocrite liar". And I thought you were a decent young woman! Take her away. And don't forget: here you must say "Respectful greetings, Mrs. Chief Warden".

✢

The guard opens a very small rectangular door in the wall. I have to bend down in order to enter a big, badly lit room, filled with a nauseating odor. Bunk beds. Three rows of them. About two steps between them. Deep silence at my entrance. I assume it is hostile. A woman hisses:
– Look at her, the brat.
Another comments:
– Don't be silly. Look at her, she is limping!
I climb with difficulty to the bed pointed out by the guard. The sheet of a dubious color is full of bed bugs. There are more of them than in all the cells at *Securitate* and Interior put together. The beds start spinning in front of my eyes, and I stretch out. I lift my feet and put them on the wall, covering them with the newspaper "Mrs. Chief Warden" has just given me saying: "Read this and don't tell me tall tales". So I read in *Scânteia*:
T means Terror. The death teams reappear with the same cast of characters. The same, but even more dangerous than in the past, because they haven't learned anything from the lesson the democracies gave Hitler.
– Hey, you with the feet up, salute me, the Chief Guard, and come down for report.
A woman gives me a hand.
– Come on kid, climb down.
The women are lined up in two rows. The guard tells them with a martial air:

119

– Good night, girls!
– Yes Ma'am, answer the girls in unison.
I feel like laughing again. As the door closes, two women approach me.
– What gang are you from?
The loud-speaker drowns us out:
"*This is Moscow: the fact that dozens of threads connect Rădescu's, Maniu's and Brătianu's terrorist organizations cannot surprise any observer who is in the least familiar with Romania's political history.*"
The women start shouting:
– Shut-up! Why do they keep bothering us with their stories!
The one next to me starts again:
– Did you swallow your tongue? What gang are you from?
The loud-speaker goes on:
"*This is a list of the terrorists: Georgescu, Adriana, the tool of the Palace Square Executioner.*"
– From what gang? I am "the tool of the Palace Square Executioner."
My neighbor seems delighted:
– Wow! So you wanted to snuff all of them? Ana Pauker too? I was with Ana Pauker in prison at Dumbrăveni[57]. She had her kitchen, personal so to speak. Lucky. After a while, maybe you'll have one too. She kept getting all sorts of packages from Russia. Nice girl, for sure. She gave me coffee with milk and cake and kept telling me about "Max", Lenin, her guys, just like that. I kept saying yes and eating her cake. After that, Russians took her. Now, look at her, she came back. She plays the big shot now and rides in a car. She pretended not to know me one day when I saw her on the street.
And with a precious air she extends her hand:
– I am Florica Ungureanu. Fifteen times in the lock-up. I just rest up, let me tell you.

---

[57] The Dumbrăveni prison: situated in Transylvania, it was used, both in the interwar period and during the communist regime, for the detention of women. After 1945, at Dumbrăveni, as well as in the prisons at Mislea and Miercurea-Ciuc, were detained women active in the anti-communist ance, as well as daughters and wives of former democratic leaders.

In the Beginning Was the End

And Florica Ungureanu shouts to the others:
— Girls! The kid is a gang chief. She is the terrorist who wanted to do all the gov'ment in.
— All right, kid. Are you a gang chief?
I feel like a caged lion. They all gather around to look at me. One of them touches me and asks:
— Are you from Puica's gang?
— Puica?
— The one that killed an actress to swipe her jewels. Next to the theater. If you got your way with Ana Pauker, you would have Stalin's jewels too.
Another breaks in:
— You fool. She is a political. Just like Ana Pauker. Ana put a bomb to kill the parliamen' and this terrorist had a gang to kill the gov'ment. They only quarrel with each other, the politicals.
— I didn't want to kill anybody.
— Don't play the prude. You can't fool us. Does the radio say or doesn't it that you are a terrorist? Yes. Well then.
Florica Ungureanu again:
— And the papers. First page. We got to see your mug.
Another intervenes:
— But yours wasn't like mine. I'm better than you. My picture on the front page, and in heavy letters: Gabi, the woman with eight fiancés.
Then with false modesty:
— I killed them all.
— Don't brag so much, you rag, yells another, who, crouched on a bucket, her skirts up, is going to the toilet.
— Go and wash your ass, whore! Your ass is dragging.
The latter jumps up and grabs "Eight fiancés Gabi" by the hair. The others run. Everybody joins the fight. The loud-speaker plays music.
At the other end of the room five bare-breasted women are dancing hysterically.
I take advantage of the hubbub to climb back into my bed. "Eight fiancés Gabi" gets out of the mêlée first and comes over. I have to share the bed with her. She shows me how to kill the bed bugs:
— Take a sheet of newspaper, spit on it, aim at the bed-bug and crush it.

While dancing, the women overturned the bucket. The windows are sealed shut. The odor spreads throughout the room.
I don't sleep the whole night. At dawn the cell boss tells me:
– Hey, terrorist, you think you're at a ball? Look at all the confetti you made. Quick, come down and sweep.
The "confetti" are scraps of newspaper. "Gabi's method". Too disgusted to keep crushing bed-bugs, all night long I threw the papers that Gabi gave me on the floor. I sweep.
The boss softens up.
– You're a decent terrorist. It's your turn for duty.
– What duty?
– Bucket duty. Let's go, pick them up.
I take two buckets, and follow the boss. We go out in the yard and stand in line in front of two primitive toilets where we have to dump the buckets. On the cement in the yard some gypsy-women delouse each other, looking through their hair, lazily stretching in the sun. When I get back to the room, they applaud. Gabi asks for silence and tells me with great dignity:
– You know, terrorist, you're OK. You aren't stuck-up.
Her declaration of friendship results in another turn at the buckets, which I have to do as a token of gratitude.

✦

How long have I been at Văcăreşti? During the day, I sleep on the floor. At night, I hunt bed-bugs, faithfully following "Gabi's method". When I have time to think, I think about the trial. The loud-speaker airs daily more commentaries from Radio Moscow.
"The chief of the T organization confessed their intention to continue with terrorist acts and called upon its members to ready their weapons for a special mission. In their fliers, the fascists dared to say that some day war between the USSR and the Allies will be unavoidable."
How could "the organization" continue with terrorist acts it never committed in the first place? I try to order my thoughts. I don't remember exactly what was in *Văpaia*. Anyway, it wasn't the most interesting flier. What did Ţeţu tell the General that day? It was stupid to take Ţeţu to the General. The whole affair is ludicrous.
The loud-speaker goes on:

In the Beginning Was the End

"The organization had underground offices and locations. The organization had a secret code. The meetings between agents were arranged by phone using previously agreed on code-words. The reports were handed in hierarchically. There were three types of reports: mission execution reports and exceptional reports. The first were handed in weekly and ended with a standard formula saying if the person reporting had weapons, and of what caliber."

I wish I still had the strength to laugh. "Three types of reports", and there are two, the standard formula indicating the caliber of weapons, all this babble, all the clichés repeated at the inquiry and repeated again now by Radio Moscow and the communist press. What did I sign? The injection? My head is burning, burning.

✢

That evening, after she wished us "Good night, girls" and waited for us to answer in unison "Yes, Ma'am", the guard tells me that tomorrow, at day-break, she will come to take me for "judgment".

Big excitement in the room.

– Listen, if they put you to the wall, leave me your shoes. They're good.

Florica wants to give me a red blouse.

– Make yourself beautiful, girl. Eat something, you look like you just got out of shit.

– Leave her alone with your rags. You want her to play the prude. Listen kid, whine all the time. Keep whining till you soften up the judge. Pretend you are fainting.

– How do I faint?

– Hit your head against the bench. Tomorrow when the dropper starts the street-cars, who else is going to be with you?

– Thirty-two men.

– Alone with thirty-two guys. Are they handsome, your guys?

– What does "dropper" mean?

– The clock, you rag. Don't be stuck-up.

I keep crushing bed-bugs.

Next day, at dawn, they gather around me to give me some last pieces of advice.

– Faint.

– Cry all you can.

– Tell them you have children who shouldn't be orphaned; that always works.

A gypsy-woman brings me some herb over which she cast a spell the day before. Another teaches me an incantation that will bring the death of the president.

I can barely stand up. The guard hands me over to some soldiers. It's day-break, the streets are empty, the city is still asleep. At the Martial Court I am led to the office of the Prison Commander. Next to him, sitting at a desk, the rat-man. The Commander gets up and leaves saying:

– See you soon, Mr. Nicolschi.

I feel extremely rich because I know his name. He gets up, tosses his cigarette and comes toward me. I don't back away.

– Listen, I'll be nice to you and give you some advice. If you don't follow it, you might regret it. You understand me, don't you? First, don't be cheeky at the trial, like you were during the investigation.

I smile, I am calm, relaxed: I know his name, I know his name!

– Next, don't say anything about the investigation before the trial. A single unnecessary word, and you've signed your death sentence. We'll kill you.

I keep smiling:

– I'm not asking for anything else. Got it?

A soldier enters:

– Can I take the detainee?

– Take her, I don't want to hear about her again.

Before leaving, I tell him quite calmly:

– See you soon, Nicolschi.

✝

In the yard the men are lined up two by two. I take my place next to Antim Boghea again, who shakes my hand.

– We were afraid for you. How was it at Văcărești?

– Not too bad. Aside from the bed-bugs.

– You were with the politicals?

– No, with the common criminals. What's the day today?

– Friday, September 7th.

In the Beginning Was the End

An officer yells an order. The column starts moving. Behind the closed gates we hear the din of the crowd. Antim Boghea says to me:
– The people who want to be at the trial.
– The trial must not be secret. Why don't they let them in?
– The C.P. probably thinks it's more prudent this way. And I understand them.
We start down a corridor and are ushered into the accused' s box. In the hall, British and American uniforms. I squeeze Antim Boghea's hand.
– They came.
– Yes. We'll have to try to tell as much as possible.
A young man behind me stirs:
– London and Washington will find out tomorrow. Their representatives are here.
I clench my teeth. I'll have to tell everything, everything.
The court is announced. Everybody rises. The court enters: General Ilie Crețulescu, Colonel Magistrate Iorgu Negreanu, and Colonel Niță Nicolau. Identification questions start. Aside from three older socialists, none of us is over thirty. The majority of the young men are Law School and Polytechnic students. Once identifications have been done, the President asks us if we have lawyers. Professor Veniamin, one of the lawyers, answers affirmatively: seventy-three lawyers have signed up for the defense. The Court retains only thirty-two.
I rise.
– I would like to report an incident. I would also like for it to be entered in the official record of the session.
The President gives me the floor. The men are staring at me.
– Mr. President, Mr. Nicolschi from *Securitate*, who during the investigation used and abused a great variety of threats, told me an hour ago in the office of the Martial Court Commander, and I quote: "One single unnecessary word and you've signed your death sentence. If you talk we'll kill you."
The President says:
– You stated earlier during the identification proceedings that you are also a lawyer. You should have answered Mr. Nicolschi from *Securitate* that there is no need for him to intervene, because

you are now under the jurisdiction of the Martial Court.
I sit down. The men pat me on the back whispering: "Well played, you were terrific", while Antim Boghea whispers in my ear:
– Maybe we're going to pay dearly, but it's worth it.

A lawyer asks for the trial to be postponed, the defense not having had the necessary time to study the dossier. Three others join him. A fourth disputes the validity of the law used to bring us in front of the Martial Court, a fifth...

I barely listen. I ponder the words, the phrases I will say, I look at the members of the British and American missions, who are taking notes. The room is spinning in front of my eyes, I would like to say everything as soon as possible. The lawyers ask for a new trial date. The session is adjourned. The Court will deliberate the issues brought up by the defense. The trial is adjourned till Monday, September 10th, at nine o'clock in the morning.

We are again gathered in the big room at the prison. I share with the men the pack of cigarettes given to me by a lawyer when the trial was adjourned, and we smoke while reading the papers. Antim Boghea has big news: Maniu, Brătianu and Titel Petrescu have asked to be called as witnesses. A young man climbs up on a chair, imitates the BBC's three muted signals, and calls out:
– Communiqué from the Great General Staff of Freedom. Victorious operations on all fronts. Retreat of the enemy troops. Strategic detail: in the hall, representatives of the Anglo-American missions. Troop morale: excellent.

We sing, we laugh, we feel very young.

✦

It gets dark, then a young man rushes into the room shouting:
– Quick, we have to barricade the door. Nicolschi and the *Securitate* team will be here in a moment. I just saw them getting out of two buses stopped in front of the barbed wire fence.
– Nonsense. The President told Adriana that *Securitate* no longer has any power over us.

I open the door, and indeed see Nicolschi and five agents on the corridor. I shout to the men:
– Everybody into my room. Let's barricade ourselves in there: they are here.

In the Beginning Was the End

We all crowd into my room. Four men block the door. Three others open the street window and shout at the passers-by:
– Save us. *Securitate* wants to kidnap us. We belong to the so-called T organization.
People stop in the street. Behind the door, Nicolschi yells:
– Open the door, you dirty reactionaries!
I tell them:
– *We'll open the door only to the military prosecutor. Let the military prosecutor come and tell us to open the door.*
The agents start pounding on the door. We all yell in unison:
– Military prosecutor!
The door breaks open.
– With or without the military prosecutor, we know how to kill you, you stinking reactionary rabble!, shouts an agent.
We all go silent. The military prosecutor enters, followed by Nicolschi.
– You must follow them. I'll go with you.
He is livid. Agents surround us while Nicolschi yells:
– Who gave newspapers to these vipers? Who allowed them to smoke?
The agents push and punch us toward the door. The soldiers watch the scene.

✢

I keep my eyes closed. I don't dare look at the men. Are they going to kill us? The men are innocent. Only I talked. Are they going to kill us all?
A sudden stop. We have arrived. Stubbornly, I keep my eyes closed. Măglaşu, a socialist sitting next to me, squeezes my hand.
– We are at *Securitate*.
I feel like shouting: Anything, but not this! I wanted them to kill me, but this I won't be able to take anymore.
I am separated from the group, pushed down the corridor. I am thrown in a cell. I fall on the ground. Nobody else in the cell. All that I lived through at *Securitate* comes back into my mind, dances in front of my eyes, besieges me. I hold my head in my hands and keep repeating endlessly: "If I am not afraid, I am free."

Varvara's phrase, Varvara "the one who is no longer afraid". But I am afraid, terribly afraid.

✢

I fall asleep at dawn. They didn't take me for interrogation. A guard wakes me up:
– Let's go, come.
The day dawns. We go into the yard. The guard pushes me.
– Faster, you shit.
We are in front of a sentry box, inside is a warrant officer. Next to him, an agent, dossiers in hand.
– Here is your dossier.
I read the statements I gave. I breathe with relief.
"I, the undersigned, confess that I was a member of the T organization, and that I took an oath to overthrow the government by force." That's all. On the table, other dossiers are open next to mine. I pretend that I am carefully reading my statement and glance over at that of a man. "I, the undersigned, admit that I wanted to kill Ana Pauker, Teohari Georgescu, Vasile Luca, and probably Gheorghiu-Dej."
"Probably". I laugh. This young man, despite all the blows, kept his sense of humour.
The agent yells:
– Have you finished reading, you reactionary slime?
The guard pushes me. I return to the cell.

✢

Another guard brings me soup in a mess tin. I throw the soup on the floor immediately after he leaves. I am afraid they want to poison me. I am afraid of everything.
Night. Steps stop in front of the cell. The door opens:
– 17, for interrogation.
In the office, Nicolschi, and three more unknown figures.
– Sign here.
I read: "The undersigned states that I read the contents of my dossier and that I was well treated during the investigation".
– Are you going to sign, bitch?

– No, I prefer to write my own.
– Have you come to your senses?

I write: "The undersigned states that I have seen my dossier in the presence of a *Securitate* agent and a Martial Court warrant officer, but not of my lawyer, and that I was mistreated during the investigation."

Nicolschi raises his hand to hit me. Another holds him back:
– After the trial.
– Reactionary leper, you're going to loose your cheek. You'll play Mata-Hari in Siberia.
– Who is Mata-Hari?
– Don't roll your eyes like an idiot... and buzz off to your cell, before I make mince-meat out of you.

I "buzz off" to my cell.

✢

I can't fall asleep. All night long, the guards pace up and down in front of the cell. I obsessively repeat Varvara's phrase: "If I am not afraid, I am free; if I am not afraid, I am free."

✢

Next day, the guard opens the door:
– Let's go.

He pushes me out into the yard. A truck. I climb in. The men squeeze my hand. One of them whispers to me:
– They are taking us again to the Martial Court.

They are quite pale, but they keep smiling. The trial will resume.

✢

It is very warm in the hall. While entering, we glance at the spectators: the representatives of the missions are there again.

The Court is ushered in. General stupefaction. The Court is not the same! The President's outburst, after my intervention, probably displeased the Communist Party. The new President is named Alexandru Petrescu. Antim Boghea tells me:

– He is the former head of prisons under Antonescu. A few months ago he was still on the war-criminals list.

The President takes the oath, placing his hand on the cross. A dull sound, the cross breaks in two! Uproar in the hall. The meeting is suspended. A newspaperman shouts:
– This is sabotage. The hand of the reaction.

A lawyer answers:
– Or of God.

The Court reappears. They skip the oath. The second session is declared open. The lawyers complain about incidents of incompetence. The prosecutor denies their basis – it concerns our recent sojourn at *Securitate* – and closes the incident by reading the indictment. Organizing of underground, subversive groups, printing and distributing clandestine fliers, organizing of resistance groups and radio stations, planning attacks against the country's democratic leaders in order to disturb the existing order, caching of weapons.

He has finished reading the indictment.

I stand up.

– Mr. Prosecutor, what weapons are we talking about? If the Tribunal would kindly compare our fingerprints with those on the weapons, this accusation wouldn't stand up.

The President intervenes:
– Accused, you don't have the floor. We'll move on to the interrogation of the accused.

The men give their statements. They don't admit to being guilty. They say they signed what was dictated to them at the interrogation under physical or mental duress; because they were hungry or they were afraid. Those that signed immediately were not beaten.

A fair-haired youth declares that he never read or distributed *Văpaia*.

– You are accused of assembling a radio station.
– I would very much like to see it, Mr. President. My technical knowledge doesn't go beyond plugging in a record player.

The President says:
– You no longer have the floor. Next.

Next is Ion Maglaşu, socialist, former chief of the maritime trade-unions. He gets up, gives his first and last names and addresses the President:

In the Beginning Was the End

– How dare you declare as material evidence a thank-you card received from the British Embassy because I signed their register on Victory Day? How dare you call me a fascist? I personally met Mr. Bevin and Mr. Attlee at the London socialist congresses. They'll be quite amazed to find out I am a fascist, since at those congresses I represented the Romanian socialist movement.

The prosecutor shouts:
– You are a traitor to the working class and a breaker of the trade-union movement.

Maglaşu raises his voice also:
– Why? Because I organized trade-union elections despite the government ban? Am I fascist, or is the government? You know as well as I do that the government is.

The President silences him. Evidently that is more prudent. The meeting is adjourned. It will resume in the afternoon. Leaving, we all shake Maglaşu's hand.

✢

We eat sandwiches in the prison room while reading the newspapers.

An official government delegation is in Moscow. Tătărescu, the foreign minister, is received by Vîşinski.

Nothing about the postponement of the trial. Editorials about T. One headline: *From The Iron Guard to the T.* Beside it in heavy letters: *The Duty to Be Free.*

I laugh.
– They have a sense of humour.

One of the young men says:
– It seems like I'm at the theatre. The play is burlesque, the roles are badly assigned, no, not badly assigned, but rather reversed. On one side, the Court: the President is a war criminal, the prosecutor killed a Jew under the Germans. On the other side: the accused, belonging to the only parties that didn't collaborate with the Germans, the parties that carried out the coup d'état on August 23rd and overthrew Antonescu's regime!

Maglaşu shrugs:
– There are no reversed parts. Everything is in the natural order. One dictatorship replaced by another. One fascism by another. In

August 1939, Molotov shook Ribbentrop's hand. In August 1939, Russia and Germany signed a pact and divided between them a few countries. Those who saw that pact as a simple diplomatic act were mistaken. It aims much further. So it's normal that we are always on the bad side... that is the good side, in the accused's box.

Somebody else intervenes:
– None of their accusations stands up. We'll be acquitted.

Antim Boghea calms him down:
– Don't be too optimistic. Let's wait and see what happens at the London Conference. This rush to end the trial as soon as possible... I can just see the Soviet delegation at the conference reading our sentences, which they probably took with them from Moscow. The sentences have been already decided. Let's not deceive ourselves.

The men protest:
– There'll be elections and then not one single communist will be left in power.

Maglașu says with a tired voice:
– What if, at Yalta, the Anglo-Americans turned us over to the Soviets? Why don't we know the decisions taken at Yalta? What if at Yalta...?

Everybody shouts:
– That's stupid. You are crazy!

Maglașu continues:
– I wouldn't want to be an ill-omen. Anyway, I hope you are right.

A man rushes in:
– Listen, guys, I found out the names of the other two that led the investigation with Nicolschi: Bulz and Stroescu.

A young man stands up and clenches his fists, saying:
– Bulz and Stroescu. Nicolschi, Bulz and Stroescu.

Another whispers:
– Three names we won't forget. Isn't it true that we won't forget them, that nothing can make us forget them?

We all repeat:
– We won't forget them.

It's like an oath, the first oath we have sworn together.

In the Beginning Was the End

+

The afternoon session starts in an incredible din: outside the communists "are demonstrating". From the street we can hear shouts of: "Death to the terrorists, death to Țețu, death to Adriana Georgescu, death to Antim Boghea, death...".

Antim Boghea leans toward me:
– You see, they don't spare any efforts.

I shrug. I have only one obsession: to be allowed to talk. I don't care about anything else. I feel like I have a fever, and I would like to sleep. But first I have to talk.

The president gives the floor to Țețu.
– I confess I printed *Văpaia*. The government had suspended the magazine *Academia* [58]. *Scânteia* had already asked for my arrest. I called *Văpaia* the official newspaper of the T organization in order to ridicule the government. I did so in order to count all the freedoms suspended by the regime. The government, not us, should be in the accused's box. I went to see General Rădescu because I admire him. He was ill. Adriana Georgescu had asked me to fill a prescription for him. You know I have a pharmacy. I asked him to let me bring the medicine personally. I wanted to meet him. That's all. If the government hadn't banned my magazine, I wouldn't have needed to print fliers.

The President silences him.
– You aren't here to insult the government.

Each of us is allowed only three minutes for our deposition. The lawyers protest in vain.

Finally it is my turn. I stand up. Where should I start? I clench my fists. I hear my voice, a white voice seemingly outside my body.
– Mr. President, I was arrested in the street. A man who looks like one of my colleagues was passing by. I called to him. He was a stranger. He is now at the Interior Ministry. Why? Under what law? Mr. President, *Securitate* took us two days ago from the Martial Court in order to force us to give statements that we were well treated during the investigation. If we were well treated, why did

---

[58] *Academia*: weekly newspaper covering social and political topics, founded by Remus Țețu. Only 12 issues were published between October-December 1944.

Securitate still need these declarations? In fact, this is how I was mistreated during the investigation: insulted. Threatened. "If you don't sign, death or Siberia awaits you"..I was beaten. My head was hit against walls, methodically. I was whipped with a sand-filled sleeve. Kept in a cell. I was starved. I was deprived of "air". Put into a lock-up. Kept hours standing on my toes until I fainted. Injections to drug me. Slapped. They spat in my face. I ask for a medical examination to be able to show the result of other interrogation methods that I prefer not to talk about in public. I ask for a medical commission including both communist and non-political physicians.

In the hall, people stand up, agitated. The lawyers shout. The President says, with a bored demeanour:

– Don't you have anything more interesting to say?

– I ask for a medical examination.

– Continue with your statement or we'll go onto the next.

– I admit I was General Rădescu's Chief of Staff and a member of Liberal Youth. I confess I was General Rădescu's lawyer and that I saw him, in this capacity, at his home where he was under house arrest. At the interrogation I gave the mandate that empowered me to do so. Anyway, I don't know of any law that places someone under house arrest just because he was prime-minister and gave an anti-communist speech. I don't know of any such law in a democratic country. I would like for you to show me the law under which General Rădescu was placed under house arrest.

– Go back to the current matter or I'll silence you.

– I am in the middle of it, Mr. President. The government decided to make Maniu, Brătianu, Titel Petrescu and Rădescu the heads of a conspiracy concocted by the Central Committee of the C.P. *Securitate* thought it would be enough to torture us to get the necessary statements in order to bring all the heads of the opposition into the accused's box. Did *Securitate* truly believe that, even if we gave these statements, we wouldn't tell the Tribunal the means by which they were extorted? We can show these methods. I ask for a medical examination.

– If you continue in this tone, I will silence you.

– Mr. President, nothing in this world will stop us from telling the truth. And the truth is that this trial is a farce staged by the government, which wants to turn the country into a huge prison.

In the Beginning Was the End

As for terrorist organizations, they are the dictatorships, not the democratic parties that believe that governments are changed through elections. We belong to parties "whose terrorist methods" are elections.

The President rings the bell:
– You aren't here to put the government on trial. Do you admit you distributed *Văpaia*?
– If there was freedom of the press, I wouldn't have had to do it.
– How do you dare say that there is no freedom of the press?
– Mr. President, surely you have read the papers that talk about the trial. You must then have seen that all the papers simply repeat the words of Radio Moscow. I assume that no more analysis is needed regarding this point.
– You are impertinent.
– No, I am telling the truth. I am asking for a medical examination.
– You show your admiration for Rădescu.

He exasperates me. I shout:
– Not admiration, but worship, Mr. President.

My words had effects.

In the hall, the communists are yelling:
– The Palace Square executioner.

I shout even louder to cover their voices:
– That is also a Radio Moscow slogan!

The uproar is such that I can't continue. To my right, a young man says:
– Every time you mention Maniu, Brătianu or Rădescu, you get an extra year.

I manage to talk again:
– I have asked you already, Mr. President, to compare our fingerprints with those on the weapons pictured in the papers. Why don't you do it?

The President is beside himself:
– I silence you.
– I ask for a medical examination. The Court has to know about certain, very special, *Securitate* investigation methods.
– You no longer have the floor.

The lawyers are also asking for a medical examination. The men stand up one by one: "I was hit, slapped, threatened".

135

The president yells:

– We will go on to the examination of the witnesses.

My head feels empty and, again, the hall starts spinning in front of me. I cannot stand up without feeling dizzy. The witnesses march past. I see and hear them as if through a curtain of thin fog. They protest: they were brought to the tribunal under arrest. I see liberal ministers from Rădescu's government passing by, about whom I had been supposed to give statements at the investigation. They are all favorable to us, but seem rather worried: Maniu, Brătianu and Titel Petrescu couldn't come to testify because trucks filled with shock teams blocked the entrances to their homes. I would like to sleep, and not to wake up again.

We are taken back to the prison. I cut off any attempt at conversation from the men, refuse to eat and go to my room, where I collapse in my bed. I would like to sleep, to sleep.

✦

Next day the examination of the witnesses continues. I didn't sleep all night, I follow their statements with difficulty.

The Editor in Chief from *Universul Literar* gives the President my newspaper articles, some censored by the Germans.

– Mr. President, the accused is not a fascist. I was in the office when, under the Germans, *Siguranța* came looking for her.

The president seems quite confused and says:

– Thank you. Next.

Next is Istrate Micescu. He starts by attacking the government. The President cuts him off:

– Mr. Professor, you came to testify for the accused Adriana Georgescu, who belongs to a terrorist organization, the members of which are gathered in the box.

Istrate Micescu replies:

– Mr. President, I see gathered in the box youths, the majority of whom were my students in Law School. There is a big difference between these young people and the rabble of loafers, yelling in the street, asking for their death. I think the true terrorists are out there. As for Adriana Georgescu, a former student of mine, I am amazed you dare to allege that she was ever a member of such an organization. She who...

In the Beginning Was the End

It is amazing the President does not stop him. He must be intimidated by Istrate Micescu, otherwise he would not let him praise me, and especially not let him ridicule the trial. Istrate Micescu is a master of irony. Sarcastic, biting, he is giving the President a master class in jurisprudence, and proving to him the lack of legal basis of all the articles of law on the strength of which we are now in the accused's box. The President is trying in vain to interrupt him. We all follow his deposition eagerly. For more than a month we have been forced to live and breathe in an atmosphere of stupidity that was for us just as harmful as the beatings and physical torture. For the first time in more than a month we are listening to an intelligent person, we see intelligence prevailing. I breathe easier; I know they can beat us, torture us, even eliminate us, but they will never be able to debase the spirit.

Istrate Micescu's testimony lasts two hours. Immediately after it ends the President suspends the session. The Court retires. A man says:
– They'll need a long break to recover their strength. Micescu destroyed them pure and simple.

Micescu comes over to shake my hand. And, when I try to thank him:
– It is I who thank you because you didn't let yourselves be debased and gave us the chance to not be either. And adds, pensively:
– ...at least, for the moment.

✢

When I enter the prison room a man hands me the newspaper:
– You must read your deposition of yesterday, the *România Liberă* version. The journalist retained only the word "worship" and embellished this theme. For the remainder, he probably slept. It's pure fantasy.
Another breaks in:
– No, he didn't sleep. Pure and simple, it's the hand of the communist cell at the paper.
I read:
Adriana Georgescu is a member of a cult... that worships Rădescu. As was to be expected, the accused, Adriana Georgescu,

denied from the start any connection with the T organization and the newspaper Văpaia, *affirming that she only found out about their existence in prison. Then she specifically confessed her adherence to mysticism, shouting in a pathetic manner her sacred devotion to the Palace Square executioner.*

Antim Boghea interrupts me:

– Stop reading that rubbish. Of course they don't mention your request for a medical examination and your statements about *Securitate*. As for the rest, I can very easily sum it up: you are one of the most dangerous terrorists in history and you stated that you didn't want to contribute to *Văpaia* because it made off-color jokes and you are too important a person to accept that.

I am amazed.

– Did I say that?

– Of course you didn't. But does it matter? They had to fill a few columns and, as the poor journalist couldn't reproduce your testimony and tell the truth...

Boghea hands me a sandwich. I turn him down, it is impossible for me to swallow anything. He continues:

– There is another article in *România Liberă*, this one humorous. The title is imprudent though, if the readers took it seriously; look: *Adriana fights for freedom*.

And as I want to read it:

– It's not worth it. The headline is the only true thing in the article.

Another man asks for quiet:

– Sit down, make yourselves comfortable. Cigarettes for everybody and listen. The article is rather long but it's typical, a classic, brilliant.

And, as the men protest:

– Believe me, it's very amusing. No interruptions. Promise? Good, then I'll start.

I sit on the bed. A man hands me a cigarette, while the other starts reading.

– *România Liberă* of September 12th:

Readers know already that the aim of this organization was to set up armed terrorist groups to assassinate our political leaders. The organization had a small printing shop...

I interrupt:

In the Beginning Was the End

– It's not even funny.

– It's coming, it's coming. I'll skip the introduction and go to the heart of the matter: the Martial Court.

The whole group of the accused was brought in front of the Martial Court. The history of the trials that have taken place in front of the Martial Court is of course very long, and the echo of judgments in our recent political life is still ringing. We all remember those trials.

At that time there appeared before the Court, as if in front of a firing squad, groups of patriotic anti-fascist fighters, ordinary people that had made a creed out of the idea of struggle and, out of their lives, sacrificed on the battlefield, the highest duty of a citizen, a banner.

In this hall of the Martial Court, inside these walls that shrank, suffocating those that fell at the hands of the reaction, behind these blind windows that smothered the protesting shouts of the victims; among these seats empty then, like an empty cemetery, were taken, in the inquisitorial atmosphere of the totalitarian regime, under the furious brows and threatening gaze of judges and prosecutors, of the Court and the clerk, of the fascist agents scattered through the room, at that time were taken the most cruel and murderous decisions.

At that time the representatives of the people were tried in the most terrible atmosphere, under the most horrible terror.

The accused at that time were alone. Alone in the box, alone in front of the Court that neither saw nor heard them, that didn't understand that the souls of the accused, chained by death, were shouting out to them.

The platoon that carried out the macabre decisions taken at that time inside these walls was, at least, outside, in the fields, under the cold, white rays of the pre-dawn sun, in the air, that at least could be breathed till the end, till death.

But in this hall of the Martial Court death at that time seemed even more somber, macabre and frightening.

It was the Martial Court of the years of terror; the Martial Court of Antonescu's dictatorship and the German occupation of Romania.

And the convicted, defenseless and without the right to appeal, were freedom fighters, patriots.

The group of Terrorists in front of the Martial Court.
In front of the Martial Court now has been brought a gang of youths from a different world. It is said of them that they belong to high society, that they are educated. And they are, most of them, very elegant. The Martial Court is trying them because they prepared terrorist acts, because they tried to revive the "death squads" of the Iron Guard. They are the elite of the reaction, those who once walked on Calea Victoriei applauding the Panzer divisions headed for London after occupying Paris, or the black shirts that wanted to attack and conquer with submarines and invisible planes the American center of New York. The reaction is regrouping and protecting these fine and elegant terrorists who can – because they are not subjected to a regime of terror and coercion – appear in front of the tribunal like at a dance soiree, in the intimate and elegant box of the courtroom.

And, for the first time, the Court is facing truly guilty people. For the first time it is facing dangerous, perfidious enemies of the people and, for the first time – in perfect accord with the people – the court must judge severely and without pity, fairly but categorically, as only the people know how.

And it should not ponder long. Guilt has been established and can be verified rapidly.

On trial here are not only a group of terrorists, but the organized remnants of an army – defeated but not destroyed – that is trying to restore our national tragedy. There are on trial here not only those in the box of the accused, but all the enemies of the people, all of the reaction.

Toward the reaction we may have neither the slightest courtesy, nor the smallest hesitation, nor the least pity, because the reaction does not hesitate to use terrorist methods in order to win, and because it would never have, as it never had in the past, neither courtesy, nor hesitation, nor pity for the people. If we lack vigilance, decision, honesty and devotion to the interests of the people, then the problem of a new terrorist and dictatorial dictatorship will arise again.

Applause and shouts fill the room. Everybody is talking at the same time, agitated.

– The style, I adore the style.

In the Beginning Was the End

– "Dictatorial dictatorship" is the pearl.
– No, no, it's the description of the *Martial Court* "before" and "after". Two pictures, same setting. Before the Groza regime the setting was sinister: "*Inside these walls that shrank, suffocating those that... behind these windows that smothered the protesting shouts... under the furious brows and threatening gaze... like an empty cemetery... inquisitorial atmosphere*" etc. etc. During Groza's regime, more sober details: the box of the accused is "intimate and elegant".
– I prefer "the white, cold rays of the predawn sun". What a strange astronomical phenomenon!
– But this is magnificent: We are "elegant like at a dance soiree". Adriana, would you rise so we can admire your toilette?

My dress is dirty and torn. I would like to laugh but I feel dirty and torn inside me as well. And, because I don't say anything:
– Didn't you discover any pearls?
– Yes, three, and very serious. First: at the interrogation, they wanted to get from me statements about the Anglo-American role in the conspiracy. In the article they talk pathetically about the Panzer divisions headed for London after they occupied Paris and... were passing through Bucharest? Let's skip the complete falsehood and retain the moral which is: we could not discredit them, let's try then to attract the other Allies to our side... Second: we were not subject to a regime of coercion and terror, which is an indirect answer to the request for medical examination. Third: "*And it should not ponder long. Guilt is established, and can be verified rapidly*"... in other words, the London conference has begun, we need the sentences as soon as possible.

And, because the whole room is now quiet and I feel guilty about spoiling their little happiness:
– But, you know, I like "dictatorial dictatorship" too.

✢

In the afternoon, when the session resumes, the President's table is laden with telegrams which he reads solemnly:
– The country's trade-unions ask for the ultimate punishment for the accused.

A lawyer says:
— Another useless expense for the CP.
Shouts and uproar in the room. The parade of the witnesses continues. The lawyers ask for a medical examination. The President does not reply and continues the examination of the witnesses. Antim Boghea tells me:
— How do you expect him to agree to a medical examination and thus to postpone the proceedings? The London conference began on September 11th. They are in a hurry. The Stalinists need the sentences before the end of the conference.
— Yes, but the Stalinists must be disappointed. They don't have the heads of the opposition. The big trophies escaped them.
— They'll be content with us. For lack of anything else... anyway, they'll have the sentences tomorrow.
— Tomorrow?
— Sure, of course.
I must talk immediately. I stand up.
— Mr. President, I ask for a medical examination.
— You don't have the floor.
— Mr. President, I ask for a medical examination.
— I've told you already that you don't have the floor.
— Still I ask for a medical examination.
— The court rejects your request for a medical examination.
The lawyers are talking, protesting. I have a moment of hesitation, then I make up my mind.
— Then I am asking the court to hear me describe the results of the interrogation methods. That, as you know, you can't deny me.
The whole room stands up. It seems that everybody is shouting at the same time. I can barely hear them: I mostly hear my heartbeats. I clench my fists frantically: if only I could resist.
The President shouts:
— The Court requires a closed session. Empty the room.
The hall is evacuated in a general uproar. The representatives of the Anglo-American missions refuse to leave their seats. Communist agents, scattered throughout the room, try to make them leave. They refuse. Another row. They stay put. The President seems furious, but opens the closed session.
Antim Boghea only has time to whisper:
— Courage! The representatives of the missions are still here.

In the Beginning Was the End

He squeezes my hand. I get up. The silence is such I can hear the sound of my steps. I have the impression that I'm looking at myself from the outside, watching the scene. It's not me reaching the front of the Tribunal's table, it's not me opening my mouth to show my wobbly teeth; it's not me grabbing the President's hand to have him touch the bumps on my head, it's not me calmly lifting the sleeve of my dress to show him the scab, my swollen, black and blue arm. Is it me, is it not me? To be honest, I don't know anymore. The silence behind me is such that I can hear the people breathing.

The President keeps silent, looks, keeps silent.

I just say:

– Then, Mr. President?

He nods.

– It happens.

I don't know how I hit the table, with all my strength, with my fist. A small, dull, unbearable sound.

– It happens. Mr. President? When you were head of prisons, under Antonescu, did it happen that the drunken agents of *Siguranța* called at night the female detainees for additional investigations of a very special kind? And, because you seem not to understand, I'll be very clear. When you were head of prisons under Antonescu, it happened too...

I can hear myself talking. I am amazed I can talk the way I do, fast, yet calm, with a white voice that dares to say all the words, to describe the whole scene. I don't see the President anymore, I don't know where I am, I don't know why I am saying all this, but I go on. I think I don't understand what I am saying anymore, even though it is very clear.

I pause. I think I added:

– That's all Mr. President.

Now, it's not just agitation, it's uproar. The President rings the bell frenetically. The lawyers, the accused, those that stayed on in the hall, all are shouting. I would like to make them stop, I would like to keep silent myself, for everybody to keep silent. The President adjourns the session. I'll have to go back to my place. It will be hard. The lawyers run toward me. I think I pushed them to the side in order to leave. I don't remember how I left the hall.

✢

Next day, the lawyers start their presentations. It's September 14th. I have a high fever, and barely listen to what they say. The thirty-two attorneys who were accepted to plead will be disbarred for sure and they risk being arrested. They know it too, yet they still dare to say what they think, everything they think.

It seems as if I am at the theater. The dress rehearsal for a play that I know by heart. In the street, communist demonstrators are shouting:

– Death to terrorists! Long live the peace!

I lean toward Boghea:

– What peace? What about the war with Japan?

– What, didn't you hear? The war with Japan ended on September 2nd or 3rd.

The president's desk is covered with more telegrams. A lawyer says:

– In this box of the accused are former officers of the Romanian Army which, while travelling 1,200 km, liberated 56 towns, 3,624 villages, lost 4,933 officers, 4,789 non-commissioned officers and 158,839 soldiers; that same Romanian Army that was cited in Marshal Stalin's daily orders and is the fourth largest contributor to the Allied war effort. Field Marshal von Runstedt declared that one of the reasons for the Germans' debacle was the loss of the Romanian resources.

My head is burning, I definitely can no longer follow what is said. My part is over, I have left the stage. I only dream of absolute, total rest. I hear the final phrase of the last attorney.

– The accused are innocent.

The session is adjourned.

A man says:

– The Romanian government delegation returned yesterday from Moscow.

– With our sentences of course.

The Court returns.

– Have the accused anything to add? Adriana Georgescu?

I stand up with difficulty.

– I have nothing to add.

In the Beginning Was the End

The men stand up one after the other. They have nothing to add. The President looks out the window. The prosecutor is staring at the ceiling. A judge is reading a newspaper. A man asks for acquittal. The President adjourns the session for sentencing. We are taken back to the prison room where we have to wait for the verdict. When we pass the barbed wire fence the foreign journalists want to approach us. The guards prevent them. Once in the room a man says:

– They were foreign journalists.

Another answers:

– Yes.

Everybody is tired. Someone asks:

– What if they send us to Russia?

Maglaşu answers:

– In Russia there are already more than 100,000 Romanian prisoners. I think that's enough for them. There are enough prisons here for us. And really, we aren't that important. This trial serves another purpose: to show the communists what not to do, the mistakes to avoid: probably from now on, for a trial, *Securitate*, instead of beating, torturing, and raping, will simply drug the accused: it's easier and less visible. The accused will acknowledge their guilt and won't accuse the judges and the government. You'll see, they'll make big strides. The T affair was the dress rehearsal. If the Anglo-Americans, warned by their missions about the way the trial took place, react, there won't be any more representatives. If not...

I look at my hands. I don't move, I stay silent. The door opens. The prosecutor appears and reads the sentences:

– Remus Țețu: 7 years; Adriana Georgescu: 4 years.

I keep looking at my hands. I hear the rest as if through a curtain of fog: 5 years, 3 years, 2 years, 1 year and 6 months, 1 year, 1 year, 6 months, 6 months, 6 months, 6 months, 2 months, 2 months, 2 months, 1 month, 1 month, 1 month, 1 month, 1 month, 3 acquittals, 5 annulments.

Months, years, the numbers dance in front of my eyes.

Antim Boghea tells me:

– You aren't going to do these 4 years. There'll be elections.

– You didn't trust the elections till today.

– If the elections are a farce, we'll find a way to get you out. You gave us a masterful lesson on resistance: we'll try not to forget it.

I smile and shake his hand.

– Let's not congratulate ourselves too much. We aren't good terrorist timber.

– I wasn't talking of terrorism, but of resistance. As for me, they only gave me three months so they can arrest me again. I am a more amusing game outside.

One of the lawyers enters the room, comes to me, and shakes my hand:

– Nevertheless you won. They couldn't get any of the political heads. As for the sentences... During the whole trial, Nicolschi sat in the next room. And then, before the elections, there is still the possibility of appeal.

Although nothing mattered to me anymore, why did I shout at the lawyer:

– What appeal? Haven't you understood yet that they own this country? Not yet?

– You forget the London conference.

– I particularly remember the one at Yalta. Since then, they do as they please.

Maglaşu intervenes:

– Not yet, not everything. But that might come.

One of us laughs.

– When I leave the prison I'll try "to start" a terrorist organization. At least I'll know why I was in prison.

Another replies:

– I'll start one with the swearing of an oath in a mystical setting.

We all laugh. We can still laugh.

The agents empty the room.

In front of the barbed wire fence a truck is waiting to take the men to Jilava. I shake hands. I make an effort to smile. Jilava is an underground prison.

Boghea adds:

– Adriana, you are very brave. But it's not over. You'll need courage from now on as well. First, you must eat. You understand? You must be able to stand up when we go together to pay a visit to Nicolschi, Bulz and Stroescu. Promise?

They all climb up. I whisper: "Promise", looking at them. Stand-

In the Beginning Was the End

ing, one of them is waving. And the national anthem breaks out, and rises, rises. Everybody is standing and looking at me, motioning to me to join them. I stiffen, so I won't burst into tears, and sing. The truck starts. After it turns the corner, I run to the prison room that is now empty. On the floor, newspapers.

A soldier enters and tells me:

– Miss, tomorrow morning we'll take you to Văcărești. I brought you cigarettes.

He hands me the pack. I shake his hand.

Văcărești... I'll have four years in which to perfect "Gabi's method", to learn to crush the bed-bugs well. I would like to cry but cannot. I stretch out in bed. What I have to do is to sleep so I won't think anymore. To sleep in order to forget. So many things to forget!

III

It's drizzling. Wet, dark weather. I am cold. The regular patter of the rain on the pavement makes me drowsy, I no longer feel capable of desperation. I am between two soldiers, in the car that takes me to Văcărești. One of the soldiers says:
– Ugly weather.

I look at the houses with windows open wide to the weather. Behind these windows, children are probably dressing up to go to school. Water for tea is boiling. A woman wakes up, stretches, maybe says while yawning: "Ugly weather".

The soldier offers me cigarettes.

We follow Dâmbovița's quay, dull and dirty as usual. And yet, above the house walls, farther than the figures of the passers-by going to their offices, to their businesses, cold and rushed, the vast expanses still exist, the sea, and the sun, and those crags which I climbed with skinned knees to watch the sky from as close as possible, as closely as possible. Will I be able to go back to those crags sometime? And, if I do return, will I still know how to climb them, to look at the sky, to jump in the sea, to stretch on the hot sand? Won't I be too tired to know how to do these things still, to know to want them still?

We arrive; the soldiers hand me to the Chief Guard, who says in a prissy tone:
– If I was the judge, I would've shot you.

I say "good day" again to the Chief Warden, who shouts:
– Here you must say: "Respectful greetings, Mrs. Chief Warden".

The scene repeats exactly. But I am too tired to laugh anymore.
– Let's go, off to the kitchen till tonight. Not to see anybody till lights out.

The guard entrusts me to the head cook. I peel potatoes, sacks of potatoes. The cook raps me on the fingers now and then.

In the Beginning Was the End

– Faster, you terrorist.

The woman that helps her is a famous thief, at least she brags as if she was.

– Leave her alone. You can see she is pale. What pains you, girl?

– My head. My thigh. My teeth.

– Maybe you have something contagious?

I shrug and drink water. I drink water all the time. The cook gets angry again.

– Don't drink so much. You are going to have frogs in your belly. You are a decent kid, you know. You have cigarettes. If you weren't a nice kid, I would have sent you to the garden.

– Is there a garden here? A real garden?

– What does that mean, a real garden? A garden like all gardens, with vegetables. What does that mean, a real garden?

Lunch. I eat in the kitchen, potato soup and a piece of bread. Gabi pushes the door ajar and calls to me:

– So, terrorist, you escaped getting riddled with bullets. You lucked out.

I don't know what to tell her. She comes near me and says:

– If you don't eat the bread, give it to me. I'll sell it.

The cook throws her out, shouting:

– You shouldn't talk to her. It's forbidden for anybody to talk to her till tonight.

I wash the mess tins, the basins, the cement floor. Then I start peeling potatoes again for tonight.

After dinner the guard takes me away "for prayer". In the yard, in the rain, the detainees, lined up and standing at attention, are singing. I take my place in the last row. The women in my row gesture, laugh. My neighbour punches me in the belly:

– Stop singing! They won't let you out of here any sooner.

The words of the prayer reach me mixed with the sound of rain, the muffled laughs of the women.

–Thy will be done, now and at the hour of our death. Amen!

The prayer ended, the guard counts us one by one before letting us inside the room, where the ceremony starts again.

– Good night, girls.

– Yes, Ma'am.

Once the door closes, they all surround my bed.

– You are the queen of the terrorists. You got away with four years.
The gypsy-woman that gave me the magic herbs beats her breast.
– I say my herbs made the judge lose his head.
Another interrupts her:
– Don't brag so much, you rag. Say, kid, did you faint?
– Did you cry, tell us, terrorist? How did the judges talk?
Gabi intervenes:
– Give her a break. You'll see tomorrow in the paper.
The loudspeaker shouts in turn:
The commitment of the Groza government to the Allied cause allowed it to...
I cover my ears. I don't want to know anything anymore.
– Why do you cover your ears?
Gabi motions to me to turn my head. A girl is sitting on the bucket, her skirts up. Next to her, a dark, thin man of a studied elegance. Probably he is the one that spoke. Gabi whispers:
– He is the prison director.
The director nears our bed.
–Stand up when I talk to you.
I get up.
– I asked you, why are you covering your ears?
– Is it forbidden to cover my ears?
He shakes me:
– Don't be cheeky, you reactionary viper. Don't be cheeky, or I'll slap you so that you'll remember it for the rest of your life. Why do you cover your ears?
– My head hurts. I have fever.
The director touches my neck.
– You don't burn enough to send you to the doctor. Anyway, you are prettier this way, with rosy cheeks.
He drowns me in all the curses in the world. Then he leaves, dignified.
Gabi helps me climb back into bed. Everything spins in front of my eyes. The women undress and stand in line in front of the bucket. Slowly the characteristic odor invades the room. Gabi kills bedbugs. The others shout and fight amongst themselves. I stare at the wall. Gabi falls asleep at last and I tear strips out of the newspaper she left me. I don't manage to crush any bed-bugs. The felons go to

In the Beginning Was the End

bed first. Then, after they stand and whisper in a corner, the thieves go to bed too. The two women in the upper bunk keep talking. One of them hid a German. "Hans got under my skin. He wasn't a German to me, he was Hans, you know, a man like any other!" I follow the love story with difficulty. Her bedmate brags that she has killed her brother, mother and sister. She was the chief of a gang.

There is always noise around the buckets. I think we are about sixty in the room. Some shout in their sleep. It will soon be daybreak. Now the whole room is asleep. I succeed in killing a bedbug. Gabi snores, making a small, steady sound that makes me think of trains leaving the station, of platforms, of all the departures. I sink into sleep.

✢

A few weeks must have passed. It's difficult for me to count the days; they are all the same. I can climb down from the bed only with Gabi's help. I still work in the kitchen. Mountains of potatoes dance in front of my eyes. The knife turns in my hand. I cut myself. I let the knife drop from my hand.

The head cook drags me to the Chief Warden's office.

– With respect, Ma'am. This one is sick. She might be contagious. I don't need her. Give me somebody else.

The Chief Warden yells at me:

– Don't you dare be contagious. I'll make out a report for the Justice Ministry and they'll let me know if she can see the doctor.

And to the guard:

– To the clinic.

The clinic must have once served as a warehouse. It is a big room with a cement floor. The ceiling is glass. Three panes are broken, and the rain falls with a small, steady patter on the cement. The guard locks the door after telling me:

– Here you have air. Maybe you'll croak sooner and we'll have more space.

I can only lie on my left side. The pain in my right thigh has reached the bone.

I am no longer used to the silence and fall asleep with difficulty.

One day the guard tells me while entering:

– So, you've been here for two weeks and you haven't croaked yet?

Two weeks... My head is burning all the time, I have completely lost sense of time. I am cold, and, as soon as I fall asleep, the nightmare returns.
– So, you opened your eyes. Before, when I came to see you in the morning, you kept them closed and were saying all sort of things. You are funny when you dream.
I had no idea I was talking in my nightmares. I would very much like the guard to shut up!
– You have a visitor. You see how nice I am. It's against the rules, but since you are going to croak anyway...
Gabi enters, smiles to the guard with a complicitous air and comes to hug me.
– You are on the doctor's list, girl.
The guard leaves.
– Say, will you give me your dress? I have a guy in the prison. Not that your dress is that great, but anyway. It's something else... It's a guy from my gang. A cool one. Will you give it to me?
– Yes.
The guard returns with two detainees, who help me to get up. I take two steps and fall. They lift me and support me. To reach the prison hospital we have to cross the street. The guard accompanies us. We enter a room where detainees are queued up. I see Gabi. My dress barely reaches down to her knees, but anyway "it's different".

✦

Radiology room. Gabi takes her dress off. Dark. Then the doctor's voice.
– 235, you have a metallic object on you. Take it off.
Gabi lets out a small shout:
– Oh! The fountain pen!
Then, she says to me over her shoulder:
– Don't let them search the dress.
Which is useless, because I can't even move without help. Once the light is on, the doctor searches the dress and finds a fountain pen and a cigarette case given to me by a lawyer at the end of the trial, from Istrate Micescu. They are forbidden items. Gabi looks at me, scared. I smile at her.

In the Beginning Was the End

The doctor tells me my lungs are in order. On the other hand, I have a pus-filled abscess in my right thigh. He adds, while writing in the register:
– We are going to operate on you. I can't keep you in the hospital without the agreement of the Justice Ministry, the general director of the prison and the political officer.
On my way back Gabi supports me:
– Don't rat on me to the Chief Warden. I didn't steal them. It was a joke. And, if you rat on me, they'll still punish you. So, you see, it's for your own good.
Of course, because they are "forbidden objects".

+

Not being contagious I return, by order of the Chief Warden, to the room and take back my place in bed next to Gabi. Gabi's hands are damp: both her lungs are touched.
I don't talk much anymore. Gabi complains because she has to kill all the bed-bugs by herself and I moan in my sleep.
Faces and figures are very dim. It seems that I am floating. Floating on a blanket of cotton-wool that touches at regular intervals rocks that stick out of the water. I hit my thigh. I am in the water, and when it reaches my mouth, the blanket jumps up and starts floating through the air.

+

I open my eyes. I no longer see the wall on which the bed-bugs were crawling every day. Next to my shoulder, a pair of feet. The feet disappear under the blanket. A voice says:
– Hey, girls, the terrorist that came in on a stretcher has opened her eyes.
There are two of us in every bed.
An old woman supports my head and helps me to drink.
– Don't croak, you're too young for that! I am on duty. Dida, a.k.a. the Rat-Woman.
The Rat-Woman has a round, dirty face. She moves her cracked hands over my face and repeats endlessly:
– Don't croak, you are too much of a kid to croak.

– Where am I?
– In the prison hospital.
I drink three glasses of water and try to get up. Everything is spinning in front of my eyes and I faint.

✢

My thigh burns. I shout. I open my eyes. I am in the operating room. My feet and hands are tied. Faces leaning over me. Somebody asks:
– Heart?
– Very weak.
– Anesthesia?
– Not possible.
My thigh is split open. A knife in my thigh. No, in my head. They are sticking a knife in my head. A voice:
– Septicemia is not excluded.
Another:
– Ready the drains. Oxygen, quick, oxygen!
The knives turn in my head. A noise very close to me, inside me, my teeth chattering inside my mouth, hitting each other, dancing. Is it me yelling all the time? I sink.

✢

In the prison hospital again. Alone in bed. The Rat-Woman wipes my face with a moist rag.
– Don't croak girl, don't croak. You are too young. Don't move. You have some tubes on your right side.
I am tied to the bed with some small straps. I keep fainting. When I open my eyes, I try to count the beds.
In the middle of the room, two buckets. The same crush around the buckets, the same line in front of the buckets. The window is always closed.

✢

The woman in the next bed is about to give birth. As soon as the doors are locked in the evening all the women gather around Bujinca's bed; she is the spiritual patron of the ward. She spins the

In the Beginning Was the End

same yarns every night: first theft, first love, first prison. Now and then she shouts.
– Shut up, you scum! I want to sleep.
My neighbour holds her hand on her belly and yells:
– I'm dying, I'm dying. Bujinca, help me!
– Stop bragging! You've been bellowing for a week and yet I see you are still here.
Another cry:
– I'm dying, I'm dying!
Bujinca, surrounded by all the women eager to hear recollections, yells:
– Shut-up, or I'll dump the shit-bucket over your head.
And, having got silence, continues her story:
– If the old man knew, I told myself, if he only knew. Sly, my old man, he found out, and that was it, "get lost, stinking whore", go to hell. Then I took off since the old man didn't want me anymore. "Whore", he kept telling me, "Whore". Well-said, I told myself, especially because the guy had no intention of "fixing it", the way the old man put it. "What do you want him to fix? I said. What's in my belly?" Then I came to Bucharest. I found a woman from the same village as me. "Come with me," she said, "I know the good neighbourhoods". After that I worked by myself, on Grivița. I wasn't making much. Then I went to the brothel. That way at least I didn't have to go after them. They came to me. I never liked petty theft. This way was much better. Then came one that liked me. The pig! He would rent me for two days from the madam, he paid well. He had a house in the country, not too far. Just the two of us was alright, but he was coffin crazy. He had a coffin in the house. We had to make love in it. I didn't like it. Oh, the swine! He must have given me syphilis. Then I became a thief, on my own. That's how I met Burtică and we set up a gang.
My neighbour shouts:
– Shut-up, Bujinca, shut-up. Stop telling tales. The baby is going to come cold out of my belly. Dead, Bujinca, dead.
Bujinca yells:
– Calve and don't bother us anymore.
The Rat-Woman kneels on the woman's belly to make the baby "come out sooner". The woman yells, yells. The guards watch through the small window. After lights out they are not allowed to

enter the room. Nobody is allowed to. Not even the male nurse.
– Come-on, Veronica, push, let's go, the Rat-Woman goads her.
A yell. A baby's cry. I don't see anything anymore. Everybody is crowded around the bed. Somebody shouts:
– It's a boy. Quick, the scissors!
They are probably cutting the umbilical cord. The baby keeps crying. A phrase keeps coming back to my mind and dancing in my head: "Light, white, asleep child wives..."
I feel like throwing up.

✢

The women keep bustling around the baby. Only Bujinca is asleep. Two women shake her:
– We have a guy in the ward. Wake up, you've got to see him.
One of them let's out a shout:
– She's cold, girls; Bujinca is cold.
Bujinca is dead. The women split into two groups. The first, gathered around Veronica's bed is busy with the baby; the second yells and moans around Bujinca's bed. They start wailing. The baby's cries echo their wails.
At dawn the doors open and the guards take out the baby and the dead woman.
The women have found another occupation now: consoling Veronica, the grieving mother crying for her baby, whose swollen breasts make her scream in pain.

✢

The General Director of the prison is named Bazalan. He comes after lunch to officially certify the death. He stops near my bed and yells at me:
– It would have been better if it was you in her place, you reactionary leper.
I close my eyes and don't answer.
Dida, a.k.a. the Rat-Woman, has been in prison fifteen times. She has syphilis, but has only two crosses, while the others in the ward have at least three, if not four, and the Rat-Woman is very proud to be so "healthy". She wants only one thing: to die while

In the Beginning Was the End

drunk. Every night she begs the two people on duty at the surgery department to bring her a little alcohol, "just to wet her whistle". Once she utters the word "alcohol" she starts crying. Being very old, she is allowed to go to the men's ward to buy cigarettes. She runs the small cigarette trade in the prison. She has grown fond of me because I look like her daughter and tells me all the time: "You must hang on. You are too much of a kid to croak". One day, coming back from the men's ward, she brings me a pack of cigarettes "from a guy that knows you". She starts crying, and asks me for a few cigarettes. I give her the whole pack because I feel like throwing up all the time and am not smoking. She sits on my bed and tells me:

– Many new politicals have arrived. They say there was a fight in front of the Palace. Some guys sang the national anthem. It's written in *Scânteia*. Big headlines. They say it was a massacre, no kidding. The cells are filled with young men.

– What's the day, Rat-Woman?

– November 12th.

On November 8th it was the King's birthday.

–Rat-Woman, get me some newspapers.

In the middle of the night the Rat-Woman creeps to my bed and gives me the papers. While I read she stands look-out in front of the small window to watch for passing guards, even though the papers, all of them, have the party's point of view.

România liberă of November 11th:

New details about the Palace Square incidents. The fascist demonstrators started in small groups from the headquarters of the political parties. Among the demonstrators two hundred prostitutes were identified.

The Palace Square aggression: first results of the inquiry. The demonstrators gave sensational statements. The position of Groza's government is decisively supported. Under the guise of a pro-monarchy demonstration, Maniu and Brătianu have organized anarchical actions against the public order. The demonstrators perpetrated fascist actions. Soldiers and defenders of the public order were killed. Yesterday, at the burial of the victims of the aggression of November 8th, 750,000 citizens called, during a huge demonstration, for the arrest of Maniu and Brătianu.

I hand the papers to the Rat-Woman. I was only able to scan the

headlines. My hands were shaking too hard. The Rat-Woman tells me, while hiding the papers under her skirt:
— At the women's ward there is a big crush too. They don't even know where to put them anymore, there's so many of them.
I would like to sleep and never wake up again.

✠

A guard comes to tell me that today is visiting day and I have a visitor: Ella Negruzzi[59]. Ella Negruzzi was the first woman attorney in Romania. She heads for my bed, accompanied by a young blonde. She tells the guard:
— We came for the appeal. Can you leave us alone. The lady with me is a lawyer.
The guard salutes and disappears. A few women in the ward have recognized Ella Negruzzi and shout to the others:
— It's Ella Negruzzi, the attorney.
In the general din, Ella Negruzzi leans over my bed and tells me in French:
— The lady is Mrs. Thayer, an American journalist. I was able to bring her in using the lawyer pass of a friend that looks like her.
Mrs. Thayer talks to me. I don't know exactly what she is telling me, but I look at her and smile. She is one of those that will be able to talk. She offers me a few packs of cigarettes.
Ella Negruzzi tells me she was sent by the Queen, who would like to know what I would like most.
— I don't want anything. I thank the Queen for her concern about me.
Ella Negruzzi adds:
— We'll do everything in our power to get you out of here. Have courage.
The guard appears. The visit is over. I can't tell if it lasted five minutes or half an hour.
Immediately after they leave, the Rat-Woman comes running:

---

[59] Ella Negruzzi (1888 – 1948): the first woman in Romania to become a barrister. Member of the Permanent Delegation of the National Peasant Party, (the leadership circle of the party), she was persecuted by the communist political police after the NPP was declared illegal in August 1947.

In the Beginning Was the End

– You have cigarettes?
And, as I hand her a few packs:
– I have to hide them. So the guards won't see them. Bravo, kid, you are "somebody".

I keep a pack of cigarettes to look at it now and then. Here, in prison, this simple pack of Camels seems like a symbol of freedom.

✣

The Rat-Woman brings me more news about November 8th. They shot from the Interior Ministry into those singing the national anthem.
– They took the bodies and buried them, saying the others knocked them off. Big funeral, quite a shindig. In the city they say it stinks. What do you think of this story?
I shake my head.
– Downstairs is filled to the brim. It is quite sad, all those young people. What if they kill them?
She starts crying:
– You have a cigarette?

✣

Veronica, the baby's mother, died. Puerperal fever.
The physicians come to see me and are amazed. I am not reacting to the Delbet shots.

✣

Every other week, the Rat-Woman and two convalescents take the blankets to the drying closet. When they bring them back, they teem with even more bed-bugs than before. The Rat-Woman says the drying closet is like a nest for them and nothing else.
I try in vain to kill the bed-bugs crawling on my body. Veronica's bed, to my right, is taken by a syphilitic: her nose and lips are eaten by the disease. She keeps her eyes closed all the time. She is the most serious case. In the ward, the girls call her "five plus five". The ones that only have three crosses look at her with a superior air.

Today the nurse removed the small straps tying me to the bed. I can lie on my left side, the drains on the right prevent me from moving. For fun, I hunt bed-bugs. "Gabi's method" cannot be used here. The Rat-Woman delouses my head and lets out a triumphant cry every time she finds a louse. Lately the girls have invented another game: every week they elect a Miss Lousy who is entitled to two cigarettes and priority at the bucket. The Rat-Woman presides over the proceedings, but even though I am her favourite she never manages to have me win.

My fever abates. The physicians come to see me more often. It seems I am a unique case: after the Delbet shots, my temperature did not shoot up like an arrow.

A physician tells me, with the most serious mien in the world:

– With you, everything is always upside-down. You are just a stinking reactionary!

The ward is closed from five-thirty in the evening till six in the morning. In the morning, the guard "takes the inventory". Sometimes a woman dies in the middle of the night, and then "there are less to count". The guard stops in front of my bed and tells me, laughing:

– Hey, aren't you ever going to make up your mind? I would love to take you to the cellar.

The "cellar" is the mortuary.

My wound is healing slowly. Today I took my first steps, and fell.

I take a shower only on my left side. We are standing in line, fifteen of us, naked, in front of the showers. The guard is present and makes comments.

In the Beginning Was the End

✦

The Rat-Woman has brought me a copy of *Jurnalul de Dimineață* [60] and a pack of cigarettes.
– From the Little Mason. You have friends among us and you don't say anything?
My head hurts too much to answer her. And I have no idea who the Little Mason is.

✦

Next day, the Rat-Woman brings me another pack of cigarettes.
– Little Mason.
– Who is Little Mason, Rat-Woman?
– I don't know. One of ours. The orderly on duty at the surgery gave me the cigarettes.
Through one of the windows I see the tree branches with hoarfrost. Christmas is coming. It is very cold.

✦

I had an attack of appendicitis. I am nauseous all the time. The nurse took out the drains.
Three women died last night in the ward. Nights seem even more endless when the women wail.

✦

A girl squealed on the Rat-Woman because she has been bringing me newspapers. The guard found a paper in my bed. The Rat-Woman spent a day in the lock-up, and I was transferred, as a punishment, to a ward with contagious detainees.
The smaller room is filled with tubercular patients. My neighbour spits all the time and covers the blanket in blood. Before, she was a thief. Now, she is a skeleton. At night I avoid looking at her. Here there is less noise. Only the coughs and the whispers break the silence.

---

[60] *Jurnalul de Dimineață* (The Morning Journal): founded by Constantin Vișoianu, one of the best independent dailies during WWII. Its publication ended in the summer of 1947.

After a few days, I start coughing too and I am convinced my lungs have been affected. In front of me is a window through which I can see Bucharest homes. I try to make up a story for each home, and suddenly I remember a street I used to take to return from school in the evening. I am gripped by a yearning for freedom that I haven't felt since being at Văcărești. It disturbs me and I try to get rid of it and return to a state of indifference, which is much easier to live with.

In the room an odor of blood and misery reigns and suffocates me. The Rat-Woman comes again to bring me a pack of cigarettes from the Little Mason.

✦

I have another attack of appendicitis. Next day I am taken on a stretcher to the surgery. The room has black curtains. I would like to be left to die. They tie my feet and hands. I am operated on without anaesthesia. I probably struggle, because two women come to hold me down.

Why don't they let me die?

✦

I have a small sand bag on my belly. They took me to a minuscule individual cell. One morning the Rat-Woman brought me a package; little stones and some dirt.

– The politicals sent you this. To get well. And for Christmas.
– Christmas?
– Yes, it's three days from today.

I don't know why, but I frenetically squeezed the Rat-Woman's cracked hand.

The first few nights after the operation I felt very bad and I was quite thirsty. I would have liked to have had her next to me, not necessarily her, even one of the tuberculars or syphilitics, anybody to put their hand on my forehead and give me water. But the cell was locked. I asked for water, shouting at the guards passing in the corridor. They always answered:

– It's forbidden by the regulations.

In the Beginning Was the End

Then there was also the nightmare that keeps recurring, always the same, always the same.

I keep squeezing the Rat-Woman's hand, who pours out her news: more politicals have come, most of them with swollen faces.

– "Tell her that other trials are prepared", they told me, and gave me this package. "Dirt and little stones," I told them, "what's the kid going to do with this?" – "The earth, the little stones remain," they answered, "water flows over them and passes. She'll understand." they told me.

I ask the Rat-Woman to bring me water. I want to be alone and look at the "earth and stones that remain".

I do not know when Christmas passed. The Rat-Woman claims I was delirious all week. Tomorrow is New Year's Day, but visiting day was cancelled and quarantine was declared: a typhus epidemic has broken out in the prison.

✦

For the last few days I have been feeling much better, but I still cannot walk. The Rat-Woman has brought me, hidden in a cigarette pack, a note. She keeps watch while I read:
Happy New Year! Don't worry about typhus. Harriman and Sir Clark Kerr are at this moment in Bucharest. The quarantine is a pretext so they won't be able to visit the prisons. We'll all be out soon. Get strong quick. Greetings.

It is not signed. I hand the note to the Rat-Woman, who tears it up and swallows it. She is very proud of her mission and tells me that, as soon as she gets out of Văcărești, she will enter "political life".

✦

I have returned to the first ward. I can only walk when supported. I have the right to a shower. Same queue, fifteen women. The same guard and the same off-colour comments.

Since last week the guard officially distributes *Scânteia* "for the political education of the detainees". A representative of the National-Peasant Party and one of the Liberal Party have joined the

Groza government. Is this the result of Harriman[61] and Sir Clark-Kerr's[62] visit to Bucharest?

✢

Yesterday the prison dentist pulled the twelve teeth that were loose. Without anesthesia.

✢

I am afraid to drink water. We share mugs, and all the women in the salon have syphilis. My gums are still bleeding and my whole face is swollen.

Emil Hațeganu, the National-Peasant minister in the government, has come to see "his men".

The Managing Director of the newspaper *Curierul*[63] has come to see me. He is very optimistic: there'll be elections.

After his departure, big agitation in the ward.

– Handsome, the guy. He's your guy?

The Rat-Woman replies, full of importance:

– Shut-up! She is a political, is a... a...

And after a moment of hesitation, says, triumphantly:

– A terrorist, you know!

✢

Scânteia announces that, on February 8th, the Anglo-Americans recognized Groza's government.

In other words: in vain I shouted the whole truth at the trial, in vain I cried with joy when seeing the representatives of the Allied missions in the Tribunal hall, in vain I have let darkness and nightmares take possession of my whole being. Is it possible that all these have been in vain?

---

[61] Averell Harriman: US Ambassador to Moscow, 1941-1945.

[62] Sir Archibald Clark-Kerr: British Ambassador to China (1938-1942), Ambassador in Moscow (February 1942 -January 1946), Ambassador in Washington (1946-1948.)

[63] *Curierul*: an independent daily led by Augustin Popa, published between September 1944 and January 1945.

In the Beginning Was the End

✢

It's spring and I am convalescing. The Rat-Woman keeps bringing, every week, a pack of cigarettes from the Little Mason. The head physician puts me on the list of those who have the right to go outside. I go down to the yard supported by the Rat-Woman and the Gypsy. Outside, the first spring sun, cold and still pale.

The Gypsy tells the Rat-Woman:
– Look at the kid. She is like a bug. You like the sun, don't you?

After Bujinca's death the Gypsy has become the spiritual leader of the ward. It is her twenty-sixth stay in prison and the thieves respect her a lot because her last break-in made her famous: she made a hit at the Finance Ministry itself. She is fifty years old; her gang is among the best-organized in Bucharest, and her face, covered with scars, stands as proof of her exploits.

The cool air makes me dizzy. I breathe with difficulty. I feel a claw in my solar plexus, a claw rummaging through my gut. I fall to the ground and can't get up. My fingers and toes curl up. The women in the yard start to yell in unison:
– Help, help, the terrorist is croaking!

The claw rises and grabs my throat. The Gypsy and the Rat-Woman take me and lay me in bed. The male-nurse comes to give me a shot. The claw is still there, and my fingers are still curled up. My throat is dry.

The claw lets go of me late at night. As I breathe better, the Gypsy, sitting on my bed, says while wiping my forehead:
– You almost kicked the bucket, girl; you've scared us very much. Don't worry, it'll get better.

✢

I am afraid to go out to the yard. As soon as I go outside the same claw grabs me and I fall down. The doctors come to see me. When I ask them what is the matter with me, they answer:
– What do you want to have? Saint Bernard's prison illness. For the moment, we'll take away your "air". Maybe it's better this way.

Indeed it is better this way. I feel better and better and, a month later, when one of the orderlies in the surgery department gets sick, the guard calls me to replace her.

Adriana Georgescu

✢

The chief orderly is a murderer. She killed her whole family in order to inherit a house. She is registered in one of the communist cells in the prison; she thinks that this way they will let her go. She is serving a life sentence.

The other orderly, Ilinca, is a medical student. She is a political. She sung the national anthem on November 8th. She was passing through the square with her fiancé, a pharmacy student, and they stopped to see the king and sing with the others. When the communists fired from the Interior her fiancé fell to the ground. And when she bent over him she only had time to hear him saying: "My true love...". He died.

She is eighteen years old, has pigtails and faded eyes. She never cries. I try to console her:

– You'll be out of here in six months. You have your whole life in front of you.

– They won't let me back in school. And, anyway, I don't care. Nobody will ever tell me: "My true love...". Only that mattered.

The chief orderly intervenes in the conversation:

– You're young, girl; the earth is teeming with men. Men are like street-cars: you lose one, another shows up. "My true love" this, "my true love" that. That's all you talk about. It's like at the communist cell: all day long the head of the cell says "Stalin" this, "Stalin" that, like you with your love.

Ilinca slapped her. Since then I haven't seen Ilinca. The head guard took her to a cell in the basement. He is very proud because, when the prison director is away, he makes all the decisions.

The director is on an inspection tour through the country to see what else can be turned into a prison: there is no more room. Movie and theater halls have thus been requisitioned, during the last week, for "the better implementation of justice".

The director returns in a bad mood and curses the politicals. It is too much of a struggle to find room for them. Obviously his job is getting, as the days pass, more and more difficult.

✢

The head physician seems pleased with me and decides to keep me in the surgery department. He sends me to the men's ward to

In the Beginning Was the End

record the temperature of those who are on the surgery list for today.
I pass between the beds, followed by the guard, and fill in the cards of the sick. I ask the guard:
– Which one is Little Mason?
From the back of the room a voice answers:
– I am.
I recognize him: he is one of my former clients. I shake his hand.
– Good day, Mr. Ionescu.
He frowns, looks at the guard who is talking to a man at the other end of the hall, and whispers:
– Don't call me Ionescu anymore, miss. Now my name is Popan. I'm sorry about the fee. I couldn't bring it to you: they took me again to count the iron bars.
And, with a long sigh:
– What can you do, it's the job.
The guard approaches us:
– You aren't allowed to talk to the detainees.
I shake the hand of "Little Mason, Ionescu, Popan" and then leave.

✢

I am washing pus-filled dressings. Seeing "Popan" again I have remembered one morning at the tribunal. I had just pleaded, and had obtained an acquittal. I was just putting the files back in my briefcase. Like any very young lawyer, I had with me two briefcases filled with files, jurisprudence, and codes of law. Meanwhile, the next trial had started.
– Ionescu Vasile.
– Present.
– You have a lawyer?
– I don't, mista' judge. I have no money, po' me. I am a mason, a bricklayer, I have a wife and five kids. I haven't done anything, mista' judge.
The President, after a moment's hesitation, appointed me counsel for the defense. I protested in vain. I asked for time to study the case, I asked for I don't know what. In reality, I was frightened. The President answered me:
– It's a very simple case. I'll leave it for last. You'll have time to talk to the client.

I took out my files and codes again. I went to Ionescu's cell. As soon as he saw me, he threw himself at my feet, crying.
– Miss, save me. I have five children, a wife. I stole a wallet. It was on the floor in a street car. I took it. I am unemployed and have five children and a wife. I had to bring them something to eat.

I returned to argue the case, law codes handy. I evoked the abandoned family waiting for the father to bring the daily bread, and bore down hard on the pathetic pedal. Ionescu, behind me, was crying and encouraging me:
– That's right, miss, that's right. It seems you've seen into my poor father's heart.

I was quite emotional and, the more I talked, the more I believed in the daily bread, children, wife, and abandoned home.

Ionescu was acquitted. I left the tribunal, both briefcases under my arm, so proud of having obtained two acquittals in a single day that I was singing with happiness on the street and didn't even think of the fee promised by Ionescu.

It never crossed my mind that he would pay it in cigarettes, at Văcărești.

✢

The news spread quickly in the ward. The Rat-Woman was my herald.

Very emotional, the Gypsy comes and gives me a hug.
– You are my sister for life! My gang is yours too. To save Fine-Skin, that's no small feat.
– Who is Fine-Skin?
– Ionescu, Popan, Little Mason, Fine-Skin, he is the chief of all the burglars in Bucharest. Our big chief.
– Does he have children and a wife?
– Fine-Skin, babies? No way.

I start laughing. The Gypsy keeps hugging me.
– So, you are a fine lawyer.
– I was a lawyer-intern, Gypsy. I got him acquitted, it happens sometimes.
– I don't have the slightest idea if it happens or not. What I know is that you are "somebody". My sister for life, I told you, and my gang is at your disposal if you need it.

The ward is very agitated. I can't sleep because all the women come to tell me their cases and ask advice for "when they are going to be outside".

From that day on in prison they all call me "Fine-Skin's terrorist" and, after the Gypsy and the Rat-Woman, I have priority at the bucket.

✦

The Chief Guard shows up in the morning in the ward, stops in front of my bed, and starts cursing.
– The Director gave me a dressing-down because I've let you work in surgery. You no longer have the right to go there, you reactionary whore!

He slaps me and leaves, dignified.

Probably the political officer has been here. He is a murderer who joined the party. He is actually the true director of the prison.

In the surgery there was a window where I could see the city silhouetted in the distance.

✦

The claw has returned and confined me to bed. All night long the women passionately discuss "the latest news": the burglars and murderers who have joined the party have been named police inspectors and are squealing on their colleagues. Four of these new inspectors have been killed by the burglars who are outside. On their bodies there was a note with the word: "Traitor". Nevertheless, the raids are producing better and better results.

At night, the Gypsy calls a war council and gives instructions that are to be sent to all the gangs in Bucharest. The women listen to her speechless. No doubt about it, she dominates them. Anyway, their society is very well organized. The hierarchy is strict, even rigid, the solidarity almost total. In the ward they are grouped by specialties: banks, safes, system X or Y, trains...

The most esteemed thieves are those who have served the most years in prison and have escaped the most times. The petty thieves are considered dilettantes. In prison they are the slaves of the professional thieves, who call them "pissers". They make the beds for the professionals, do the laundry and do "bucket duty" in their place. They only dream of one thing: to become professionals. When they get out of prison, they go to one of the addresses given them by a thief whom they have served and start their apprenticeship; they call this "going to school".

The Gypsy's slave is very much envied by the other petty thieves. Whenever anybody dares to point out something to her, she utters, with a very dignified air:

– Once I get out of here I'll join Gypsy's gang.

This is for her the true title of nobility.

As for the prostitutes, they always end up by becoming thieves. It's a less exhausting profession, they say.

One of them, Milica, changed her trade in prison last month. Now she belongs to Gypsy's gang.

Afterwards, she told me:

– I was fed up with that stinking trade. There was no way to rest, not even when I had my period.

✦

The doctors say my nerves are deteriorating. The claw returns at least once a day, and I faint often. The General Director has ordered that I be taken to an individual cell, so that I "can croak in peace".

The cell on my right is occupied by a half-mad political. Once night falls, he starts whistling like a train. He also yells and strikes the door with his fist. The guards rain curses on him and then he starts again to whistle. The distant, muted cry of an owl accompanies him.

The cell on the left has been occupied since yesterday. I am not allowed to leave the bed, but I crawl anyway into the corridor to try to see the newcomer. I don't have to go too far. A woman stands in the corridor, her back towards me. A woman, or at least what is left out of a woman: a skeleton looking out the window. I get closer, she looks at me suddenly: it is Maria Antonescu, the wife of the former Marshal. I thought she was in Russia. Her face is green, her eyes aimless. I back away one step. She asks me with a dim voice:

– What did you do to get here? You seem so young.

– I am a political.

Political...
– Yesterday they shot my husband.
The guard comes running and cursing and pushes me back into the cell.

✦

I am called before a medical commission. The physicians have a funereal air. My blood pressure is 70 over 40.

✦

One of the only results obtained by Mihai Romniceanu, the Liberal representative in Groza's government, is to get me transferred, as a detainee of course, to a hospital.

The room is very clean, but they had to change the mattress on my bed. The first one seemed too soft, and I felt as if I was sinking and suffocating.

For more than a year, at Văcărești, I didn't have a mattress.

✦

Mihai Romniceanu comes to see me and tells me that General Rădescu has managed to get out of the country by plane and has reached Cyprus.

It is one of my first joys, but I don't have the strength to enjoy it fully. I am so sick that I feel beyond life.

After Romniceanu leaves, the nurse enters the room, and, while pretending to take my temperature, whispers as she leans over me:
– Careful. Microphone in the room.

✦

I see Mihai Romniceanu again after the elections that took place on November 19th, 1946. The opposition won almost eighty percent of the vote. When the results became known it seems that madness took hold of everybody at the Interior Ministry, starting with Teohari Georgescu. They thought that everything had been prepared so well. The President of the Electoral Commission had communist leanings. Forty-five names entered on the electoral lists had been erased. The motive invoked: fascists.

Each voting station was presided over by a communist, while the opposition parties were allowed only one representative for every four or five polling stations.

Members of trade-unions and professional organizations had been forced to go to the polls accompanied by communist political officers.

Soldiers had been forced to vote in their barracks under the strict supervision of political commissioners.

Teohari Georgescu and the central committee of the C.P. went to the Soviet Embassy to ask Kavtaradze[64] the same question the Provincial Prefects had telegraphed them: "The opposition has won an 80% majority. Advise by telegraph what to do." Kavtaradze contacted Moscow, and Moscow said: the opposition votes are to be assigned to the government coalition, and vice versa.

It was, of course, the ideal solution, only somebody had to come up with it. And because he didn't figure it out, Teohari Georgescu was forced to make public the results of the elections a day late.

Maniu, Brătianu and Titel Petrescu have sent a protest note to the Anglo-Americans. How many protest notes have they sent by now? And with what result?

I suddenly recall a scene from the trial. I was in the Martial Court prison. A man was saying:
– There'll be elections and then not a single communist will be left in power.

Was Maglaşu the one that answered:
– What if, at Yalta, the Allies have given us up to the Russians?

✢

In April 1947 I am still in the hospital. Few pieces of news are arriving from outside, but still I have learned something: the conflict between Lucreţiu Pătrăşcanu and Teohari Georgescu is becoming more and more acute. Lucreţiu Pătrăşcanu is beginning to be considered a possible deviationist by the Central Committee of the C.P.

---

[64] Serghei I. Kavtaradze: Soviet Ambassador to Romania, 1945-1952.

In the Beginning Was the End

I remember this rumour when I find out later in April that I have been pardoned by the King. Lucrețiu Pătrășcanu is the Minister of Justice.

✦

I prepare to leave the hospital and the prison. I am free. I try a few times to say the word "freedom", to remember a phrase about freedom, to think about freedom. I am not able to. I find in myself neither an explosion nor shouts of happiness. I find almost nothing but a fear of the city waiting for me outside, this city and this life which are no longer familiar to me.

PART THREE

"Roses have never been so blue"

I

Ever since I have been pardoned I walk the streets all day long like a mad-woman; all the time in the streets. At night, I resign myself only with difficulty to the idea of going home. I am obsessed with walls that seem to fall on me, with the door that closes behind me. Another obsession: avoiding human beings. Aside from a few "political" mates from Văcărești, whom I meet secretly in the evenings, I don't see anybody. Only with them am I able to talk; we use the same words, we have lived through the same reality that isolates us from the community of the living.

Because I am alive I still need air. I walk the streets in search of it. I have a mad desire to make up for all the "air" periods that have been denied me for the last two years.

What is most serious though, is that I am not able to find myself again, to be true to my own self.

✢

For the last two days I have had fever and have had to stay in bed. Typhus is raging through Bucharest. Probably I have typhus. I decide to go to a hospital where I know the head physician.

I meet him in the waiting room.

– What is happening? What do you want?

– Nothing, Radu, at least nothing special. I have typhus and I have come to check myself in.

– How do you know you have typhus?

– You forget that I was a nurse once and most recently an "or-

derly" in the surgery department at Văcăreşti.
– I'll take you to the professor so he can look at you.
The professor wears glasses. A little hard of hearing, he listens carefully to my chest for a long time, shaking his head.
– If you had come tomorrow, I would have taken you directly to the morgue. The heart is too weak, surgery is excluded!
I don't understand too well.
– An operation for typhus?
The professor looks at Radu with surprise:
– Is the patient delirious?
Radu laughs.
– She has always had obsessions. She is convinced she has typhus.
– I would have preferred it to be typhus! None of the organs is in its place: the stomach is sagging, the kidneys are displaced, as for the lungs, let's not even talk about them. The infection is so generalized that septicemia can set in at any moment. If we can get a large amount of penicillin, we still have a chance to save her.
– How many units are needed?
– A million for now. A few million to really save her.
– I'll call the International Red Cross; they have received American aid.
I follow their conversation with difficulty. Again I have the feeling that my head is swelling like a balloon and my teeth are growing endlessly.
Before letting me go, the professor turns toward me with a reproachful air.
– Obviously I don't have the right to ask you what kind of life you have led to get in this sad condition...
I keep silent, Radu answers for me:
– She was in prison, professor.
The professor turns red, takes off his glasses, wipes them and says, while looking through the window:
– Oh, well, then...

✦

Another hospital room. Radu gives me the first penicillin shot. I take advantage of a moment when the orderly is not nearby to ask him:

– Radu, couldn't you register me under a false name?
– Do you want me to lose my job? What if the head of my cell finds out?
– Did you sign up with them?
Radu shrugs.
– I have a wife and three children. What do you want me to do? The physicians that didn't join the party no longer have the right to practice medicine.

✦

Every time Radu comes to give me a shot, he feigns complete indifference. He doesn't want anybody to think that he is paying more attention to me than to other patients. He is the head physician of the hospital, but he is afraid of the political official in his department. The official is a mechanic, but this does not prevent him from donning a white coat and accompanying Radu on his rounds to see patients. Radu is a graduate of Bucharest Medical School, but the mechanic has been a party member since March 6th, 1945. By virtue of that his opinion is more important than that of the head physician.

✦

The head physician's assistant treats me with a kindness that seems suspicious to me. He is never satisfied with the care that I receive. He thinks the orderly doesn't pay enough attention to me. That there isn't enough ice, or enough disinfectant.

While filling in my hospital release card, he asks me in a whisper if I would want to leave the country, to escape abroad. Everything is prepared. No risks. A plane will be available for the political chiefs of the opposition. A seat will be reserved for me. I tell him that the professor has prescribed me six months of total rest. The few million units of penicillin have stopped the infection, but, in order to be completely cured, I need these six months of absolute rest.

The assistant seems disappointed. He leaves me his phone number and asks me to call him if I change my mind. I take the piece of paper with his address. I don't want to seem too harsh. Thanks to the assistant many of my colleagues have been able to enter the hospital at night to see me. He seemed well acquainted with our people. Still, this secret departure story seems rather strange to me.

+

I am at home again after two months in the hospital. I am still in bed. One of my British friends comes to see me. I ask him all of a sudden:
– What would you say if you found out I had reached Constantinople?
– You aren't able to stand up and you want to swim across the Black Sea?
– Not swimming. By plane.
He covers his ears.
– Don't tell me more. I don't want to hear any more! You know very well that I can't get mixed up in such things, but let me give you some advice anyway: don't ever see again the person that proposed this to you. Maybe he is honest, but he just as well might not be, and then I don't see how you could survive a new interrogation in the state you are in.
Before leaving he adds:
– What an idea, to come to see you on July 13th!
My friend is a very superstitious Irishman.
I don't call the assistant. I have torn up the little note he gave me.

II

Dull knocks at the door tear me away from sleep. It's difficult for me to understand what's happening. I have had fever all night and I am still heavy with sleep. Somebody has opened the door. Two men enter the room:
– You are being arrested. Get dressed!
I ask myself if this is the usual nightmare coming back. Maybe I am not awake yet? A man shakes me:
– Are you deaf? Get dressed!
The other intervenes:
– Don't shake her. We are lucky we found her.
– I just got out of hospital. Where do you want to take me?
– You'll see. Come on, get dressed.

It is high summer, but I am shivering. I put on long pants and a sweater. Now I know how to dress; I am used to prisons. The same drive through the city as it is waking up. We enter the yard of the police headquarters.

A long corridor. Another office. A gray-haired, jovial man is rubbing his hands while saying to the two agents:
– Bravo, boys! Good job.
– Why did you arrest me?
– You'll see. Take her, boys! I'll fill out her card.

Another office. A large portrait of Stalin has replaced the King's. Three men who are roaring with laughter meet me.
– Văcărești didn't do you any good, you infamous terrorist. You wanted to bolt by plane together with the liberal chiefs.

They hand me a sheet of paper:
"I, the undersigned, declare that I wanted to join the heads of the Liberal party, namely..."
I interrupt:
– No way. I won't sign anything.

This can't be real. My nightmare must be continuing even when

I am awake. This must be the past coming back to perfidiously insinuate itself into the present, this must be a hallucination.

They yell like they did before, with the same voices, the same words. I am waiting for the blows to start. Now I know that I will faint before they have time to do me any harm. The blows don't come. I read again the statement that I have to sign. I look with indifference at Stalin's portrait, smiling and holding children in his arms.

The gray-haired man enters the room:
– Well?
– Nothing yet.
– Did you search her?
– We'll do it right away. Undress.

I clench my teeth so I won't tremble. They rummage through my clothes while I am standing, naked, in the middle of the room. I manage to tell them rather calmly:
– It's useless, you know. I dressed after I was told to come here. After all, I wouldn't take with me messages or secret documents when coming to the police.

They start cursing me again, but don't hit me. They throw me my clothes. I get dressed.
– Now be kind and sign. Otherwise you know very well what awaits you. Have you by any chance forgotten?
– And you, have you by any chance forgotten that I know how to talk at a trial?
– If you don't sign, we'll kill you.

I know this, I know this by heart, this is the only thing that I know. I want to scream because everything is repeated identically. But instead of screaming, I shrug.
– You know very well that I am not going to sign anything.

✢

Two guards take me to the basement. At the end of a corridor they open a door:
– Come on, get in.

I see in the semi-darkness a group of women looking toward the ceiling. I follow their gaze. Above them, near the ceiling, there is a window. A small, square, barred window that opens toward the yard, through which one can see the feet of the sentries passing at regular intervals.

All the women are standing still, on their toes, almost mesmerized by this small bit of air. The cell is saturated with a humid stench. The scene is absolutely unreal, I have the feeling that I am looking at a painting which might be titled: In Search of Air. Who might have painted it? Who could have captured that semi-darkness heavy with human breath, those dark silhouettes stretched out directly on the cement, huddled on the covered toilet, yearning towards the window, those emaciated necks, the grimaces on their faces, all these subterranean humans who, in order to move, take the shape of rats and moles?

I let myself get swept along, grateful to forget for a moment the obsessive thought: will the interrogations be carried out in the same way as at *Securitate*? Will indeed everything repeat exactly as in the past?

I try to get closer to the window. The odor is so strong that my head starts spinning again. I bump into bodies. A woman gets up, ready to curse, but, recognizing me, she falls into my arms:

It is Milica, the prostitute that joined the Gypsy's band at Văcărești.

– You came back to count the bars, you terrorist? You lucked out!

She shouts to the others in the cell:

– Girls, she is Fine-Skin's terrorist! Gypsy's friend!

Huge excitement, because everybody knows at least Fine-Skin's and Gypsy's names. They are the two stars in their world. Milica tells her version of my story: I am head of a gang, I wanted to kill Ana Pauker and the government, my story was in the papers, I got Fine-Skin out of a big mess and a big man came to see me in prison, my guy, a cool guy. They all come to hug me.

– Who did you want to kill this time?

– Nobody.

Milica intervenes:

– She always says that, don't believe her.

From a dark corner of the cell a woman nears our group. She has dark eyes, a wrinkled face, and her dress, now rumpled, must have been very elegant.

– Look, the stuck-up twit is coming too, says Milica nodding in

her direction. You know, terrorist, this nitwit is kind of thick. She speaks in a language we don't understand. She probably thinks she is a great lady.
– Wait, Milica, let me see for myself.
I approach the woman. She asks me:
– Do you speak French by any chance?
– Yes, ma'am.
She lets out a small shout:
– Finally, I couldn't take it anymore, if you only knew...
She hesitates for a moment, then:
– Why are you here...?
– Probably because, of all the prisons in Bucharest, it's the only one I don't know yet.
– Strange. You have, how should I say, such a decent air. How can you live like this?
I burst out laughing:
– Do you think I am a whore?
She seems slightly scared, so I feel obliged to comfort her. But before I have time to do it, she says:
– Maybe you are a foreigner like myself? I was arrested in front of the legation. Following the legal thievery which they call here monetary reform or "stabilization", I was left penniless. I went to the Italian legation to ask for a loan, but I was arrested before being able to enter. For three days I have been sitting in this miserable cell. And these whores fight all the time, tear each other's hair, yell. One of them, the redhead in the corner, wants to hug me all the time. I can't tolerate this promiscuity. How can you have such a vile profession?
She has started to cry.
– Calm yourself, ma'am. If it helps, I am a political prisoner. Have you been interrogated?
– Not once. I don't know how to notify the legation so they can get me out of this hole. Are you really a political?
– Yes. As for the whores, they aren't quite that terrible, you know. I'll translate for you.
I don't have time to translate for her because a guard comes to take us to eat, he makes us go out into the corridor in a column. I am next to two workers who have been arrested because they missed three demonstrations. Fifty women from their factory were arrested

at the same time. The older one keeps crying. Her five month old baby has been left home alone. At the end of the corridor, a warrant officer gives me a mess tin. A guard does the men's roll-call. We are separated from them by a row of policemen and the bucket of soup. The roll-call is divided into three categories: common law, sabotage, politicals. After that the women: thieves, prostitutes, politicals. The workers are in the political category. When they call my name at the end of the list, I hear a man's voice shouting:

– Say, Miss Adriana, you've come back again?

The guard yells:

– Shut-up! The one who talked stand forward.

And Fine-Skin gets out of the line and stands at attention.

– You miserable son of a bitch! What do you mean by "miss"? You are using words from the "feudal" era. You aren't just a burglar, you are a reactionary on top of that. You know you are not allowed to talk to the women.

Fine-Skin winks at me.

– We are like brothers, mista' guard. We were together at Văcărești. At Văcărești I was in the trade-union, mista' guard.

– Are you one of those that joined the trade-union in order to be freed sooner?

– I was in the trade-union and they let me go. Then, I got it on the chin again. What do you want, mista' guard, it's a hell of a job! But I am not a reactionary; I am a progressive; I am in the trade-union.

–Well, we'll see. What's your name?

– Lache Ion, mista' guard.

I can't help laughing: he has changed his name again. While we are standing in line in front of the soup bucket, Fine-Skin looks at me. He touches his ear, which in the language of the detainees from Văcărești means: "Do you have a message for the outside?". I touch my forehead, which means: "Yes." I am able to relay this way Giovanna's, the Italian's, name, and ask him to alert the legation. I am sure he will do it. The guards, who treat the politicals quite badly, are quite indulgent with the common-law ones, with whom they have all sort of dealings. And Fine-Skin has always found a way, even at Văcărești, to transmit to the outside anything he wanted.

I've thanked Fine-Skin by touching my chin.

Adriana Georgescu

✦

After we have gulped down the soup that looks even more like dishwater than the one at Văcăreşti, and have eaten our piece of gluey bread, we are locked up again in the cell with the usual ceremony:
– Good night, girls.
– Yes, sir, mista' guard.

Once the guard has locked the door, the two workers start moaning. One of them complains in a loud voice:
– We were better off back home in the country. What did we want at the factory? They told us that this government thinks only about us.

Milica shouts:
– They fool us, this government, that's what they do, and then they throw us all into the slammer. They want us all to drop dead. I shit on this government.
– Shut-up, another breaks in, look: she's started again.

The worker that left her baby at home has started to sing a lullaby. Her crossed arms seem to cradle a real baby. The girls surround her and watch her speechless.

I am stretched out on the cement next to Giovanna, to whom I explain the scene.
– It's not possible that they took her child away. Not possible. They must respect women!

I don't even try to explain to Giovanna how women are respected during interrogation. But I tell her that Fine-Skin is going to alert her legation.

Milica comes near us:
– What language are you talking with the stuck-up twit?
– French, Milica.
– Is she French, the stuck-up twit?
– No, Milica, she is Italian.
– Italian? The idiot! I had an Italian guy in Brăila. He was cool. He sang, then we went to bed together, then he sang again, and we went to bed again. Mario was his name, blue eyes that looked like the sky. I had a family, I wasn't on the streets, it was the first time for me. One day I tell him: "Mario, I got knocked-up." "Very good," he says, "very good". For three days, we only talked about the kid.

In the Beginning Was the End

One evening: "I go to town, I'll be back at night". Do you think he came back? He never even sent me a flower. Oh, the scum! And Milica leaves, shaking her head, to go tell the girls that the "stuck-up twit" is Italian.
– What did she say? Asks Giovanna.
I try to translate as faithfully as possible.
– I think it's disgusting, absolutely disgusting. And you?
– Oh, I, you know, I've gotten used to it.
She looks at me with a strange expression. I don't think she is quite convinced that I am not on the streets as well.

✢

There have probably been new raids in the prostitutes' neighbourhoods. During the night the door opens a few times and groups of gaudily made-up women with aimless eyes are pushed into the room. The newcomers step over the bodies stretched on the floor and lean over them to look for possible colleagues. One of them feels my legs.
– Are you one of ours?
Milica, on my left, intervenes:
– Leave her alone. She is the terrorist who was with the Gypsy at Văcărești, Fine-Skin's terrorist, you know!
Shouts at the other end of the hall:
– Are you here, terrorist?
Three colleagues from Văcărești, Gypsy's sworn sisters who have been thrown into the slammer, come to hug me and give me cigarettes. I give one to Giovanna, who looks at me more and more askance; she must be convinced that I am in the same profession. She turns her back to me, pretends to be asleep, and stops telling a story about Napoli, Valle del Infierno, and a great love.

✢

I have been at the police headquarters for five days. I am hungry all the time, I feel feverish and I am once again familiar with bed-bugs. Giovanna was taken one day by the guard and has not returned. Fine-Skin probably relayed the message.
The room is getting more and more full. Spots on the cement

floor have become precious. I have to remain stretched out all the time to keep my share of cement at night. When I move, Milica guards my spot, but anyway I move very little, and only to get food and to vomit. I smile, thinking of the professor who recommended six months of absolute rest and a total change of air. As for the change of air, his wish was fulfilled.

I haven't been called for interrogation again.

✢

A few days ago another mute joined us in the cell. She sits all day long crouched near the window with her large green eyes riveted on the bars. She doesn't move, she doesn't talk to anybody. Milica thinks that she is the police director's informer, that she is here to "rat" on us, that she is a Communist. I don't agree. She has the look of someone who has walked to the end of the road of exhaustion, of someone who has reached that final point from where no return is possible. I try to calm down Milica and promise to go and "take a closer look to see what it's all about". I find some pretext to sit next to her. I offer her a cigarette.

– Political?

She answers in a very flat voice.

– Yes, political. Are you afraid of me too? I know that all the women take me for a spy.

– I know you aren't a spy. I am not afraid of you. I am also a political.

– I know. Radio Moscow has talked enough about you and the attempt you had planned on Ana Pauker's life.

– I didn't...

She interrupts me.

– I believe you. I know the way they stage trials. I was a member of the party. But, for once, I regret that their declarations weren't true. I would have wanted you to kill her.

Her voice seems to be beyond hate. I ask her:

– What is your name?

– My real name is not important anymore. I changed it at fourteen for a Party name: I have kept it. Names sometimes have a longer life than the beliefs that inspired them: thus my name is Vera Zasulici.

In the Beginning Was the End

– Well, but Vera Zasulici was...
– Yes, the girl that wanted to kill the Tsar. I would have been willing to kill many people in order to reach justice and love. Empty words! In the end I reached hatred. The Party... you see yourself. I have resigned from the Party. Now they'll eliminate me. They don't tolerate heretics. But I am going to fight against them to the end. It's the only way to remain faithful to my truth. This way, at least, I can recite to myself, at the end of the road, these verses of Aragon that I liked so much:

> *Oh friends, if I am to die*
> *You'll know what happened.*

She stops and stares at me. I continue:

> *And, if I could do it again*
> *I would take the same road.*
>
> *Under the fire of your arms*
> *Let a better future sing.*

I shake the hand that Vera extends me. I didn't think that oaths could be that simple.

✦

I calm down Milica. Vera is one of ours. Milica spreads the news through the cell that Vera has joined my gang. The prostitutes offer her cigarettes, the murderers talk to her, but Vera keeps quiet.

Next day a guard comes to take her. Before leaving, she shakes my hand, and I see her smile for the first time while she tells me:
– Don't forget: *And, if I could do it again...*

✦

I have been transferred to the Interior Ministry. More formalities. A guard searches me and breaks out laughing:
– The terrorist has lice.

We pass by the cell that I shared two years ago with "Varvara who is no longer afraid" and her mother. We stop a few steps farther. The guard pushes me inside a cell where two very thin women say to me, in place of a welcome:
– Are you sabotage or political?

– Political.
They seem glad and come over quickly to hug me:
– Are you going to give us some of your food?
– Don't you get anything to eat?
– Oh yeah, soup and more soup, with a small piece of bread at every meal. But the politicals are very well fed. They get meat.
I suddenly remember Antim Boghea's words before sentencing: "Probably from now on they'll drug the accused; it's easier and less obvious." I remember also the slips of paper I received from the politicals via the Gypsy, at Văcărești: "If you go through interrogation again, stay away from meat: it is laced with drugs that make you sign anything like an automaton".
I understand now why they didn't beat me. Of course, "it's easier and less obvious".
The two women seem surprised by my sudden silence.
– What's with you? If you don't want to share your food with us, that's alright. But stop shaking like that.
My nervous tremble has returned. My teeth chatter, making a dull sound. I find it impossible to talk. And even if I stopped trembling, what could I tell them?
The door opens. The guard brings us the evening meal: three pieces of gluey bread and three mess tins. In their tins, a blackish liquid; in mine, a meat dish they look at greedily. One of them whispers, after the guard leaves:
– Let's climb up onto the upper bunk. We'll sit with our backs facing the door so you can give us a little of your meat without the guard noticing. Only a little taste.
The other is staring straight at my tin. A small thread of saliva is flowing out of her trembling mouth. She says with a broken voice:
– You know, I am so hungry. Aren't you too?
– I have a high fever, I am not hungry.
Anyway, it's true. I feel like vomiting all the time. We climb on the bed, I hand them the tin and close my eyes. I can hear the dull sound of their jaws tearing up the meat. I don't know how to stop them from eating without telling them that the food is laced with drugs. They ask me:
– Can we eat it all? You are sure you don't want any?
– No.
When I open my eyes again, they have emptied the tin. We re-

In the Beginning Was the End

turn to our places. The guard enters and takes away the tins. If only he doesn't realize! If the food was drugged, I'm sure I'll be called for interrogation tonight. From my bed I watch the two women, who are talking with strange, dim, flat voices.
- Are you warm? I am very warm.
- Yes, I am very warm. I am perspiring.

They both talk at the same time, without stopping. I try to memorize the sound of their voices so I can imitate it at the inquiry. Are they going to take me for the interrogation? Probably, since the food was drugged, because these two women are sweating while I am shivering.
- 15, for interrogation.

The guard is standing on the doorstep.
I get out of bed and follow him.

✢

I enter the office. Three men. I am startled. One of them was an inspector at the Interior Ministry while I was Chief of Staff. He comes toward me, offers me a chair, gives me a cigarette. I stare at him. He lowers his eyes. Another one talks:
- I hope we are going to get along very well.

I'll have to talk, to talk endlessly, with the dim, flat voice of my cellmates.
- It was suggested to you to run, to leave the country by plane, and you didn't turn in the individual who made this offer to you.

I don't answer the question. I start to talk about my illness, my stay in the hospital, the physician's recommendations, in jerky, incoherent sentences. I am inexhaustible. I see one of them winking to the other two, probably to say: "the drug has worked".
- Come on, write here, be a good girl, write what we are going to dictate to you.
- I don't know how to write, I don't know how to write, I don't know how to write...

For a few minutes I keep repeating these words and they don't beat me. One of them frowns, pushes a button and tells the guard who enters:
- To the lock-up.

The guard takes me with him.

✦

I relive all the sensations I felt the first time I was in lock-up. My legs are rubbery, I can hear my heart beating. Are they going to send me to *Securitate*? Am I going to meet again Nicolschi, Bulz, Stroescu and the guards?
Again circles are spinning in front of my eyes. I faint.
The two women pounce every time on my food, which I continue not to touch. They are always delirious after eating, but do not seem to understand anything.
My fever rises, my teeth chatter almost all the time.
When they aren't delirious, my cellmates watch me with a strange expression on their faces; they probably tell themselves that I am crazy. They avoid me, they are almost afraid of me. I am afraid they'll tell that I am giving them my food and thus reveal my stratagem.
We don't talk at all.

✦

Another interrogation. Same men. They want to make me declare that the chiefs of the Liberal party intended to escape together with those of the National-Peasant party. I understand, from their questions, that the latter have been arrested and their party has been outlawed. My statements are to serve to also outlaw the Liberal party.
I pretend to be delirious, and for this my fever is quite helpful. In reality, I am quite lucid. The investigators seem dismayed: I mumble endless sentences about penicillin, about hospital, and I don't sign anything.
One of them, no longer able to take it, takes my head between his hands and starts hitting it against the walls. Another one comes to save me and whispers:
– Stop hitting her. You know what we were told.
Once he lets go of me, I fall to the ground, repeating machine-like:
– I don't sign anything, I don't sign anything.

✦

Back in the cell, I think I am going to faint in earnest: the two women are no longer there. Did they talk? How am I going to

In the Beginning Was the End

manage from now on with the food? Declare a hunger strike? They would give me shots. I go round the cell looking for a place to hide the food. Under the bed I find some *Scânteia* back numbers. I have a solution, and I am waiting calmer by the meal time.

When the guard brings my food, I pretend to pounce on the tin with a famished air. Once he leaves, I climb onto the bed with the tin and a sheet of newspaper. I empty the tin on the paper, make a package and place it inside my pants between my legs. The package is damp and greasy and I feel like vomiting. I knock as hard as I can in the door.

– I need to go to the toilet.

Once there, I throw the package down the toilet and flush a few times.

The guard accompanies me back to the cell.

– Have you finished eating?

I hand him the empty tin.

I go to bed immediately. For the last few days I have only eaten a little bread, and I feel weaker and weaker.

✢

At night, the interrogations continue. They no longer hit me. I don't sign anything and talk endlessly. When they keep me standing for more than an hour I lose consciousness. I hope that after a month of this kind of treatment I'll die. The three investigators are increasingly nervous: the trial is probably imminent.

✢

Every day the guard brings a copy of *Scânteia* to the cell. Before tearing it up to pack up the food, I scan a few headlines. Today on the front page is a headline in heavy, red letters: *New Details About the Tămădău Affair.* A picture: in front of a plane, the National-Peasant chiefs, suitcases in hand. With them is the assistant who suggested I escape with them. I am convinced he is an agent provocateur.

Maniu was arrested. He didn't want to run away. He only authorized the main people in his party to do so. Maniu wanted to stay to the end in the country in order to bear witness. They'll never be able to make a victim out of Maniu. Undoubtedly history is reserving a larger role for him: he will become a martyr. I realize I have started to cry. I didn't think I still had the strength to do it!

✢

I am afraid that soon I will no longer have the strength to go to the toilet to dump the packages. I can barely stand up, and every night the guards have to support me when they take me to interrogation. Once I reach the office, I collapse to the ground. The investigations last for three, four hours every night. I don't sign anything.

✢

Today's *Scânteia* is dated September 7th, 1947. In other words, I have been in prison for more than a month, and for about two weeks I haven't eaten anything except for a little bread and water... I thought that when someone goes on a hunger strike, even a limited one, after two weeks they die.

I no longer have the strength to go to the toilet, and hide the food packages under the mattress.

A few nights later, the guard opens the door and stands to one side to let pass my former Interior Ministry colleague, the police inspector. He tells me:
– Follow me.

Why did he come in person for me? He is accompanied by two soldiers who hold me up in order to go down the stairs. The guard has disappeared. The inspector tells the soldiers:
– We don't have a car available. You are going to walk.

We go out into the street. The inspector is looking at us from the doorstep. Where are they taking me? To *Securitate*? On foot, all the way to *Securitate*? What if they turn me over to the NKVD[65]?

---

[65] NKVD: The People's Commissariat for Interior Affairs of the USSR. Repressive security service responsible for the labour and concentration camps. Later known as the KGB, its organisational model and its brutal methods of repression were emulated by all political police organisations in the countries of the Soviet bloc.

In the Beginning Was the End

They told me a few times, during interrogation, that if I don't sign anything they would hand me over to NKVD. My teeth are chattering. We have turned the corner. A car is parked near the curb. Is it the NKVD car? As we pass by the door opens and two arms pull me inside. I try to shout. A hand presses my mouth. I have been abducted. Who has abducted me? What are the soldiers doing? The yellow circles float in front of my eyes.

I faint.

III

I am afraid to open my eyes. I am afraid of light, I am afraid to face the stares of those that have abducted me. If I see NKVD uniforms, I am going to break into tears. I don't want to cry in front of them.

Marc's voice:

– Hey, bring some water.

Maybe they arrested Marc to confirm what I say. He has been hiding for a year. Did they catch him? I mumble, keeping my eyes closed:

– Did they arrest you?

Marc starts laughing.

– In other words, dear resistance-fighter, we do everything possible to get you out of that mess, and you don't find anything better to do than to faint?

I open my eyes. In the room, Marc and the five young men whom I used to meet every night after I was pardoned. I don't understand anything.

– Where are the soldiers?

– Maybe you would have liked us to bring them also? It wasn't enough that we got her out from the Interior Ministry, we also had to abduct her personal guards.

I want to shake their hands, I get up and collapse to the ground.

The men lift me, laughing.

– If you had stayed one more week at the Interior Ministry you would have been quite ready for the Văcărești hospital.

– But where are the soldiers?

–Tell us how you managed not to sign a statement.

– How do you know?

– You think you are still in the time of the "T organization"? We have evolved in the meantime.

– But from whom did you find out?

In the Beginning Was the End

– We have our people at the Interior Ministry. We have our people just about everywhere.
– Whose place is this?
– "Conspiratorial domicile". And now, let's be a little more serious. The Communists urgently wanted to implicate the Liberals in the Maniu trial. They put their hopes in you. How were you able not to talk? Because they would have drugged you anyway.
– I haven't swallowed anything. I hid the food and threw it down the toilet.
– Smart girl... but this means that you haven't eaten in...
– Two weeks, I believe.

Marc comes to me and takes my pulse. Then he turns toward the men:
– Of course, it's very weak. Victor, go fetch the doctor. You, make some tea. Victor, the doctor must be here in half an hour at the latest. You can take the motorbike.

Then leaning over me:
– Well played, girl, you played hard. Now you must rest. You deserve it in abundance.

I have started to cry while Marc has been talking.

✦

I have been in bed for three weeks now. The men come every night with fresh news. Lucrețiu Pătrășcanu is increasingly regarded by Moscow as being a dangerous heretic and a nationalist. Russians walk the streets in civilian clothes. These Russians dressed in civilian clothes requisition flats, buildings, sometimes whole neighbourhoods. They have brought their families from Russia and want to be comfortable. People have to leave their homes within twenty-four hours and have the right to take with them only a small suitcase with strict necessities.

Victor says:
– And nobody protests. The King, now more than ever, is the prisoner of the government.

Marc replies:
– Yes, but it's good he is here.

Since I got out of bed and can move through the room I feel useless, alone in the apartment. I can hear the door-bells through-

out the building. The door-bells have replaced the stamping of the boots down the prison corridors. They startle me every time.
One day Marc suddenly appears:
– Here are your papers. I need a picture. Put on your pigtails. They are in the closet.
I have dyed my hair black. I put on my pigtails and pull the curtains. While Marc is taking pictures, I wonder where he found a flash.

✢

At night Marc brings my papers. He laughs:
– You'll have to become familiar with the new name. Important detail.
Otherwise, everything is fine.
– I would like to go out at night with you and distribute fliers.
– Are you crazy? You will faint every time you hear steps on the street.
– I would rather distribute leaflets than remain here alone, listening to the door-bells. The walls depress me.
– I'll ask the men tonight. Anyway, it's too risky. You wouldn't be able to withstand another interrogation.
– Listen, Marc, promise me that you won't tell anybody what I'll confess to you now. I have some cyanide with me. If they arrest me, I'll swallow it.
– Who gave you the cyanide?
– One of the men. No, Marc, don't ask me which one of them, I couldn't tell you. Forgive me. You must understand how much this is necessary for me, at least from the psychological point of view.
Marc goes away furious.
Knocks at the door. The familiar signal. The men come in one after the other. I have never seen them so angry. When they are all there, one of them says:
– Maniu was sentenced to forced labor for life.
A few moments of silence, we can hear our own breathing. I whisper:
– How did it happen?
– The same tribunal president as for the T organization. Your president, Alexandru Petrescu. In the audience: the foreign press

In the Beginning Was the End

and the party bigwigs. As for the staging, progress has been made since the T organization. Two categories of defendants: the drugged ones, who have talked like automatons, accusing themselves of the most horrible crimes, and the ones who were not drugged – among them Maniu – telling the truth, turning from accused into accusers. For the foreign press, an impression of almost perfect veracity.

– How was the indictment worded?

– Agreement with imperialist forces to overthrow the democratic regime, attempt to flee abroad, connections with "those in the mountains". The Communists distributed petitions in all workplaces calling for the death of Maniu. They demanded that employees sign them. The outcome: a few thousand more unemployed – those that refused to sign.

Victor is pacing the room with large steps:

– But the peasants are going to revolt. For fifty years, Maniu has been their defender, moreover, an irreproachable defender.

Marc intervenes:

– Exactly, the Russians probably want to use a revolt in order to provoke a civil war and annex the country. This must not happen. Nobody from outside is going to help us.

The men are silent, stunned. Victor continues:

– Adriana, you are the only one among us who knew him personally. How was he?

I shout:

– Don't talk in the past tense! He is still alive.

Marc puts his hand on my shoulder:

– Sure, he is still alive; and, one day, he'll come out even greater. But, for the moment, we are left a little lonelier. That's all.

✢

The men have understood that the walls depress me. Aside from Marc, who voted against, the others have decided that I can go with them at night to distribute fliers.

Before the first outing, Marc gives me instructions with a somber air.

– We go in groups of two spaced well apart. You'll be with Victor. If you hear somebody walking behind you, don't speed up, don't run. As for the rest, Victor will show you.

And, as I was heading for the door:
- One more thing: as regards the cyanide, try to use it only psychologically. Good luck!

✦

It's raining, the streets are empty and poorly lit. We walk close to the walls. Victor squeezes my hand:
- Here.
I see the mail-box of a house. I take two fliers out of my pocket and put them in the box. My hand is shaking. Victor is three steps away throwing manifests in the yard of another house. I join him. The process is repeated in front of every house, and my hand no longer shakes. At the end of the street, I sigh with relief: we haven't met anybody. Victor whispers to me:
- Quick, into the alley.
He has pulled me by the hand. We have entered a dark area. A moment later, a patrol goes by. When we come out, Victor whispers:
- Just in time!
- But our papers are in order.
- It's more prudent this way.
We go down another street. We go by another person. I squeeze Victor's arm. The danger seems to me to float in the air, it can come from anywhere; it's watching me slyly, in the guise of a man, a car, or the sound of steps. Even the man we passed seems like a monster to me. At the end of the sixth street I no longer feel the rain, and I have gotten used to the passers-by, the cars, the muffled respiration of the street which gradually becomes once again a street like any other.
That night, for the first time in two months, I slept deeply.

✦

I am alone in the house and I busy myself at the stove preparing the men dinner. I am startled: the bell has rung next door. I take my shoes off and go and press my ear to the wall with the flat on the right. Shouts, a child crying, voices: the flat has been requisitioned. I remain motionless: they have rung our bell. Once, twice, three

In the Beginning Was the End

times... they go away. Are they going to come back? I spend the day in a chair, trembling and starting at the slightest noise. In the evening Marc arrives first. I tell him what happened. He says simply:

– It doesn't smell good. Maybe they are going to requisition the whole building. Take your raincoat; we are leaving.

We go down the stairs and walk outside. In front of the door, a sergeant. Marc accompanies me to the corner.

– I'll stay here to warn the men. We have to avoid being caught like rats in a trap. You go to this address. The password is: "Roses have never been so blue". They are going to answer: "Or gray". You have it? Repeat.

I repeat.

– Well, now repeat the address.

I tell him the address again.

– Are you going to find it by yourself?

– Yes, Marc.

– Then, see you soon. Good-bye.

It is the first time I have been walking on the street by myself. It is only nine o'clock in the evening. I have to walk slowly, but I feel like running.... I avoid the big avenues, I have my head wrapped in a shawl, I walk, I walk. I am there. I pass once in front of the house, I look at the number, turn the corner, come back and enter. I stop on the first floor. The door is ajar. A gray-haired woman. I whisper:

– Roses have never been so blue.

The door opens widely.

– Or gray. Come in. Go straight to the kitchen. The children haven't gone to bed yet. They must not hear you. This way. I'll come in a quarter of an hour, after I've put them to bed.

She opens the kitchen door and tells me:

– There's soup on the gas stove. If you haven't had dinner yet, help yourself.

I sit next to the stove to warm myself up. She comes back after a little while. And, since she says nothing, I ask her:

– Did you listen to London this evening?

– No, we no longer listen. The children might talk about it at school.

– Talking at school that you are listening to the radio? Why?

– Where do you live? Talking at school, pure and simple. They teach them to do this: to talk about what their parents are discussing with each other, if they listen to BBC or Voice of America, if they have hidden food or gold, and who knows what else. For each piece of information they receive a good mark. You understand? Last week, one of my husband's colleagues was arrested because his son said that he had cursed the government. Praise the Lord, mine haven't gone that far yet, but can I be sure?

She has started to cry:

– Last week, I trembled for a whole day. They had asked me to tell them a story, I started to make up a fairy-tale, the small one – he is seven – interrupted me: "Tell me, were they reactionary fairies?" I said, surprised: "What do you mean? – Well, at school they told us that all the fairies are reactionary... I wanted to know if yours are too". The girl – she is eleven – loves history. Before, we used to do homework together in the evening. Now, no way. Every time I tell her a date, or a fact, she contradicts me: "At school they told me...." They are distorting history. What can I do? The prayers I used to make them say are reactionary. The Christmas tree has become the "winter tree". As for Father Christmas, he no longer exists: "Father Stalin" sends the toys.

And, because I am laughing:

– I assure you it's all true, every word, honestly. On the other hand they study, even at their age, Marx, Lenin, and Stalin... and they learn to hate. Russian is compulsory. If we don't get out of this disaster soon, we'll need quite a few years to re-educate our children. For now, I no longer know how to talk to them or what to talk to them about. I feel like I am going crazy. You have no idea what this means. You can sleep here. My husband is out in the country for a couple of days. Tomorrow morning, until the children go to school, you'll have to walk on the street for a quarter of an hour.

– I can't go out during the daytime.

– Well, then I'll hide you in the closet for fifteen minutes. Let me get you a mattress.

I couldn't sleep at all in the kitchen of "the house with children that denounce".

In the Beginning Was the End

+

Next evening, Victor and another man come looking for me. Victor, who knows my host, tells her:
– You don't know whom you have taken in. Your husband must meet her, he who...
The woman interrupts him:
– No, Victor, I don't want to know anything. It's more prudent.
We say good-bye to the woman, and leave. On the way the men tell me what has happened. Two apartments in the building have been requisitioned. As for them, they spent the whole night moving stuff into the cellar of a party member, but who is one of ours. The stuff is in the cellar now but the party member can't give us shelter. We will have to scatter to different addresses for a week or two.
– To whom are we going, Victor?
– You'll see. Don't worry, there are no children in the house.
We arrive. A very small house with a yard. A small, empty street lit by a single street-lamp.
– As you can see, it's an ideal place.
Our host is an officer who has recently returned from Russia. Immediately after we settle in the living-room he starts to talk.
– They took me prisoner after the armistice. I was in Iași. After the armistice, the Russians took 24,000 prisoners.
– In Russia... how is it?
– Excuse me, but it's difficult to talk about this. Well, not difficult, but painful.
– But how did they let you go?
– I've pledged loyalty to the Party and agreed to join the Romanian Communist division. You have to understand: I was cold, I was hungry, I was ill.
And, as the silence stretched out:
– I am ashamed. It would have been better to die there. Now I am even more afraid.
– Why?
– I am afraid of the political officer of my unit, who joined the Party before me. He is afraid of me because I am a former prisoner in Russia. And both of us are afraid of the unit commander, who in turn is afraid of us. Have you seen how people look at the officers

from the Communist division? With what contempt? Victor tries to console him. The officer shrugs and leaves the room. I wait for him to go away and say:
– Do you think we've been prudent to come here?
– Don't worry. It's quite safe. Marc will come in a few minutes, and Marc goes only to the very safe houses. I'll go out and signal to him that everything is in order and he can come in.

Ten minutes later, when Marc enters with Victor, he finds me with my teeth chattering and runs toward me.
– Why are you trembling? It's not that cold.
– It's not a matter of temperature. It's the nerves.

Marc lights a cigarette, and ponders.
– We'll try to get you across the border. You are too weak to be useful here.
– What do you mean, get me across the border? How much does a guide cost?
– About fifteen hundred dollars.
– You're crazy! With that money we can make fliers for at least a year.
– How much longer do you think you can run from house to house dropping fliers in the mail-boxes? What if they grab you again?

I touch the cyanide in my pocket. Marc, who has followed my gesture, shrugs:
– Anyway, for now you have to get your strength back. Tomorrow you'll go to a mountain town.

And turning to Victor:
– Everything set with the transportation?
– Yes, tomorrow morning at eight.
– Good, tomorrow at eight in the morning somebody will come looking for you. His name is Ion. You'll hold hands and he'll explain everything. He is going to be your boyfriend for a day.
– Marc, you know this is not at all funny.
– You're right, it's not funny. You are going to pretend you are in love with him during the ride. It's a foolproof method.
– And how are we going to go?
– You'll see tomorrow. I have prepared a little surprise and since you have a sense of humour you'll appreciate it for what it's worth. You'll be there for a month. I'll send somebody to bring you back.

In the Beginning Was the End

Good luck!

We shake hands. After they leave, the officer returns and brings me a mattress, sheets and a blanket, and then goes out, wishing me a good night. I am not able to sleep. An owl is calling in the garden, reminding me of the one at Văcărești; the moment I close my eyes figures, making faces, move toward me. I chain-smoke and stare at the ceiling.

When I light the last cigarette in the pack, the day has dawned.

✢

Ion came for me. We climbed into a truck filled with workers. Every Sunday the "trade-union" organizes "political agitation" trips to the Prahova Valley. Ion is a worker. He introduces me to the political chief as his "sweetie". Workers are allowed to take with them their wives, fiancées and girlfriends, provided they also do "political agitation" on the way.

December is coming to an end. It is drizzling lightly and the colours of the freshly painted portraits of Marx, Engels, Stalin and Ana Pauker are running. Once we reach a town, we have to swing the placards, posters and the red flags and to chant in unison: "Stalin, Stalin!" Marc was right, the situation is not lacking in humour.

The workers are chanting the slogans rather lackadaisically. Now and then, the man in charge gets upset and yells:

– What the hell, comrades, more enthusiasm or I hit you on your snouts with the bearded ones.

The "bearded ones", Marx and Engels, continue to lose their colours melancholically.

When the truck stops in some town, passers-by move away in a hurry. I move my lips to pretend that I am chanting with the others. The political chief slaps me on the back.

– Not too bad comrade, but put more heart into it.

Ion intervenes:

– She's timid, comrade. She is from the country, this is her first time in the city.

– Ah, that's it! She is cute, your sweetie. And then, with a very serious air: you'll have to educate her politically, comrade.

– Yes, I do, comrade. I was just telling her about the great comrade Stalin.

The chief goes away satisfied. Ion keeps telling me "Stalin's biography", in other words, giving me instructions for the woman I am going to stay at, whose husband is a guide.

We reach small town X. The man in charge, who already knows that I live in the area, stops the truck and tells me, while extending his hand:

– Good-bye, comrade. Make good use of what comrade Ion has taught you.

I smile.

– Sure, comrade.

Ion climbs down and kisses me on the cheek.

– Good-bye sweetie. See you soon.

I take out my handkerchief and wave it frenetically while the truck moves away, covered with red flags waving in the wind.

✤

I try to walk calmly and not to speed up every time I see an agent or a uniform. I know town X a little, and have no difficulty finding the working-class neighbourhood where my host lives. A very blonde woman opens the door. In the room, three children are playing.

– Ion has...

– Sure. Don't you have any luggage?

– No.

– Can you do the laundry and take care of the children?

– I'll do whatever I can.

– You must. I am a washerwoman, so you'll give me a hand with the laundry, and take care of the little ones. If you don't break too many things and are sparing with the soap, we'll get along quite well. I was told that you shouldn't go out. Do you have instructions for my husband?

– Yes, but what about the children?

– Don't worry. They don't go to school, they are too young. The twins are three, the other one is five.

I relay to her the instructions, she loans me a peasant-woman's dress, helps me carry a folding-bed into the kitchen, and shows me the house: two rooms and a kitchen. Her husband is in Austria.

– He'll have to rest a little when he gets back. He has taken too many across lately. With this miserable life of ours he sure is not lacking clients. I've been told we'll need to do something for you also. We'll see when he comes back. Now you have to start working.

So I start working. I wake up every day at six, dress the children, cook lunch and dinner and wash the laundry my host brings home. The boy, who is five, is after me all the time to tell him "funny stories". And, when I tell him that I don't know any:
– Why don't you ever laugh? Haven't they taught you to laugh?

✢

Tonight, I didn't sleep at all. One of the twins is sick and I had to take care of him. When I go out to get some water, I freeze on the doorstep: in the yard are five men with searchlights. They are headed toward the house in front. I close the door quickly. They start to shout, and the children wake up and are crying. Their mother is away for two days in the countryside nearby, at a sister who is ill. She will come back in the morning. I try to quiet the children. They stick their noses to the windows to see, and the one who is ill is crying.

What if they've come to arrest me? What if they find me?

Muted knocks in the door. I have to open: the children are crying, and certainly can be heard from outside. I try to control the nervous tremble that has taken hold of me and open the door.

– Economic police. We have to search. We've found a flour storehouse next door.

– Come-in. I won't be able to accompany you. The child is sick.

– We'll hurry up. Come on boys, in the cellar. You, Vlad, stay here.

The man remains in the room. I've taken the child in my arms and swing him slowly. The other two children have come and are holding my skirt. I don't know where I find the strength to sing them a lullaby. The economic police belong to the Interior Ministry and are often used to root out the underground. What if the flour storehouse is only a pretext... One of the children pulls my skirt.

– Sing more. Sing another one.

The inspector, who returns with his men from the cellar, stops when he hears me singing.

– Hey, boys, what do you say? We aren't usually received with songs. Come on, let's do it: the closets, under the beds, the children's clothes. The two rooms and the kitchen from the bottom up.

He sits on a chair and looks at me. I keep singing while swinging the small child. I would like to run, to shout, to get away, but I keep singing.

Ten minutes later, the men return.

– We haven't found anything, comrade inspector.

The inspector is rubbing his hands while he moves toward me:

– I know that this isn't a reactionary house. But we had to search anyway; it's the job, what can you do, and the country is teeming with economic saboteurs! You are a pretty girl, and have nice pigtails. One doesn't meet girls like you every day. Can we go out some evening, go to the movies? What do you say?

I put on my most modest air and tell him:

– I'd like that.

They leave. While shutting the door behind them, one of them, undoubtedly impressed by his boss's attitude, adds:

– Excuse the inconvenience.

Silence, then I can hear from the yard the shouts of a man they are taking with them. After a few minutes, his wife comes in, disheveled and in her night-gown, she drops to her knees in front of me and starts crying. Her husband works at the factory and only returns very late in the evening, after the political meetings at the trade-union. At lunch, at the mess-hall, he gets very little to eat: soup, bread, sometimes dried vegetables. She has to feed her man something. She had thus laid in a few provisions: ten kilos of flour, five of sugar, three liters of cooking oil, all bought on the blackmarket. And now, look, they have taken it all. What if they throw her husband in prison.... He isn't a party member.

I follow her story with difficulty. What if the search was only a pretext?

What if I have been followed, and they didn't arrest me tonight because they think the men might come to visit, and it would be better to grab the whole group? What did these words mean: "Can we go out together?"

The woman continues to cry. The children, infected by her hysteria, are crying too.

I take the woman next door, give her a glass of milk, force her to drink it and to lie down on the bed, and put a cold compress on her forehead. I then go to put the children to bed, but they don't really want to go to sleep and keep asking me for more songs.

I feel like going out into the yard to see if they have left an agent in front of the garden gate. I can barely keep myself from doing so, and spend the rest of the night taking care of the sick child, who is screaming, of the woman who is yelling, and of the other two children who are crying.

✣

The woman has gone back to her house to get dressed and to find out "what they did" to her husband. When my host returns, I motion to her to talk softly: the children are still asleep. I ask her:
– Is there anybody in front of the garden gate?
– Who do you want to be in front of the gate? Are you crazy?

I tell her about the sabotage next door. She doesn't seem scared at all.
– They do this, by neighbourhoods, every week. When they catch you with a kilo or two of flour they force you to either join the "voluntary" work brigades, or to spy on the others for them. If you turn them down, you are sent to prison. Just before you arrived here they arrested a foreman from the factory, and he resisted. He refused to work for them, so they've thrown him in prison. Before they took him away they paraded him through the whole town, with his hands tied and a placard hanging from his neck: "I stashed two liters of cooking oil. I am a reactionary saboteur". An agent was pushing him, punching him. We all went out on the door-steps to watch. That night the agent that hit him was found dead in a ditch not far from here. They arrested four more people the next day, but since then they don't parade anybody with placards through the neighbourhood. It costs too much, one dead guard a week! Don't be afraid, they won't find anything here. I am not that stupid, with my husband travelling. How's the little one?

I reassure her and add:
– Still, I must go. The inspector has promised to come some evening to take me out to the movies. What if he comes tonight?
– Where do you want to go?
– Bucharest.

– The men said you have to stay here and that they'll come back for you.

– I know, but it's better for everybody if the inspector doesn't get to know the house very well.

– Maybe you're right. I'll tell the inspector that I fired you because you were too lazy. There is a bus for Bucharest tomorrow morning. You can sleep here one more night.

– What if he comes tonight? No, it's better if I leave right after dark.

At nightfall, I shake her hand, take my things and walk through the small streets toward the forest. After half an hour I reach the edge of the woods. I go in as far as possible and lie on the ground, my luggage under my head. The night is cold and I have to get up now and then and run in place to warm up. It's dark and I can feel the forest teeming with animal life. I am not afraid. For a long time now I have only been afraid of humans.

+

Next day, I wipe my face with dew-covered leaves. I haven't slept all night, and heading for the bus-station my legs feel heavy. I touch the cyanide in my pocket: when the bus leaves they usually check the travelers' papers.

On the plaza there is already a queue. I get in line myself, bag in one hand, money and papers in the other. I force myself to think of something else, to have an expressionless, impassive face. My turn comes at last, I buy the ticket. Next to the ticket collector is an agent:

– Papers?

I hand them to him. For a second I remember Marc's words when he brought me my identity card: "Take your pigtails from the closet. I'll photograph you". Now I am wearing the pigtails. The agent returns my papers. I try to breathe steadily.

– Why are you going to Bucharest?

– My feet are swollen. I am going to the hospital.

– Good, get in.

– For once, the swollen feet were good for something too.

Next to me, on the bus, a priest. He asks me:

– Where are you going, my daughter?

In the Beginning Was the End

– To Bucharest, Father, to take care of my feet. They are swollen, you see.

He doesn't glance at all at my feet. He continues to look at me seriously and tells me, after a moment, lowering his voice:

– May God take care of you, my daughter, may God help you.

✣

I get out of the bus on Victory Square. It is day now and I have to avoid walking on the streets. I go into the first pub and call Marc at the factory, even though he had explicitly forbidden me to do so. There's nothing else I can do; I have returned without an address, without a password. Finally, I hear Marc at the other end, who answers in a very calm voice:

– Sorry sweetie, but I can't see you before tonight. Please don't make a scene. You know how much I hate that and I don't like seeing you jealous. Work comes first; I can't leave the factory before this evening. So, I'll see you tonight at eight, in front of the movie-theater where we saw the film with the Romanian Communist brigade that returned from Russia. I've forgotten the name of it, but I'm sure you remember it. Don't go in without me, wait for me in front of the theater.

I understand, I play the game, make a small scene, then hang up. The theater with the Communist brigade must be the house of the officer who has returned from Russia. Will I be able to find it again? What am I going to do until tonight at eight? I go into the first church. I kneel in front of the icons, and start praying. After an hour, a deacon comes and starts fidgeting around me and looking at me. I have to go. Leaving the church, I see the time on a clock. It's twelve o'clock. I can't stay on the streets for eight hours, it's too risky. I decide to go visit some friends whom I haven't seen in three years.

I ring the bell. I see Mihaela at the door. I breathe out, relieved, I was afraid she might have moved. She doesn't smile:

– You? I thought you were in prison.

– Can I stay here till tonight?

– Yes, but what's with you?

– I am hiding.

She hesitates for a moment, then tells me:

– Come in, we are eating.
When we enter the living-room, her husband gets up quickly.
– You! You are no longer in prison?
Mihaela intervenes, slightly irritated.
– She is hiding. She is going to stay with us until this evening. Mihaela goes out to bring another place-setting from the kitchen. After offering me a chair her husband sits down.
– Are you still working?
– Thanks God, yes.
Maybe he has joined the party? I don't dare ask him the question. Mihaela returns. She wants to serve me some soup. I turn her down.
– Aren't you hungry?
– No, not at all. If the smoke doesn't bother you, I'll light a cigarette.
There is something phony, artificial in the atmosphere. I feel that I am suffocating. They both jump at the slightest noise on the stairs, at every passing car. Mihaela's husband gets up from time to time and looks out the window, moving the curtain carefully to the side.
– Are you sure you haven't been followed?
– Don't worry, I haven't been followed.
Inside me, my stomach is sinking. The men are right, I am too much of a marked person. My friends are afraid of me, and I am afraid of the fear I inspire in them.
After lunch, Mihaela's husband leaves... taking the back stairs. Seeing that I look at him:
– It's more prudent this way.
I chain-smoke. Mihaela is knitting and doesn't ask me any questions. The chair I am sitting on feels like it is burning. After it gets dark, I sigh:
– I am going.
While seeing me off at the door, Mihaela says only:
– Good-bye, and don't forget... you haven't seen us.

✦

Marc is waiting at the street corner. It is ten minutes to eight. He takes me by the arm and pulls me in another direction.

– Our friend no longer lives here, but I didn't know how to give you an address on the phone. Why didn't you stay there? What happened?

I tell him the story about the economic sabotage, the night spent in the woods, and my wanderings during the day.

– It was very risky, but maybe wiser when all is said and done. I was ready to box your ears because you called, since you knew you must not do that.

I burst out crying. Marc puts his arm around my waist suddenly.

– Don't worry, sweetheart, I won't leave you.

An agent, who had stopped for a moment, goes away, but not before looking at Marc knowingly.

We keep walking. Marc tells me softly:

– Sorry, but this always works. Why are you crying?

I tell him the scene that took place at my friends'.

– You must understand them, replies Marc. The whole city is divided into spying sectors. There is a person in charge for every building. Soon there will be such persons for every apartment. Since nobody really knows who these people are, everybody is scared of everybody else. As for the last words of your friend, it's normal now. When two friends meet on the street and one of them is a little suspicious, the other tells him: "Good-day, don't tell me anything. You haven't seen me". Anyway, the spying is bearing fruit. New waves of arrests are taking place in the city.

– But this mutual distrust is even more dangerous than the use of force.

– Exactly. They are trying to completely distort us. But don't worry. It's a double-edged sword. They've already started to inform against each other inside the party. They've already started to fear each other.

I stop crying.

– Where are we going, Marc?

– "Underground house". We still have a few. You'll eat well, take a sleeping pill and sleep. Meanwhile, I'll work on your papers. These ones have done their duty.

We reach the "underground house" dripping wet. We have walked in the rain for more than an hour.

I've been in this house for two days and can no longer go out at night:
The building has a concierge. On the third evening, while I am talking with Victor, Marc enters at a run. Two of the men have been arrested.
– Victor, we have to hurry. They had the linotype. If they drug them, they might talk. We have to change all the identity cards, this very night, all the addresses.
He hands me an identity card.
– Your papers! Thank God I did them yesterday, at least yours are ready. Start with her, Victor. I'll give you an address which only I know. The password: "Never two minus three". The answer: "Four plus four is four". Take the motorbike. Don't return here. Pass by and warn the men. As for you, Adriana, you mustn't stay more than two nights in the same place. I'll take care of that. Did you dye your hair?
I have taken advantage of three days of forced immobility to dye my hair red.
– Come on, get going. Victor, repeat the address. We'll meet again in two hours at Mircea's. Good-bye.
On the way Victor is grumbling:
– They're arresting everybody. Not only those that print and distribute leaflets, but anybody... any excuse is good enough for them. Those that criticize the government while standing in the bread-line are arrested. The workers who don't want to go to the demonstrations are arrested. The officers who have been removed from the army are arrested. The professors who refuse to join the party are arrested. Those who...
I interrupt him.
– I'd like to come with you to warn the men.
Victor shouts at me:
– That's all we need! You're going to stay put, you hear me? I'll come by tomorrow to bring you fresh news.
We have arrived. I understand why Marc kept this address secret: my host is an influential party member.
He smiles when replying: "Four plus four is four". He keeps smiling when Victor tells him that we are in a state of alert. He

shows me to an easy chair.

– Come-on miss, get over it, you're white as a sheet. Mister, tell Marc to find her another house for tomorrow night. I am expecting some "comrades" for dinner who might recognize her. It would be rather unwise. Agreed?

Victor left at a run. The "comrade" returns to the drawing room, and offers a case with cigarettes.

– Would you like some coffee, tea, liqueur? I'll serve everything myself, I don't have a maid; not that it's more democratic, but it is wiser. Once you recover a little, I'll show you to your room. Stop trembling, for a night and a day you're safe here... at your enemy. Secrecy has its good points, doesn't it?

✢

For the last two weeks I have changed address every other day. The other men are doing the same. The net is getting tighter, and Marc is beginning to run out of addresses. All the hosts welcome me kindly, but at every sound of steps on the street, at every ringing of a phone, we fall silent and stare at each other intensely. In every house where I stay, the air seems to get thin. All my hosts smile, want to help me, take care of me – for the last week I have had fever again – and feed me. And I, who don't have a ration-card, feel that each mouthful of food that I swallow is a sacrifice imposed on the others. I, for whom anxiety is almost second nature, recognize it in others before they show it. Prison seems like a dream to me next to this "free life" of a hunted animal.

And when one evening Marc tells me: "It's impossible for me to keep you in Bucharest. Tomorrow a friend will take you to the country-side", I feel like crying with happiness.

✢

Marc's friend is none other than Sandu, in whose house I had lived at Câmpulung while hiding during the German occupation. He came to pick me up on his motorbike, and my surprise pleased him greatly. He told me, laughing:

– We didn't think then that we would meet again in secrecy. Just between the two of us, the first one was like child's play compared

to this one. What was your name then? Johanna Müller I think.
– How is Jana?
He hesitates, and then tells me with a sigh:
– She's in Paris. Let's not talk about that anymore, please.
He rubs his forehead and continues on a lighter note.
– So, are you in shape for the trip?
– Where are we going, Sandu?
– It's a surprise just as big as the one you had when you saw me. It's going to take a while, so make yourself comfortable.

Sandu took me to Câmpulung, to the house of the old woman who had hosted us when the Russian troops arrived. The woman hugged me, crying. Her son, who was at that time "somewhere on the front", never returned home. More than three years have passed and she is still waiting.

Sandu went back the same day. I have been left alone with the old woman and a young girl, Mărioara, who helps her with the garden. Entering the house, all the memories came back and surrounded me. All the efforts I had made since my first arrest, all those slow, patient efforts to eliminate memories, to not remember anything that could affect me, that could crush me by reminding me of my former life, all were erased in one day by this house, this house that had known me as a different person.

For a week now I have been without fear, and my insides feel as if they are made out of ash. Because here fear and anxiety have disappeared, just like the feeling that I am a burden and a danger for others.

The day after my arrival I thanked the old woman for her hospitality, and asked her if I was a burden to her. She replied:
– Listen, girl, don't be silly. I ain't very smart, but I think that to some extent you were in prison for all of us. So there is no reason for you to thank me.

And, just like that, these words in their calm simplicity have re-established in me a difficult balance.

✛

In the evenings, when they come back from work, the three of us gather around the fire-place in the old woman's room. Mărioara and I sew; my host lies on the bed "to rest her tired old bones", and

we start talking. The old woman asks me about prison and the city, Mărioara crosses herself and laments:
– They're asking for more wheat than we have in all the village barns put together. For a while I bought from the neighbours to give to the state. Now the neighbours don't have anything more either, and the state asks for more and more. When they don't come asking for wheat, they come, they say, for "agitation", and gabble: saying Stalin has brought us happiness and all sorts of things like that. As if we couldn't see ourselves what their Stalin has brought us: misfortune and famine, and typhus, and fire. I think that if they keep coming to "agitate" here, an accident might happen and we are going to agitate in earnest. Last week they wanted to remove the King's portrait from the school and replace it with Stalin's and his ilk. The men wanted to take their pitchforks and kill them. Vasile, who's got smarts, no joke, told them: "Leave it to me". He went together with the men to the Communists at the town hall and told them: "The icon has been here for as long as we can remember. So it must stay here in order to have God on our side. The King is in the city. We can't go there to see him. So we have to leave the picture where it is, so we know he's on our side. Stalin, whoever wants to see him can go to you at the town hall and look at the picture". The mayor shouted: "Yes, but Stalin gave you land". Vasile told him: "Yes, but he takes the wheat we make. So with land but without wheat we are like a woman without a child, like a man without limbs; just like we didn't have it."

Mărioara has paused. The old woman is lamenting for the son that has never returned. In the hearth the fire dies without any of us trying to rekindle it.

✢

One evening, while we are talking around the fire as usual, Mărioara gets up quickly and goes to the window motioning to us to keep silent. She turns toward us and whispers:
– There's a motorbike in the yard. Put out the lamp.
While I make the wick of the gas lamp smaller, my hands tremble. Mărioara, still at the window, keeps watch. She adds:
– A man is coming this way.
We hold our breath. A voice from outside:

– It's me, Adriana, open up.

It's Marc. I run to the door and open it wide. Marc is standing in front of me, smiling. I introduce him to the two women. And while we are trying to take off his windbreaker:

– I can only stay for half an hour. I'd like just a little warm water to wash up. And I'd like to talk to you for a moment, Adriana.

We go next door.

– What has happened Marc?

– Don't look gloomy, because this time at least I am bringing you some good news. In a few days you are going to take a cruise on the Black Sea to Constantinople.

– Marc, have you gone mad?

– Well if I've gone crazy, I am in any case a reasonable madman, a well-organized madman. Everything is well-arranged. A medium-sized ship, in good working order. Stock of fuel assured. Departure guaranteed. Pleasant company: three people you know, but whose names I can't reveal to you yet; that's the way it is when one "conspires".

He is laughing all the time. I don't manage to say a word, because my teeth are chattering. Marc comes to me and shakes me.

– This isn't the moment to tremble, girl. Do you have a pair of long pants?

– Yes.

– Good, then put them on quickly. In half an hour we have to go. As for your things, you might as well leave them here. A complete outfit is waiting for you at the harbour. Meanwhile, put on your warmest sweaters. I've brought you a lined windbreaker. You're going to freeze a little, but it's not going to last long. In town X we'll change our gear and take the train. Tomorrow evening we'll reach our destination. While I am washing, say your good-byes to the two women and tell them you are going to Bucharest. Not one extra word, you understand?

I leave Mărioara my dress and overcoat. She makes us sandwiches and forces us to down a couple of glasses of liquor, one after the other.

My head is spinning when I bid farewell to the old woman, who blesses me with a serious air on her face.

In the Beginning Was the End

✦

I am sitting next to Marc on the train. The ticket-collector is accompanied by two agents in civilian clothes who are checking papers. They pass every hour. The compartment is badly lit. Across from me, a woman is grumbling:
– They've seen my papers three times already. If they were forged I wouldn't travel by train and have to show them every five minutes.

I squeeze Marc's hand who smiles and tells the woman:
– You're right, ma'am. But you never know. Maybe it's more prudent this way. There are so many enemies of the people.

The woman doesn't know how to retract her words; she probably thinks that Marc is an agent provocateur. In the corner, next to the door, a man who is trying to sleep shouts at us to be quiet.

Another verification, this time a longer one. An agent asks everyone about the reason for their trips. I am afraid that I will start trembling again. When our turn comes, Marc says:
– My fiancée and I are going to a cousin's wedding.
– What does your cousin do in town Y?
– He is a worker. The political officer of the harbour.

The agents returns our papers bowing slightly. Immediately after they have left the compartment, I whisper:
– Are you crazy? What if they check-up on this?
– I don't care. The political officer of the harbour will confirm this. Thanks to him I was able to arrange your departure. He is waiting for us at the station.

The woman pretends to be asleep, but she looks at us furtively, anxiously. She takes advantage of the first stop to change compartments.

Thereafter the agents don't ask for our papers anymore. The trip seems endless.

✦

On the platform in station Y, a man leaves a group and beckons to us. After shaking his hand, Marc introduces me:
– Petre, this is my fiancée. Are we expected at your place?

– Sure. Let's hurry, to avoid the line at the controls.

Two police checkpoints. Petre tell the agents plain and simple: "They're with me", and we pass. At the second checkpoint, I see one of the agents who was with the ticket-collector on the train. He points at us with his finger, and a man on his left asks Petre:
– Are they with you, comrade?

Petre replies calmly:
– Yes, comrade.

I stare with a preoccupied air at the station clock. We go through. The streets are empty and quiet. I tell Marc:
– Marc, I'd like to see the sea.

Petre answers:
– You'll have all the time in the world to see it on the way to Constantinople. For a few days you'll only see the water. Now, we have something else to do.

We hurry along. Marc and Petre are talking about the political structure of the port. I can barely hear them. I listen only to the sea roaring somewhere in the distance.

✦

I don't get out of bed. It's cold, and I am not allowed to make a fire during the day. The street captain knows that this house is occupied by workers and seamen who work during the day. Smoke might seem suspicious.

The house is occupied by four workers and three seamen, all Party members. Two of them are married. Their wives work at the factory. They work in the harbour. The house has a total of three rooms. We don't have to guard against them, they are on our side. The three other people with whom I will run away, and whose names I don't know yet, are staying with other workers four houses away. Marc and Petre commute between the two houses and the port.

They have been gone for almost three hours, they should have been back at nightfall; it's dark already and they haven't come back yet. I sit motionless, chain-smoking and listening to the sea. The day after tomorrow it will be New Year's Day and I will be on the ship. Tomorrow I will leave my country. I try to repeat this sentence to get a feel for it. But I am simply not able to. I am completely empty, the despair, the violent feelings have disappeared. I

In the Beginning Was the End

have just decided to get out of bed and turn on the bed-lamp, when I hear the entrance door being slammed. Marc and Petre enter the room. I tell them "Hello"; but they don't answer me. Marc turns on the switch. In the harsh light of the lamp I see their white faces.
— What's happening? Have you been followed?
— No.
— Then, what is it? Why are you standing there like stones? Why are you silent?
Marc looks away. Petre whispers:
— The King has abdicated. They forced the King to abdicate!
I sit on the bed. Marc keeps standing with his back toward us. Petre is standing motionless. How long did we stay like this without uttering a word?

I am crying now, and Marc comes over and puts his hand on my shoulder. He tells me in a flat, dim voice, without looking at me:
— The men will come at any moment. I don't want them to see us crying. I don't want them to see us crying. We have to find the words to give them courage, now that we are left completely alone.

Somebody knocks at the door. Marc hands me his handkerchief.
— Come-on, swallow your tears. They've come!

The workers file in one by one, with muffled steps as if in a sick person's room. They all whisper, and all the faces are pale. One of them says:
— Now we are in no-man's land.
— Don't say that, replies another one, don't say that! They've taken the King from us so that we won't keep fighting. They aren't stupid; but they aren't going to defeat us with this strategy. I say that, tomorrow even, we should blow up something, no matter how small, in the port.
— They're going to catch you.
— Maybe they're going to grab me, but they aren't going to grab the whole country. Let's not collapse now. A little sabotage, that's what we need now. What do you say, Petre?
— I agree, I am for sabotage. But we'll have to prepare everything well.

Petre spoke loudly. The evil spell seems broken. They have all started to talk, and they light their cigarettes. Marc leaves the group and approaches me.
— As for the departure, there's nothing that can be done. They've

doubled the guards, and have replaced our people with others of whom we can't be sure. Of course we couldn't have predicted this.

– It doesn't matter Marc, or, at least, it's not this that matters now...

Marc looks at me for a moment, and then tells me in a changed voice:

– Listen to me well, girl; right now, fatigue is a luxury. The same goes for despair. We can't afford such luxuries, or we are going to be lost, and many others along with us. What do you think?

– You're right. When are we going back to Bucharest?

– Tomorrow morning. Tonight we are going to organize the work here. You light the fire and make us some strong coffee. We'll have to stay awake the whole night.

I make the coffee, hand out the cups, and sit on a bench next to Petre, who is explaining the action plan.

The two women who have also returned are crying in the room next door. I remember all of a sudden the long nights in the ward at Văcărești and the harrowing rhythm of the wails.

Marc spreads on the table a map of the harbour and with his fingers traces some red lines that dance in front of my eyes. I have to copy the maps onto tracing paper.

The dawn finds us all gathered around the table. The room is filled with the acrid smell of cigarette butts and, when I open the window, the roar of the sea enters the room. One of the seamen listens for a moment in silence, then says, shaking his head:

– She doesn't seem too happy either. When the sea roars like that, it means that a storm isn't far.

✢

Today I should have been on the ship, on the high seas, far from the Romanian shore. It is the last day of 1947.

On the train taking us to Bucharest, I keep my eyes closed. I let Marc answer all the controls. The story is different now: I am pregnant, and Marc is taking me home to Moldova. The game is risky; we might meet one of the agents who saw us get off the train the other day in port Y, and then... But we have no other choice, we must return as soon as possible; without Marc the men are probably going stir-crazy.

In the Beginning Was the End

The compartments are almost empty. The few passengers are looking silently out the window, or pretending to sleep like me. Next to me Marc is reading the papers that announce the creation of the Romanian Popular Republic.

✢

The men have found a small, somewhat run-down house on the outskirts of Bucharest, and have turned it into a second-hand store.

In the cellar we have installed the linotype, a radio and the stock of paper, all hidden behind all sorts of odd things: old clothes, a collection of odd shoes, silverware, old paintings, family portraits, broken easy chairs, precious souvenirs and useful objects all covered with dust.

The owner of the store is one of ours, and also the owner of a precious Party card. While he sells his wares upstairs, in the cellar we print leaflets to be distributed at night. The linotype is hidden under a Louis XV style piece of furniture, and the radio is installed in an Empire desk. The cellar is connected with the next house through a corridor. This house is also occupied by friends. There is a makeshift cover over the corridor entrance. The working conditions are ideal.

I only leave the cellar when I go through the corridor to the neighbouring house where I sleep. I sleep very little anyway, and spend most of my days and nights in the cellar where, behind a folding screen, I have laid out a little corner for myself: a three-legged easy chair that tips dangerously every time I sink into it, a small, rosewood desk, a few candles and an icon in the purest Byzantine style, a stone-still Virgin staring at me with her inscrutable gaze.

We print leaflets all day long. Evenings the men go out to distribute them, and I listen to the foreign radio broadcasts and take notes. It has been two months since the King left the country.

Late at night I go to the house next door where I have a mattress in the bathroom.

At dawn I return to the cellar and wait for the men to start our work.

This way three more months pass.

Victor was arrested during a raid. Marc takes over; in just two hours the store is closed, the linotype and the radio moved to a different location, the whole group scattered into the country-side. Marc has again run out of addresses in Bucharest. He needs a one month break to find new ones and reorganize our work.

Travel by train or by bus has become too dangerous, so Marc entrusts me and my new papers to a truck driver, who locks me up in a chest that was supposed to be filled with... dried prunes. This way I arrive at village Z where a friend of Marc's is expecting me.

When I enter the yard of the house at the address that was given to me, a young red-head comes to meet me. I tell her:

– When the trees have leaves...

She responds:

– ...it's a first order equation.

And, without any change in the tone of her voice:

– Welcome. Here you're my cousin, and you've come to recover after pneumonia. That's all. My name is Monica, I used to have a small property here but they took it from me. I am staying with a peasant. I've put another bed in my room. Marc passed through here two months ago and told me that, if things got worse, he'd send you here. So I have been expecting you any day. What happened?

– They arrested one of ours. We all scattered.

–You can rest here. Marc told me you shouldn't go before he personally comes to take you back. Would you like to go inside? Let's organize our communal life.

We cross the yard. In front of the entrance, a tree in bloom. For the past few months I have been living in a cellar and I haven't seen any trees. And, since I am frozen in my tracks, Monica follows my gaze and adds with a suddenly changed voice:

– Yes, they've bloomed. Easter is coming.

✦

Days I have to stay inside. Once it gets dark Monica takes me out for air.

Less than a week has passed since I arrived when, one evening, I hear the sound of steps behind us. Somebody is following us on the village lanes. Monica glances behind quickly and tells me:

– Don't worry. It's the warrant officer from the police station. He was raised by my parents. He is devoted to us.

The officer catches up with us. I frantically squeeze Monica's arm.
– Good evening, Ma'am.
– Good evening, Dumitru.
He walks alongside us. He hesitates a moment, then says:
– Ma'am would you like to come to the station?
I grip Monica's arm even tighter, just about ready to fall. She says, laughing:
– Why, Dumitru, do you want to arrest me?
– God forbid, Ma'am. He raises his arms toward the sky and adds: I would just like to show you something.

We follow him to the station. He steps aside to let us enter into a small room, locks the door, offers us chairs, rummages through a drawer, takes out a sheet of paper, and hands it to Monica. I see her turning pale while she is reading. I can no longer control myself and snatch the paper from her hand.

Attention, to all railroad stations, airports, border stations, police stations; immediately arrest Georgescu Adriana, former Chief of Staff of the Executioner of the people, currently wanted by the police.

I place the sheet of paper on the desk and, as the officer is staring at me, I say calmly:
– Why are you looking at me like that? Do you think it could be me? All you have to do is check my papers.

He checks my documents carefully and smiles while returning them:
– Well done, these papers. Except that, together with the notice, I've received this: take a look.

A small poster with two photos of me, face and profile.
The cyanide is in the pocket of my blouse.
Monica gets up.
– What do we do, Dumitru?
– You see, Ma'am, the village people know that somebody is staying with you. They are on our side, the peasants. But what if there is a traitor among them, or at the village hall? One can never be sure. I am risking my skin with this story. I have to post this flier at the station.
– Where do you want her to go, Dumitru?
– If I only knew... I am only asking you not to keep her here any longer. If there is a snitch around here, we will all go to prison. If it

was only the name, I wouldn't say anything. But with the photos... I'm not going to arrest her, ma'am. I know what gratitude means and, after all, you know yourself that we think the same way. But I can't risk my skin. We have to take her back to the city.

– Can you lend me the station's gig?

– I'll harness the horses and in a quarter of an hour I'll be at your house.

Once we get out of the station I ask Monica:

– What if he is setting a trap for us?

– I don't think so. He is somewhat of a coward, but he is quite devoted.

– What are we going to do?

– I'll take you to town, and you can get on the train for Bucharest.

– You want me to take the train? They must have received the picture at the station as well.

– I'll dress you up in peasant garb. Headkerchief and all. I'll buy the ticket myself and go through the controls. You'll cross a small garden at the end of the platform, behind the public toilets. There is no control there. We'll meet on the platform and I'll give you the ticket.

– What about the controls on the train?

– After you've left the station, you don't have to worry anymore. They won't have sent your picture to the ticket-collector.

I am convinced of the opposite and, while Monica is looking for a peasant outfit for me, I try to figure out the best way to swallow the cyanide before being caught.

Half an hour later the gig is in the yard. Monica climbs up on the front bench, tells me to join her, shakes Dumitru's hand and whips the horses.

– We'll have to hurry now to get there before the train leaves.

Once out of the village she starts driving like a mad woman. I grab the bench with both hands in order not to fall off. Meanwhile, Monica, leaning forward and with a tense face, is humming a song about a village feast and the wind roaring through the forest.

✦

We arrive too early and, while Monica is waiting in line for the ticket, I remain hidden in the park next to the station. Half an hour

later, I decide it's time to go, crawl on all fours to the fence, climb it, go around the toilets, and reach the end of the platform. A little farther, Monica, sitting on a bench, is reading the paper. I sit next to her. She gropes for my hand, shakes it, and passes me the ticket. She whispers in French:
– *Bonne chance!*
She folds the paper calmly, gets up and heads for the toilets, pretends to go in, goes around them and disappears. She has left me a basket with two geese in it, gaggling and stirring. When the train comes into the station, I grab the basket and head for one of the third class cars. The train is overcrowded, and I have given up trying to find a seat when a man in uniform looks out of a compartment and tells me:
– There's a seat inside. Don't you want to sit down?
My heart is pounding, but I tell myself that sitting next to a man in uniform might be helpful. Thus, I settle next to him. Only inside the compartment do I realize that he is wearing a station chief's uniform. He tries to start a conversation:
– What's in the basket, girl?
– Some geese.
– Are they expensive?
– I've to take them to the co-operative store in Bucharest.
The word "co-operative" shut him up. He doesn't say anything anymore. The agents accompanied by two soldiers pass by in the corridor. One way or another I have to talk to the station chief, to make them think that we are together.
– Are you going to Bucharest?
– Yes, girl.
– Are you ill?
– No, I am not ill. He lets out a long sigh. My woman left me for another man, a scoundrel, I can't call him anything else. I am the station chief.
He sighs once more and asks me:
– And you, girl, aren't you afraid to go like this on the train?
The compartment is badly lit, so he couldn't have seen me turning pale.
– Why should I be afraid?
– You're a pretty girl. Aren't you afraid that somebody is going to kidnap you? One never knows.

I sigh and whimper as best I can. The station chief takes my hand in his. I let him do so.
– You've pretty hands. You don't work much in your house. Your skin is very white.
– Because... because I was ill and I was bedridden for a few months. I had typhus.
– That's why you are so thin. You're lucky you got well.
The train has left the station. I whisper:
– Yes, I am lucky.
The station chief starts to tell me his life-story:
– ...In the end she left me a note: "I am going to Bucharest with him who treats me like a lady and not like a rag." "He" is the railroad inspector who has come to check my station, and then... I don't have the slightest idea if he treats her like a lady, but I know I am going to have a few words with this inspector. I am going to him; I have his address in Bucharest. The whore must be with him. To do this to me, I, who took her without a dowry, who gave her culture and an education. When we got married, she didn't pretend to be a big lady. She bragged all the time: "I am getting married to the Station Chief, I am getting married to the Station Chief".
I pretend to listen to his story with interest. In reality I think only about the controls. I yawn, excuse myself, yawn some more and tell him, while withdrawing my hand:
– I'd like to sleep, mista' Station Chief. You know, with this illness, I don't have much strength anymore. Can you show my ticket when the ticket-controller comes?
– Sure, girl, sleep well.
He pats me lightly on the cheek with a protective air while I give him the ticket. I hide my face in the seat so that one can only see two pig-tails and a nose coming from under the head kerchief. I don't move the whole night. The chief of station covers me with his coat and shows my ticket to all the controls, telling them with a satisfied air:
– The lady is with me.
Much later, he shakes me:
– Hey girl, get ready, we've arrived!
I open my eyes. The outskirts of Bucharest parade sadly in front of the windows, in the pale light of dawn. The controls in the station are next...

In the Beginning Was the End

— You have beautiful eyes, girl.

He takes me by the hand. I let him and, when the train stops, we get off together. On the platform, I pretend that I am not feeling well.

— Mr. Station Chief, I am dizzy. Must be because of my illness. I can't walk straight anymore.

He puts his arm around my waist, a protective look on his face. I lean my head on his shoulder and we start walking down the platform entwined like that. We approach the police barrier. The Station Chief tells me:

— Must be a bad illness. Your legs are trembling.

I don't answer and sink my face deeper in his coat. At the control he shows both tickets and his identity card:

— For my lady and me.

We pass. The Station Chief laughs loudly:

— I said that so we would pass quicker. But it wouldn't be that bad if it was true, would it girl? You're neat, and I like it when you call me "mista' Station Chief". You're respectful. Nowadays, the young people don't know about respect. I like to be respected. Hey, say, what do you think about the two of us?

And, as I pretend to be confused, he laughs even louder.

— You're timid. But maybe if we see each other more often, you could get over it. What do you say?

I try to seem moved when I answer him.

— Yes, mista' Station Chief.

He caresses my face with a satisfied air.

We part at the tram stop in front of the station, not before having decided to meet in the afternoon "to go to the movies".

✤

The basket with geese in it is obviously not the ideal way to pass unnoticed on the street. Everyone I cross paths with stops to ask me:

— How expensive are the geese, girl?

I answer invariably:

— I am taking them to the co-operative store.

Once they hear of the co-operative, people frown and keep walking. I could go into the yard of some house to sell the geese, but I would be running the risk of being arrested: the stores are state-owned, and all food from the countryside must be sold at the cooperative. With my false papers an arrest must be avoided at all costs. I don't know what to do. I have reached Bucharest at midday; there isn't anybody I could call, and anyway I only have Marc's number, and he hasn't been going to work for two months. Might he be in Bucharest? And how could I reach him?

Passing in front of a building, I suddenly remember that I have some friends who live there. I haven't seen them in almost three years. I hesitate for a moment – the scene at Mihaela's is still fresh on my mind – but finally I decide to go up. I take the back stairs. I ring the bell on the first floor. The door opens a little and I can see Mira's tousled mug. She glances at the geese and tells me:

– We won't buy anything, girl. Don't you know it's forbidden to sell birds?

I burst out laughing, push the door and enter while taking off my head kerchief. Mira looks at me dumbfounded.

– Is it you? What did you do to lose this much weight, you poor thing?

I stop laughing. I fall in a chair.

– Can I stay with you until tonight Mira?

– You'd do better if you didn't ask stupid questions. Here, you are at home.

– Do you know that I am in hiding? That I have false papers?

– I imagined that you weren't walking the streets dressed like this just for fun. Anyway, I knew you were in hiding.

– What about your husband, would he agree also?

Mira starts laughing.

– How could he not agree when you bring him geese? I don't even remember for how long we've only been eating potatoes. We're going to make a real feast!

– Let's talk seriously Mira, do you think he'll agree?

– What are you afraid of, Adriana? Let's talk seriously if you want to. We don't have much to lose anymore. Horia refused to join the party. The result: he was removed from the Writer's Society, he can no longer publish, not even an article, not one line, and his books are banned, removed from circulation and the libraries. That's the way it is!

In the Beginning Was the End

– But how do you make a living?
– We translate books and articles from English and German. Other authors, who have joined the party, sign them and pay us a pittance. But we manage. And we still have the apartment and our library. They'll probably take them some day, but until then... Come-on, don't look gloomy. We live like everybody else, and probably not worse than everybody else anyway.
– So, do you think I can stay here until tonight then?
– Of course. Only tonight we have a guest for a potato dinner. Don't worry. He is a former jailbird like you.
I stand up. I am sure Mira doesn't know Marc and the boys.
– Who is it?
– Guess. A prisoner of long ago. A notorious Anti-Nazi belonging to the "Transylvania Group". Do you remember the Transylvania Group, the resistance network? Did you know that the twelve men arrested in 1941 and freed in 1944 were the leaders?
– Yes, I know. Which one of them?
– He is a specialist in radio broadcasting. Can't you guess?
– Yes, I know, indeed...
How could I not know him? Sandu belonged to that network. At Câmpulung he kept talking about his bosses who were in prison, and especially about Ştefan C., the great radio specialist. Sandu even ended up thinking that Antonescu was alright, because he had not turned the group of twelve over to Hitler. Sandu and his twelve legendary heroes... Câmpulung and the days of our resistance...
– Have you guessed?
– Ştefan C.
– It wasn't difficult, but you deserve a reward anyway. Do me a favour and take off this costume and put on one of my dresses.
I hesitate for a moment, and then ask:
– Could I take a bath?
I say the word "bath" with piety. Mira takes me by the hand and pulls me toward the corridor laughing with abandon.
– Why didn't I think of this before? I could have prepared it after you came. There isn't enough water for a bath, but it's sufficient for a shower. A shower on the outside... and on the inside, that's what you need!
I follow her without really being able to fall in with her mood, but laugh when appropriate: a shower on the inside...

✦

I have taken a shower and I have clean underwear and a clean dress. If I could stay in this bright and friendly house, I would even sleep on the floor.

✦

Mira was right, her husband receives me with open arms, without even a trace of reticence. The two of them almost succeed in ridding me of my fear. When we hear the door bell ring, Mira says calmly and without starting:
– Must be your prison colleague, Adriana.
Ştefan C. enters in the living room. He is quite dark-haired, and is wearing a black leather jacket. And, as Mira introduces me under the first false name that comes to her mind, he starts to laugh:
– What did you say: Sanda Dănescu?
Mira can barely control her laughter.
– Yes, Sanda Dănescu.
– Listen, Mira I thought you trusted me. It's true she has changed a lot, but I recognized her anyway.
I intervene:
– Where did you meet me?
– At the Interior Ministry.
– Were you locked up at the Interior Ministry?
– Not yet, and I hope never to be. I didn't meet you as a detainee, but as Chief of Staff instead. You were insufferable. You kept smiling and repeating like an automaton the same sentence: "The audiences are suspended, the audiences are suspended".
He mimics the whole scene, and now all four of us are laughing with abandon. This joyful dinner, without stress, without obsessions, seems to me like a memory from long ago that has come to visit and to warm me up a little.
Once we finish dinner I tell Horia and Mira:
– It's time to go.
Horia looks at me astonished.
– Where do you want to go?
And Mira picks it up:

In the Beginning Was the End

– Yes, where do you want to go, and to whom? Don't you feel well here?
– Can I stay with you?
– As long as you want.
– But, Horia...
– What language do you know best?
– Italian, French...
– Perfect, I'll get some translations from Italian for you. You'll do the translation, and an author who is a party member will sign it. This way you won't have any remorse, since you'll contribute to the common expenses. Are we agreed?

I feel like crying. I didn't think that I would ever again feel like crying for joy, for regained inner peace.

Before leaving, Ştefan takes me aside and asks me:
– Do you have any message for Marc?
– What?!
– You don't have to shout. I just asked: "Do you have any message for Marc?" He thought you were at his friends. I warn you that for at least a month he won't be able to help you. He must vanish himself for a "little rest" in the country-side. Try to stay here for a month. When he returns he'll take care of you again. I'll tell him you're here. No need to talk about this to Horia and Mira. Did anything serious happen in the countryside?
– No, nothing serious, but I had to leave, the police have sent my picture to railroad stations, airports...
– We know. Marc wanted to send somebody looking for you, but it's just as well you've returned on your own. Anything else for him?
– No, nothing. Is he in any danger?
– Not really, but anyway, he'll do well to leave the scene for some time, and you'll do well to stay here. Do we agree?
– How did you know Marc?
– That's another story, too long to tell it now. Anyway, you know that people in the underground always end up meeting each other.
– Are you underground?
– Not yet for the time being, or not completely.

Then, in a loud voice:
– I'll pass by tomorrow evening. I'll try to get the Red Cross car and take you out for a ride. And, looking at me: for "air", isn't that right, comrade detainee?

And leaves while I am explaining to the others the meaning of this word that seem strange to them: "air".

✢

We sit on pillows, our backs against the bookcases. We talk softly, not because we are afraid, but in order not to disturb this peace that is taking over the room, this peace inside us.

Horia tells the latest news from the literary world: the authors who have joined the party have to apply self-criticism after self-criticism, to publish at least once a month an article in which they declare that "Stalin is the greatest writer in the universe, that he is their guide, model, beacon illuminating the darkness in their minds", to put their books, before publication, through three levels of political censorship, and especially to disown any past links with France and the West.

– Why France in particular?

– Because the French influence was by far the strongest in our country. Have you forgotten that we used to be the second or third largest market for French books in the world? That the majority of our intellectuals studied in France? But now all this will change. Teohari Georgescu has told us that the light is no longer coming from the West, but from the East. Anyway, I agree with him on one point only, or better said, one author. I am talking about that writer, who more than forty years before the outbreak of the revolution predicted its later development, its Apocalypse-like present aspect, about the one who has given the best description of what we are going through now, I am talking about the prophet...

Mira smiles.

– Dostoyevsky and *The Demons* again. That's his obsession.

– No, it's not an obsession, replies Horia, going to the bookcase and taking out a book. Everything is in here, absolutely everything, phrase by phrase and point by point; it's a faithful description of the phenomenon, a description made more than forty years before the phenomenon took place, because you aren't going to make me believe that Neciaiev, who organized the first revolutionary committee among the Moscow students and who planned and executed Ivanov's murder, was of Verhovensky's caliber. No, Neciaiev was only a pretext through whom Dostoyevsky foresaw how history was going to unfold, but who didn't contain history in him. And

In the Beginning Was the End

notice that Dostoyevsky isn't only forty years before his time, but much more than that, as he has not only predicted the revolution, but its aftermath and the current situation as well. Listen, I feel like sending this text to Teohari Georgescu as a reply to his slogan: "Light comes from the East". Listen how Verhovensky describes to Stravoghin Şigaliev's system, Şigaliev being the theoretician of their revolutionary group:

Şigaliev is a genius. I set aside a role for him. He has discovered "equality"... Everything is in there. He has invented a new spying system. In the society that he envisions, each member is spying on his neighbour and is asked to inform against him. Any member belongs to everybody else and all members are the property of anyone. All slaves, and all equal in slander and murder, but, above everything else, equality. In the beginning the level of education in science and arts will be low. A high level is accessible only by superior spirits, and we don't need superior spirits... They'll have to be banished or sentenced to death. Tearing out Cicero's tongue, gouging out Copernicus' eyes, Shakespeare's stoning, that is Şigalievism... Listen, Stavroghin: the leveling of mountains, that's a beautiful idea that has nothing ridiculous in it. I am for Şigaliev. There is no need for education, we are fed up with science... but we need docility. Only what is necessary is necessary, this is going to be from now on the slogan for the human race. But we need convulsions, and we, the bosses, will make sure that we have them. We need masters and slaves. Total obedience, absolute lack of personality... Listen, first we'll unleash the revolt... We'll proclaim the destruction. We'll start the fire. We'll create myths. The world will walk upside down like never before. Night will cover Russia, the earth will cry for its former gods.

In the room the silence settles in heavy, unbearable. Horia gets up slowly, closes the book, puts it back in the bookcase and says in a dim voice:

– Earth will cry for its former gods...

✢

I sleep in the living-room, on the sofa next to the bookcase. At dawn I hear soldier's songs and rhythmic steps. I wake up startled and run down the corridor, where I bump into Mira, who looks at me surprised:

– What is it?

– A regiment on the street. The German goose-steps. There must be some event.

Mira puts her arm around my shoulders and takes me back to the room:

– Where have you been? They've been passing like this, in front of our windows, singing fighting songs for a year now. They go to the training grounds. All the streets are filled. All the factories are producing for the war. They never say so exactly, but the whole country is preparing for war.

– But according to the peace treaty we don't have the right to rearm more than...

– What does it matter? Can anybody come here on the spot to check-up on Moscow?

– What about the Anglo-Americans?

– If they ever protest, Moscow will no doubt reply that it is an army... for peace, or some such nonsense. And then, you know they aren't going to protest. Haven't you heard the anecdote on this theme making the rounds in Bucharest now:

It seems that in a small sea, the Silver Sea, all the sardines have been caught one day. One of them, who witnessed the massacre, manages to escape and goes to warn the sardines in the neighbouring seas, the Gold and the Diamond Seas. Who, upon hearing the news, hold council after council. The little sardine, concerned for her sisters, struggles, agitates, asks for a quick intervention. But her efforts are in vain. Time passes. Finally, one day, the sardines from the Gold and Diamond Seas decide to go and save their sisters, the sardines from the Silver Sea. They swim noisily upstream and finally reach the site of the massacre. No trace of either the sardines or the fisherman. After a long search they find their sisters, or better said the cans that contain their sisters. Optimistic and enthusiastic they have the cans opened and shout to awaken their sisters who seem to be asleep. And then they realize that their sisters from the Silver Sea are not only dead, but cooked in oil.

✢

Late at night Ștefan comes in a car "to take us for air". And, because we don't have any cigarettes and all the tobacconists are closed, he makes a detour, stops in front of the building where he

In the Beginning Was the End

lives, and goes upstairs for cigarettes. While I am talking with Mira I look at the gray, gloomy building: a masterpiece of bad taste.

Ştefan returns with the cigarettes. We drive on the badly lit streets for more than an hour. Ever since yesterday I have a crazy feeling of safety. When we are saying good-bye, in front of the door, Mira invites Ştefan for dinner for next day. Ştefan replies:

– I won't be able to come. I am leaving for Moldova tomorrow for two weeks.

Once back in the apartment Horia tells me:

– Tomorrow you are going to get the Italian texts. Don't get too excited; they are all Marxist, moreover Marxist in the Stalinist vein.

✢

Three weeks later, around midnight, I am typing the final draft of the translation, while Horia is reading, Mira is sewing, and all three of us are half listening to the BBC broadcast: something about a horticultural exhibit in London.

A knock at the door, then the doorbell. Horia closes his book. Mira gets up. We look at each other for a moment. Horia whispers:

– It's midnight. It can only be the police or, at best, a requisition commission. Adriana, go down the back stairs. Get in the garbage bin. It's empty. Pull down the lid.

The doorbell again.

– If in fifteen minutes we don't come to get you out of there, try to disappear.

Horia opens the door for me, while Mira sits in my place to pretend that she was typing.

I get outside and easily recognize the garbage bin belonging to our flat: for the last two weeks I have taken out the garbage. Before getting inside I take the cyanide out of the pocket of my dress and hold it in my hand. I pull down the lid. Soon the odor that emanates from the bin penetrates deeply inside me, and in the dark the circles start spinning again in front of my eyes. They have the same colors: yellow, red, yellow, red.

I think that more than half an hour has passed when I decide to get out; if I don't breathe fresh air very soon I might faint. What might be going on upstairs? As they haven't come for me, it must be the police. I go out through the back door and around the building. An empty truck, nobody in the street. After the street corner I start running like a madwoman. That's exactly what I shouldn't do, but it doesn't matter anymore! I've reached the end of the second street; I go down the third, still running, I don't meet anybody, I keep running. At the end of the fifth street I stop distraught. Where can I go? To whom? I am in my dress and canvas shoes, that's all I have. Marc probably isn't in Bucharest, and anyway I don't even know his address. The men are scattered. After this month, in which I have lost the habit of breathing, moving and acting like a hunted creature, I feel even more helpless. Maybe I have used up whatever was left of my strength; maybe I shouldn't go any further. And in the first place, where should I go and to whom? Suddenly I remember Ştefan. Could he have returned from Moldova? I remember that grey, gloomy, building in poor taste. Will I be able to find it again? I start walking very fast. I have decided to find that building again. I have a rough idea of the neighbourhood: it's almost at the other end of Bucharest. I will make a last attempt. If I don't find it, too bad...

I was sure that the excessively poor taste of the building would help me remember it. I found it relatively easily. I don't know Ştefan's floor, but I have decided to throw caution to the winds and ring at all the doors starting with the last floor, the fourth. I take the lift, go up, ring the door bell.

A tousled, red-haired young man opens the door.

– Is Ştefan C. at home?

I wait patiently for him to tell me: "Which Ştefan C.?" Instead, the boy opens the door wide.

– He should come any moment now. Are you the cousin who was supposed to come from the countryside?

– Yes.

– Did you leave your luggage in the taxi?

– No, it's at the station.

He invites me into a room occupied across its whole width by a large table. On the table, three dismantled radio sets. The boy follows my gaze and tells me while laughing:

– Ştefan's toys.

As I don't answer he continues:

– Take a seat. Are you cold?

My teeth have started chattering again. I am trembling so hard that I am not able to answer him.
- Are you ill, are you cold? It's possible Ștefan might be a little late, he is having dinner at some friends nearby. Do you want me to go looking for him?

He looks at me increasingly surprised. My teeth are chattering and I am not able to articulate a single word. He leaves. I hear him closing the door, running down the stairs.

It's one thirty in the morning. My teeth keep chattering wildly.

✢

Ștefan enters, followed by the boy who let me in before.
- Ah, is that you cousin?

Then turning to the boy:
- Can you make some hot tea?

Once the boy has left, Ștefan tells me:
- Do you know what he told me? "There is a mad woman with chattering teeth who says she is your cousin. You must come immediately. I am afraid to be alone with her. Her eyes are wild". What happened?

And, as I am still not able to articulate a word:
- Well, let's get something to help you.

He goes next door, and comes back with a tea cup and a cachet.
- Swallow this right away. It's a sedative.

After fifteen minutes I manage to tell him the whole story of what happened at Mira's and my race through the night. I add:
- Can I sleep here tonight?
- Not only tonight. As long as you need and it is possible. On one condition: you are not to scare my friend again. Tomorrow I'll try to find out what happened to Horia and Mira. For the time being, take my room. I and my colleague will sleep in the hall.

And he leaves with his friend, who seems barely more reassured.

Next day Ștefan brings me news about Horia and Mira. The requisition commission that came to take their library only left at dawn. They needed all that time to write the report, to list the title of each book, and to load the two thousand volumes of the library in the truck.

– They didn't do anything to them?
– No, nothing else. Anyway, for this time it was enough... They seem to be in shock and stand next to the empty shelves without moving. Horia asked me to tell you that he won't be able to send that letter to Teohari Georgescu; they've taken the famous *Demons*.

✢

Ştefan has gone for two weeks to the countryside with the Red Cross of a foreign mission. His friend has gone back home. I am alone in the house. For the month since I have been here I haven't been outside.

A few days before Ştefan is supposed to come back I start having fever again.

This morning I wake up with a violent headache. I dreamed that somebody was knocking at the door. No, I didn't dream. There are knocks at the door indeed. I don't move. I can hear voices behind the door.

– The spy hasn't come back yet.
– We can break down the door, occupy the flat, and wait for him.
– No, comrade. It's better to take him by surprise. This one is an Anglo-American spy, and he is clever.

I grab the sheets. I feel that if I don't grab the sheets I'll fall out of bed. Spy? Ştefan's mission ends tomorrow, and he will return to Bucharest.

Beyond the door the two agents keep talking. They have decided to bring more comrades and form two permanent teams in front of the two doors of the apartment, the front door and the service door. One of them has left. I can hear the other one endlessly pacing in front of the door. I must warn Ştefan, at any cost... but for the moment I don't want to get out of bed, the agent might hear the noise.

Around noon I receive some unhoped-for help: in the flat next door they are playing the radio so loudly that the whole building is filled with noise. I take advantage of the hubbub to put on my dress and my shoes, and go to the kitchen. The kitchen window looks over the roof. I sit down and wait for nightfall, a pack of cigarettes in front of me.

When I have finished the pack it is dark. I check my pockets once more: my papers, the cyanide, a handkerchief, a few coins. Everything is ready. I climb on a chair, open the window and go out on the roof. Moving slowly, crawling on all fours, I go around three windows, also kitchen windows. Through the fourth I see the service stairs. When I have probably gone half the way around the building I reach a second service staircase, not the one leading to Ştefan's flat. The staircase seems empty. I break a window pane with my fist and open the window. My hand is bleeding. I see the Gypsy's face. The Gypsy's face, very accurately. I jump through the window, run down the stairs, I slip, I somersault. I manage to grab the rail and get up, I stifle a moan: a sharp pain in my ankle. I go down the stairs biting my lips, my ankle hurts very badly.

I have reached the ground floor. I go out into a yard. A dog comes running toward me. I lean over and pet him: if only he doesn't bark! The street door has a glass pane. I press my face to the glass. I don't see anybody on the street. The dog is licking my bleeding hand. I take out my handkerchief, wrap my hand in it, open the door, go out. Behind the open door the dog has started to bark.

Now I have started to run. A house, two houses, the street corner, my ankle hurts too much, I try to hold onto the walls. If I fall nobody will be able to warn Ştefan. I have bitten my lips so hard that I feel the taste of blood in my mouth. Where should I go? To whom? Marc, where could Marc be? I don't know where I am anymore, I no longer recognize the city; everything has started to spin in front of my eyes. I try to cross the road; in the distance a motorbike is approaching me, coming at great speed. I want to run, the pain in my ankle makes me let out a cry. I have fallen on my knees, I try to get up, the motorbike is coming, is coming, it is here, it is... A sudden sound of brakes. I have fallen again. Who is leaning over me? Looks like Victor. Victor was arrested. Victor is in prison. It can't be him. I am dreaming. I say to him:

– Are you in prison?

He seems scared. I have started to laugh, softly at first, then more and more loudly.

– You are in prison, aren't you.

– Shut up, shut up at once.

I keep laughing. He slaps me. He whispers:

– Forgive me. Listen: be calm, calm. I'll put you on the back

seat. Come on, easy. That's it. Grab me tight.
I lean my head on his back. I have grabbed his coat with my hands. We are speeding. I feel the rush of the air, I feel the rough cloth of his coat, I feel my hands clenching, clenching.
The motorbike stops in front of a yard. Nobody in the street; all these empty, empty streets. Victor takes me in his arms, he rings the doorbell. The door opens: inside, people, cigarette smoke, warmth. Everything is spinning. I whisper:
– Ştefan C. must be warned... Police are waiting for him at his house. He is coming back tomorrow from the countryside.
I lose consciousness.

+

When I come to, I see Marc, Victor and somebody else, who is putting compresses on my forehead, leaning over me. I whisper:
– He must be warned...
Marc tells me to be quiet:
– We'll do it, don't worry.
They give me something to drink. The other man touches my ankle. I let out a cry. Marc takes my hand:
– He is a doctor. It's going to hurt some. Your ankle is broken. Come on girl, a little courage.
I cry out again. Marc squeezes my hand. He keeps talking to me. I don't understand a word of what he is saying.
I think I fainted. I come to again. I ask:
– Is Victor in prison?
Marc keeps talking. The doctor gives me a shot. He no longer seems to be working on my ankle. They are all sitting around the bed. They make me drink something bitter again. Only at dawn do I manage to get my head straight and understand what they are telling me: Marc returned three days ago, has reorganized the group and they have found a house. The first meeting was tonight. As for Victor, he managed to escape from prison two weeks after his arrest, even before going through interrogation. He was going to the meeting when he ran into me. He touches my forehead:
– As for you girl, you excel at novelistic situations! For me to get to the point of slapping you! But I was afraid you were going to wake up the whole neighbourhood with your laughing.

In the Beginning Was the End

I try to smile. I ask him:
- And my ankle?
The doctor answers:
- It's in a cast. Now, one more small shot for your heart, and I let you sleep.
Outside the pale light of dawn.

✢

The men were able to warn Ştefan. He comes to see me two weeks later. He is also in hiding. The agents are still waiting for him at his house... He tells me very calmly:
- I have money for a guide. Everything is taken care of. I am leaving tomorrow and I am taking you with me.
I make an effort to smile while showing him my leg: the cast is still on. He frowns:
- Everything is arranged. Tomorrow is the last day.
- I can't move. Go without me. You must get to the other side. You know very well that you'll be more useful there than here. Go.
He paces up and down the room. I chain-smoke. The discussion lasts more than an hour while next door the other men are making leaflets.

✢

Ştefan left yesterday. He has promised to write.
The men bring me the latest news every day: the factories have been nationalized. The owners weren't replaced with qualified workers, but instead with party members without any technical competence. The owners were arrested only after they brought the new worker-owners up to speed as to how the factory functioned. The whole national economy is shaking. The Communist newspapers call the lack of preparation of the new owners "economic sabotage", and ask for severe punishments to serve as an example. The former owners, the new owners and the workers are all trembling with fear. Anyway, everybody is trembling with fear. Only the agent provocateurs and the snitches move up the ladder peacefully... until they are in turn denounced.
Scânteia declares that *"for the freedom of the people we must*

fight against the sabotage of the reaction".

I feel increasingly tired. Now and then I see in my mind's eye the look on Vera's face as she was leaving the cell, and hear her last words: *"And if I could do it again..."* I whisper again the continuation: *"I would take the same road".*

✦

Two months later a boy brings me a postcard from Ștefan:
"My dear Rebecca, Our friends from the Joint have received me quite well. Your birthday is in a few days. Many happy returns for you and the children. I am sorry I have left, but you know that my dearest dream was to go to Palestine. I will write to you soon from Tel-Aviv. Until then, my best wishes and my great affection. Long live the Romanian Republic!"

Lately a few groups of Jews have been allowed to leave the country and go to Palestine. I smile at the clever way Ștefan got the postcard through censorship. I also smile thinking about my birthday: it is today and I had totally forgotten about it. I am especially happy because he has reached Austria: the postmark is from Vienna.

✦

For the last two months I have once again been running from house to house. The group had to scatter. We have almost run out of addresses. I can't sleep more than one night in the same place. Marc no longer knows where to send us. We no longer know where to go. I no longer know where to go. On the city grapevine circulates the rumor that a state housing office is in the works. In reality this office "in the works" has already started its activity. Commissions come to measure the living space for each house – a room for a family of two, two rooms for larger families – and they name ex officio the people that are going to share the apartment with the current lodgers from that evening on. Another decree, this one official, directs apartment owners to hand in to the office a complete list of lodgers, as well as their biographies, and provides for penalties for those who don't. Under these conditions it becomes almost impossible to hide.

When I go to a house I increase the fear of those who receive me. Fear of walking on the streets and of coming home, fear of taking an assigned job. Fear of talking in front of the children. Everything follows from fear.

At night, walking the streets in search of another place to stay, I have trouble recognizing the city, my city. All the statues have been knocked down. The streets are named after Soviet heroes. The buildings are draped with red flags and Stalin's portraits.

In the city there is a large outbreak of suicides.

✢

This is the last address that Marc could give me. I must leave the house tomorrow evening... to go nowhere. The people that have taken me in tonight have a stiff and silent way of moving, as if there is a dead person in the house. Five people sleep in two rooms. I don't want to share the bed with one of them and go to the kitchen instead, sit on the window sill and gaze at the stars. While trying to recognize the constellations I talk softly to myself. It's obvious that I can't continue living like this. It's obvious that, more than anything else, I want to die. It's obvious that if I don't die I will go mad. Already, beside the familiar and faithful nightmare, I have started to have visions. Once I close my eyes, even when awake, I see faces: from Varvara's to Vera's, going through the Gypsy, Milica, Giovanna and Nicolschi – all the faces coming toward me bearing smudges of black blood. Usually they all grin, even the Rat-woman who wants to set fire to my hair with a cigarette that looks like a torch. When I open my eyes and the visions leave me, I find myself laughing in a strange way, or praying to God to save me, to allow me to rest.

That evening I look at the stars and tell myself that I should no longer hesitate, that the moment has surely come, the moment I was trying to postpone, to postpone...

Knocks at the door. The previously agreed-upon signal. Somebody in the house went to open it. Marc is here.

– I've met somebody who was looking for Ştefan.
– And?
– I've brought him with me to talk to you.
I shout:
– Marc, you are irresponsible. What if he is an agent... They are

going to arrest everybody in the house. They are going to arrest all these innocent people. You've gone completely mad. You know that Ștefan has been in Vienna for two months.

Behind Marc, a voice:
– Really, he has been in Vienna for two months?

Marc backs away. I collapse in a chair. Probably I am dead and am in the next life. In the next life, Ștefan is here in front of me and approaches me, limping.

– Good evening Adriana. Has your ankle healed? Can we go soon?
– What's wrong with your foot Ștefan?
– Nothing very serious. It's a little swollen. I've been too much the globetrotter.

Am I alive, am I dreaming, have I died?
– How did you come back from Vienna?
– On foot, with a compass. The same way I went there.
– Did you come on foot, alone?

He laughs:
– Yes, like a grown-up, imagine that.
– But why, why did you come back?

He keeps laughing.
– You disappoint me. I thought you were a smart girl. Haven't you understood yet? I came for you.
– You're insane too, you're insane! What if they arrest you, if they arrest you because of me? How can you risk your life for me?

Ștefan puts his hand on my shoulder and tells me in a voice that has suddenly turned very serious:
– Calm down. Don't confuse yourself with words. In reality things are quite simple. I came for you. In one week you're going to be on the other side.

I keep repeating, like an obsessed woman:
– But why risk your life? Why didn't you stay there where you were free?
– Let's say, if you want, that I didn't feel free there as long as I knew you were in danger here. Let's say that at that price freedom didn't seem desirable.

I dare to utter out loud the phrase with which I am obsessed:
– Ștefan, am I dreaming, have I died, or is this for real?
– I think it's real. But, anyway, if you prefer to think it's a dream,

let's say we're dreaming. For the time being, if you could give me a little coffee, I'd prefer it to be real, because I really need it.

While I am lighting the fire to heat him some coffee, Ştefan adds:

– In three days, to the hour, to the minute, we'll be in Hungary.

✢

Ştefan has rested the whole day. We are going to leave tomorrow morning. Marc comes to bring me the last set of false papers and a man's suit. He doesn't want to go with us; he has his work, he is responsible for the group. I can barely restrain a terrible desire to cry. We shake hands. Marc's laugh sounds fake.

– Come on, kids, no tears. See you soon, come back soon. We'll wait for you until the end.

On the doorstep, he turns back one more time:

– You know, Adriana, of all the passwords there is one which was my favourite. I made it up one evening when everything seemed even more absurd, even more unreal than usual. It's the first one I gave you. Do you remember it? "Roses have never been so blue." From now on nobody will use it here. It's yours. If I ever hear it, I'll know you've reached safety on the other side of the world.

And, opening the door:

– And come back soon so the roses will some day stop being blue, isn't that right, kids?

✢

The rest no longer is history.

The long and dusty road past a village, the cornfield where we stopped for a whole day listening to the wind rustling the stalks and waiting for nightfall, the compass in Ştefan's hand, the calm emanating from his whole being, the motorbike noises and the headlamp that came on suddenly and which we had to avoid, the dogs barking around us and somewhere, quite far, the peals of a small country church sounding softly, somewhat muffled and seemingly praying, and in the end the final road through darkness and mud, the light that served us as a landmark trembling in the distance, the final road and somewhere behind us the country getting farther away, the land of my country running through my fingers and becoming distant: for all these events I can't really find the words.

The roads that lead to the secret border crossing are made of a special dirt and mud that only those who have been there are able to know and understand.

Yes, the rest no longer is history.

✢

I reached Vienna at the end of August 1948.

In the Beginning Was the End

ACKNOWLEDGEMENTS

Adriana Georgescu wishes to thank all those who, at the risk of their own liberty, helped by hiding her before she escaped from Romania. She addresses special thanks to Anita and Dinu Hariton, who, although parents of young children, risked their safety by hiding many other fugitives, including Alexandru Paleologu, and also to the British Military Mission in Bucharest, which hid her in the attic, at the intervention of General Rădescu – who also took refuge at the British Mission before managing to fly out of the country.

The author also wishes to pay tribute to her late husband, Frank Lorimer Westwater (1909-1969), captain and instructor in H.M. British Navy. Two of the ships on which Captain Westwater served during WWII were sunk by the enemy; the first time he was the only surviving senior officer, being saved by a passing ship in the Atlantic, the second time he was found, almost dead from exposure, on the shores of Gibraltar. He received numerous awards (Star, Atlantic Star, Defence Medal, War Medal, and, in 1954, the Order of the British Empire). F.L. Westwater studied mathematics at the Universities of Edinburgh and Cambridge, and worked as a scientist and researcher in Sir Fred Hoyle's team at the Institute of Theoretical Astronomy at Cambridge University. He is the author of four books published by English University Press.

Adriana Georgescu

The Geography of De[tention]

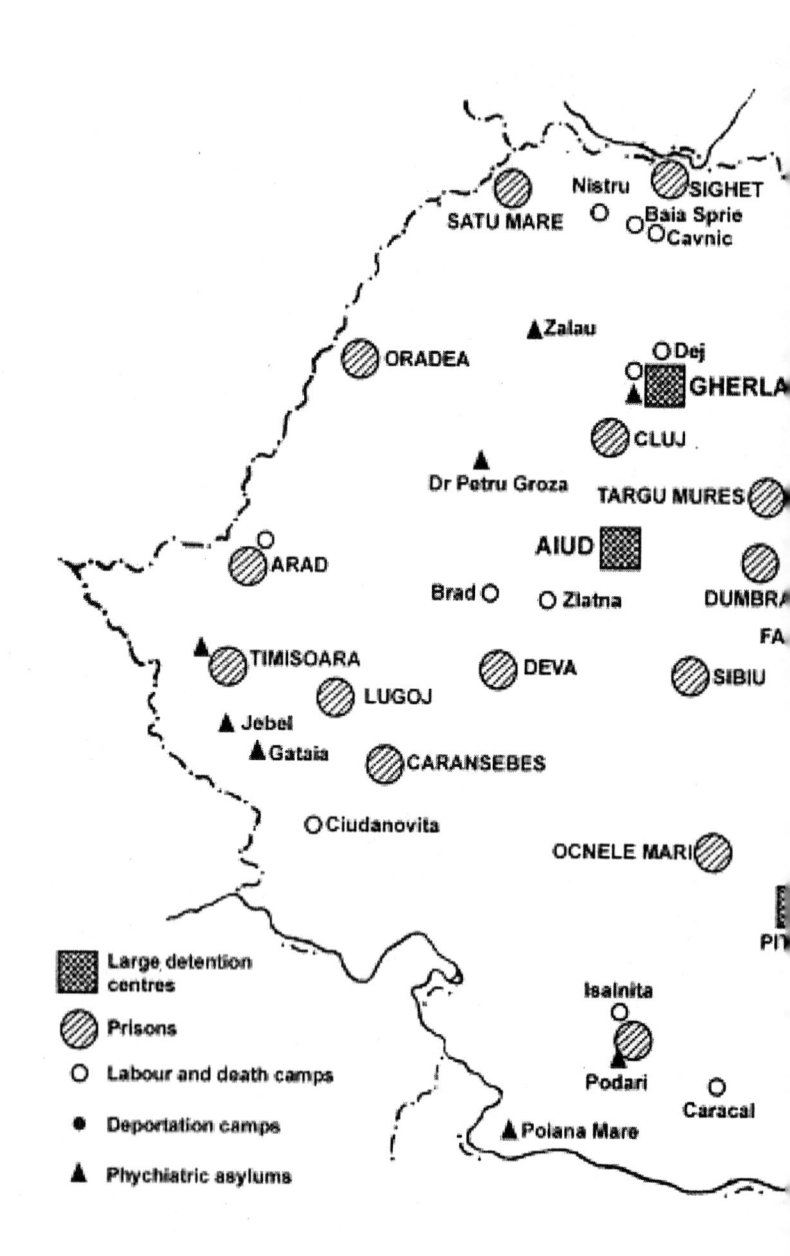

Nistru
SIGHET
SATU MARE
Baia Sprie
Cavnic
▲Zalau
ORADEA
O Dej
GHERLA
CLUJ
▲
Dr Petru Groza
TARGU MURES
AIUD
ARAD
Brad O   O Zlatna
DUMBRA
FA
▲TIMISOARA
DEVA
SIBIU
LUGOJ
▲ Jebel
▲ Gataia
CARANSEBES
O Ciudanovita
OCNELE MARI
PI
Isalnita
▨ Large detention centres
◎ Prisons
○ Labour and death camps
● Deportation camps
▲ Phychiatric asylums
Podari
O Caracal
▲ Poiana Mare

In the Beginning Was the End

ion Centres in Romania

M.VLADEASA
M.ZARANDULUI
MURES
MURES
TIMIS
M.POIANA RUSCA
OLT
M. FAGARAS
M.CERNEI

In the Beginning Was the End

Areas of activity of anti-communist resistance groups between 1945-1960

Tiparul executat la
S.C. LUMINA TIPO s.r.l.
str. Luigi Galvani nr. 20 bis, sect. 2, București
Tel./Fax 211.32.60; Tel. 212.29.27